THE WAYFARER'S WEIRD

THE WAYFARER'S WEIRD

Wild Tales of Uncanny Rambles

Edited by

WEIRD WALK

BRITISH LIBRARY

This collection first published in 2025 by
The British Library
96 Euston Road
London NW1 2DB
bl.uk

Cataloguing in Publication Data
A catalogue record for this publication is available from the British Library

ISBN 978 0 7123 5548 3
e-ISBN 978 0 7123 6864 3

Photographs by Fay Godwin on pages 2 and 288 © The British Library Board
Cover design by Mauricio Villamayor with illustration by Sandra Gómez
Text design and typesetting by Tetragon, London
Printed in England by CPI Group (UK) Ltd, Croydon, CR0 4YY

MIX
Paper | Supporting
responsible forestry
FSC® C013604

CONTENTS

INTRODUCTION

In our previous collection of weird fiction related to rambling in the British landscape, *The Haunted Trail*, we often selected stories whose locations were decidedly gentle and bucolic – all the more unsettling when the shadow side of the rural idyll should emerge, of course. In this anthology, we frequently find our protagonists in more extreme terrain when they encounter the numinous, strange and horrifying. It is, in that sense, a much wilder collection of tales. Temporal boundaries have also been expanded for *The Wayfarer's Weird*, as we have drawn upon later stories than the 1950s, where *The Haunted Trail* left off. It has been a wonderful thing to explore more recent takes on the terrors that lurk out there in the fields, forests and hills of these isles.

The appeal of Britain's wild places is longstanding. Although it has often been said that people of earlier ages were indifferent or outright hostile to more remote and harsh environments, the truth is more complex. As Dawn Hollis shows in *Mountains Before Mountaineering*, premodern people were capable of rich and varied responses to the rugged landscapes they inhabited and travelled through. The natural environment was more than a simple backdrop for human affairs, or a place fraught only with danger. Hollis notes that the sixteenth-century botanist Conrad Gessner, for example, was happy to recommend walks in the mountains "for the sake of suitable bodily exercise and the delight of the spirit".

If the idea that before the late eighteenth century nobody appreciated the attraction of wild places is false, it is certainly true that the Romantic period turbocharged a desire for wilderness. A sense of rapture in the presence of the natural world abounded at this time. The right kind of remote, rural spot could be not just picturesque, but awe-inspiring. When the Gothic novelist Ann Radcliffe visited the area around Keswick in 1794, she was struck by the beauty of the fells:

> The colouring of the mountains was, this day, surprisingly various and changeful, surpassing every thing of the same nature, that we had seen. The effect of the atmosphere on mountainous regions is sometimes so sublime, at others so enchantingly beautiful, that the mention of it ought not to be considered as trivial, when their aspect is to be described.

With wild places very much in vogue, poets, artists and the well-to-do flocked to areas such as the Lake District and the Wye Valley to be confronted with the sublimity that Radcliffe mentions. Of course, exploration on foot was a key part of enjoying the landscape. In 1818, a 22-year-old John Keats and his friend Charles Armitage Brown completed a remarkable tour through northern England and into Scotland, walking some 600 miles in the process, including a hike to the summit of Ben Nevis, where whisky was drunk and a sonnet composed. When writing to his brother, Keats compared the exertions of the climb to "the task of mounting ten Saint Pauls without the convenience of staircases".

Some would take this passion for hiking further – Samuel Taylor Coleridge was also a prodigious walker, but in 1802 he made England's first recorded rock climb when he descended Broad Stand (a steep wall of slabs linking Scafell to Mickledore in the Lakes). Coleridge reported that upon finally reaching the bottom after some nerve-wracking moments, he lay, in true Romantic fashion, "in a state of almost prophetic Trance and Delight". Female poets were active in mountaineering too: Dorothy Wordsworth and her friend Mary Barker made one of the first recorded ascents of Scafell Pike, the highest mountain in England, in 1818. Like Keats on Ben Nevis that same year, Wordsworth and Barker would write at the summit, composing celebratory letters to fellow hillwalker Sara Hutchinson.

In many ways, Romanticism set the stage for the modern appreciation of being in the natural world, especially its wilder places, and echoes of such sensibilities can be found in some of the weird tales in this book. (Indeed, authors of uncanny and esoteric fiction can also count mountaineers in their ranks: Algernon Blackwood was a committed hiker and climber, while Aleister Crowley was part of expeditions to scale K2 and Kanchenjunga in the Himalayas.)

By the time our first story was published in 1879, there was already a long history of fascination with Britain's moors, mountains and windswept coasts. However, in a space as geographically tight as Britain, resettled and explored by humans since the close of the Ice Age, there are no truly untouched areas. In fact, some of our most treasured wild landscapes are the result of human action, with both ecological and societal costs. Austere Welsh uplands have gained much of their treeless character through the expansion of sheep grazing, while the uninhabited nature of many Scottish glens can be traced to the injustices of the Highland Clearances.

Unforgiving, wild environments have the power to remind us that we are part of, rather than distinct from, nature. But these are also very human places. It is because of the hardships and joys experienced in these landscapes, and the folklore, history and legend embedded within them, that weird fiction can thrive in this difficult earth. Although, for our reading pleasure, the walkers in this book suffer less than ideal rambling experiences, we hope these atmospheric tales inspire you to engage with our strange, storied landscapes, to plan a route, prep your gear and head off into the hills with some pals. As the aforementioned Conrad Gessner wrote, "And so let us conclude that from mountain ramblings undertaken with friends the highest of pleasures and the most satisfying of all sensations are to be enjoyed."

WEIRDWALK.CO.UK

REFERENCES AND FURTHER READING

Kerri Andrews, *Wanderers: A History of Women Walking* (London: Reaktion Books, 2020)

Stephen Hebron, *The Romantics and the British Landscape* (London: The British Library, 2006)

Dawn Hollis, *Mountains Before Mountaineering: The Call of the Peaks Before the Modern Age* (Cheltenham: The History Press, 2024)

Robert Macfarlane, *The Wild Places* (London: Granta, 2007)

ACKNOWLEDGMENTS

Thanks to Mike Ashley, James Machin and Mark Valentine for sharing their knowledge so generously, and to Martin Pratt for researching William Croft Dickinson's military service. Thanks also to the British Library team for all of their work on *The Wayfarer's Weird*.

WALKING NOTE

The brief location notes in this book are intended to prompt further exploration and research.

The Ramblers website gives the following useful guidance when planning a mountain or hill walk:

Rather than choosing a set route a long way in advance, be flexible and have a plan B (or C!) ready just in case. Always consider the needs of the least experienced walkers in your group. Ask yourself three questions to ensure it is suitable and enjoyable for everyone in your group:

1. Have we fully considered the weather conditions and whether this will make the route more challenging?
2. Do we all have the correct clothing and kit?
3. Do we all have the right knowledge, skills and ability for this walk?

If you can't answer yes to all these questions, then choose an easier route or wait for the weather to improve.

Before setting off, share your route and expected finishing time with a reliable person. Tell them when you're safely down.

Further tips for hillwalking can be found at ramblers.org.uk

A NOTE FROM THE PUBLISHER

The original short stories reprinted in the British Library Tales of the Weird series were written and published in a period ranging across the nineteenth and twentieth centuries. There are many elements of these stories which continue to entertain modern readers; however, in some cases there are also uses of language, instances of stereotyping and some attitudes expressed by narrators or characters which may not be endorsed by the publishing standards of today. We acknowledge therefore that some elements in the stories selected for reprinting may continue to make uncomfortable reading for some of our audience. With this series British Library Publishing aims to offer a new readership a chance to read some of the rare material of the British Library's collections in an affordable paperback format, to enjoy their merits and to look back into the worlds of the past two centuries as portrayed by their writers. It is not possible to separate these stories from the history of their writing and therefore the following novel is presented as it was originally published with minor edits only, made for consistency of style and sense. We welcome feedback from our readers, which can be sent to the following address:

British Library Publishing
The British Library
96 Euston Road
London, NW1 2DB
United Kingdom

1879

THE WRAITH OF BARNJUM

F. Anstey

Thomas Anstey Guthrie (1856–1934) used the pen name F. Anstey for many humorous novels, short stories and parodies over a long writing career. He rose to prominence with the successful fantasy novel *Vice Versa* in 1882, where a father and son swap bodies after encountering a magical stone from India, much like a Victorian *Freaky Friday*.

Guthrie was also a staff writer on *Punch*, and his skill as a humourist can be seen in this unusual ghost story, which a young Guthrie saw published in *Temple Bar* magazine in 1879. "The Wraith of Barnjum" pairs a withering satire of fickle London high society with a "back from the dead" narrative that sends up late-nineteenth-century interest in the supernatural.

The tale begins with unlikely companions Bunting and Barnjum scaling the heights of Cader Idris, before Bunting's patience violently snaps, setting the story's strange events in motion. One of the most popular mountains in southern Eryri (Snowdonia), Cader Idris' distinctive peaks and strenuous hiking routes have drawn visitors for generations. The mountain's name translates as "Idris' Chair". In legend, Idris was a wise giant practised in the arts of poetry, philosophy and astronomy, who was said to have used the mountain to recline while he observed the movements of the heavens.

I frankly admit, whatever may be the consequences of doing so, that I was not fond of Barnjum; in fact, I detested him. Everything that fellow said and did jarred upon me to an absolutely indescribable extent, although I did not discover for some time that he regarded me with a strange and unreasonable aversion.

We were so essentially unlike in almost every particular – I, with my innate refinement and high culture, my over-fastidious exclusiveness in the choice of associates; and he, a big, red, coarse brute with neither sweetness nor light, who knew himself a Philistine, and seemed to like it – we were so unlike, that I often asked him, with a genuine desire for information, *what* had I in common with him?

And yet it will scarcely be believed, perhaps, that with such good reasons for keeping apart, we were continually seeking one another's company with a zest that knew no satiety. The only explanation I can offer for such a phenomenon is, that our mutual antipathy had become so much a part of ourselves, that we could not let it perish for lack of nourishment.

Perhaps we were not conscious of this at the time, and when we agreed to go on a walking tour together in North Wales, I think it was chiefly because we knew that we could devise no surer means of annoying one another; but, however that may be, in an ill-starred day for my own peace of mind, we started upon a journey from which but one of us was fated to return.

I pass by the painful experiences of the first few days of that unhappy tour. I will say nothing of Barnjum's grovelling animalism, of his consummate selfishness, his more than bucolic indifference to the charms of Nature, nor even of the mean and sordid way in which he contrived to let me in for railway tickets and hotel bills.

I wish to tell my melancholy story with perfect impartiality, and *I* am sure that I am not reduced to exciting any prejudice to secure the sympathies of all readers.

I shall pass, then, to the memorable day when my disgust, so long pent up, so imperfectly concealed, culminated in one grand outburst of a not ignoble indignation, to the hour when I summoned up moral courage to sever the bonds which linked us so unequally.

I remember it so well, that brilliant morning in June when we left the Temperance Hotel, Doldwyddlm, and scaled in sulky silence the craggy heights of Cader Idris, which, I presume, still overhang that picturesque village, while, as we ascended, an ever-changing and ever-improving panorama unrolled itself before my delighted eyes.

The air up there was keen and bracing, and I recollect that I could not repress an æsthetic shudder at the crude and primitive tone which Barnjum's nose had assumed under atmospheric influences. I mentioned this (for we still maintained the outward forms of friendship), when he retorted, with the brutal personality which formed so strong an ingredient of his character, that if I could only see myself in that suit of mine, and that hat (referring to the dress I was then wearing), I should feel the propriety of letting his nose alone. To which I replied, with a sarcasm that I feel now was a little too crushing, that I had every intention of doing so, as it was quite painful enough to merely contemplate such a spectacle; and he, evidently meaning to be offensive, remarked, that no one could help his nose getting red, but that any man in my position could at least *dress* like a gentleman.

I took no notice of this insult; a Bunting (I don't think I mentioned before that my name is Philibert Bunting) – a Bunting can afford to pass such insinuations by; indeed, I find it actually cheaper to do so, and I flattered myself that my dress was distinguished by a sort of studied looseness, that would appeal at once to a cultivated and artistic eye, though of course Barnjum's hard and shallow organs could not be expected to appreciate it.

I overlooked it, then, and presently we found ourselves skirting the edge of a huge chasm, whose steep sides sloped sheer down into the slate-blue waters of the lake below.

How can I hope to give an idea of the magnificent view which met our eyes as we stood there – a view of which, as far as I am aware, no description has ever yet been attempted?

To our right towered the Peaks of Dolgelly, with their saw-like outline cutting the blue sky with a faint grating sound, while the shreds of white cloud lay below in drifts. At our feet were the sunlit waters of the lake, upon which danced a fleet of brown-sailed herring-boats; beyond was the plain of Capel Curig, and there, over on the left, sparkled the falls of Y-Dydd.

As I took all this in I felt a longing to say something worthy of the occasion. Being possessed of a considerable fund of carefully-dried and selected humour, I frequently amuse myself by a species of intellectual exercise, which consists in so framing a remark that a word or more therein may bear two entirely opposite constructions; and some of the quaint names of the vicinity seemed to me just then admirably adapted for this purpose.

I was about to gauge my dull-witted companion's capacity by some such test, when he forestalled me.

"You ought to live up here, Bunting," said he; "you were made for this identical old mountain."

I was not displeased, for, Londoner as I am, I have the nerve and steadiness of a practised mountaineer.

"Perhaps I was," I said good-humouredly; "but how did *you* find it out?"

"I'll tell you," he replied, with one of his odious grins. "This is Cader Idris, ain't it? well, and you're a *cad awry dressed*, ain't you? Cader Idrissed, see?" (he was dastard enough to explain) "That's how *I* get at it!"

He must have been laboriously leading up to that for the last ten minutes!

I solemnly declare that it was not the personal outrage that roused me; I simply felt that a paltry verbal quibble of that description, emitted amidst such scenery and at that altitude, required a protest in the name of indignant Nature, and I protested accordingly, although with an impetuosity which I afterwards regretted, and of which I cannot even now entirely approve.

He happened to be standing on the brink of an abyss, and had just turned his back upon me, as, with a vigorous thrust of my right foot, I launched him into the blue æther, with the chuckle at his un-hallowed jest still hovering upon his lips.

I am aware that by such an act I took a liberty which, under ordinary circumstances, even the licence of a life-long friendship would scarcely have justified; but I thought it only due to myself to let him see plainly that I desired our acquaintanceship to cease from that instant, and Barnjum was the kind of man upon whom a more delicate hint would have been distinctly thrown away.

I watched his progress with some interest as he rebounded from point to point during his descent. I waited – punctiliously, perhaps, until the echoes he had aroused had died away on the breeze, and then, slowly and thoughtfully, I retraced my steps, and left a spot which was already becoming associated for me with memories the reverse of pleasurable.

I took the next up-train, and before I reached town had succeeded in dismissing the incident from my mind, or if I thought of it at all, it was only to indulge relief at the reflection that I had shaken off Barnjum for ever.

But when I had paid my cab, and was taking out my latchkey, a curious thing happened – the driver called me back.

"Beg pardon, sir," he said hoarsely, "but I think you've bin and left something white in my cab!"

I turned and looked in: there, grinning at me from the interior of the hansom, over the folding-doors, was the wraith of Barnjum!

I had presence of mind enough to thank the man for his honesty, and go upstairs to my rooms with as little noise as possible. Barnjum's ghost, as I expected, followed me in, and sat down coolly before the fire, in my arm-chair, thus giving me an opportunity of subjecting the apparition to a thorough examination.

It was quite the conventional ghost, filmy, transparent, and, though wanting firmness in outline, a really passable likeness of Barnjum. Before I retired to rest I had thrown both my boots and the contents of my bookcase completely through the thing, without appearing to cause it more than a temporary inconvenience – which convinced me that it was indeed a being from another world.

Its choice of garments struck me even then as decidedly unusual. I am not narrow; I cheerfully allow that, assuming the necessity for apparitions at all, it is well that they should be clothed in robes of some kind; but Barnjum's ghost delighted in a combination of costume which set the fitness of things at defiance.

It wore that evening, for instance, to the best of my recollection, striped pantaloons, a surplice, and an immense cocked hat; but on subsequent occasions its changes of costume were so rapid and eccentric, that I ceased to pay much attention to them, and could only explain them on the supposition that somewhere in space there exists a supernatural store in the nature of a theatrical wardrobe, and that Barnjum's ghost had the run of it.

I had not been in very long before my landlady came up to see if I wanted anything, and of course as soon as she came in, she saw the wraith. At first she objected to it very strongly, declaring that she would not have such nasty things in *her* house, and if I wanted to keep ghosts, I had better go somewhere else; but I pacified her at last by representing that it would give her no extra trouble, and that I was only taking care of it for a friend.

When she had gone, however, I sat up till late, thinking calmly over my position, and the complications which might be expected to ensue from it.

It would be very easy to harrow the reader's feelings and work upon his sympathies here by a telling description of my terror and my guilty confusion at the unforeseen consequences of what I had done. But I think, in relating an experience of this kind, the straightforward way is always the best, and I do not care to heighten the effect by attributing to myself a variety of sensations which I do not remember to have actually felt at the time.

My first impression had not unnaturally been that the spectre was merely the product of overwrought nerves or indigestion, but it seemed improbable that a cabman should be plagued by a morbid activity of imagination, and that a landlady's digestion could be delicate sufficiently to evolve a thing so far removed from the merely commonplace; and, reluctantly enough, I was forced to the conclusion that it was a real ghost, and would probably continue to haunt me to the end of my days.

Of course I was disgusted by this exhibition of petty revenge and low malice on the part of Barnjum, which might be tolerated perhaps in a Christmas annual, with a full-page illustration, but which, in real life and the height of summer, was a glaring anachronism.

Still, it was of no use to repine then; I resolved to look at the thing in a common-sense light – I told myself that I had made my ghost, and would have to live with it. And after all, I had much to be thankful for: Barnjum in the spirit was a decided improvement upon Barnjum in the flesh; and as the spirit did not appear to be gifted with speech, it was unlikely to tell tales.

Luckily for me, too, Barnjum was absolutely unknown about town: his only relative was an aunt resident at Camberwell, and so there was no danger of any suspicion being excited by chance recognition in the circles to which I belonged.

It would have been folly to shut one's eyes to the fact that it might require considerable nerve to re-enter society closely attended by an obscure and fancifully-attired apparition.

Society would sneer considerably at first and make remarks, but I was full of tact and knowledge of the world, and I knew, too, that men have overcome far more formidable obstacles to social success than any against which I should be called upon to contend.

And so, instead of weakly giving way to unreasonable panic, I took the more manly course of determining to live it down, with what success I shall have presently to show.

When I went out after breakfast the next morning, Barnjum's ghost insisted upon coming too, and followed me, to my intense annoyance, all down St James's Street; in fact, for many weeks it was almost constantly by my side, and rendered me the innocent victim of mingled curiosity and aversion.

I thought it best to affect to be unaware of the presence of anything of a ghostly nature, and when taxed with it, ascribed it to the diseased fancy of my interlocutor; but, by-and-by, as the whole town began to ring with the story, I found it impossible to pretend ignorance any longer.

So I gave out that it was an artfully-contrived piece of spectral mechanism, of which I was the inventor, and for which I contemplated taking out a patent; and this would have earned for me a high reputation in the scientific world if Messrs. Maskelyne and Cooke had not grown envious of my fame, declaring that they had long since anticipated the secret of my machine, and could manufacture one in every way superior to it, which they presently did.

Then I was obliged to confide (in the strictest secrecy) to two members of the Peerage (both persons of irreproachable breeding, with whom I was at that time exceedingly intimate) that it was indeed a *bonâ fide* apparition, and that I rather liked such things about me. I cannot explain how it happened, but in a very short time the story had gone the round of the clubs and drawing-rooms, and I found myself launched as a lion of the largest size – if it is strictly correct to speak of launching a lion.

I received invitations everywhere, on the tacit understanding that I was to bring my ghost, and the wraith of Barnjum, as some who read this may remember, was to be seen at all the best houses in town for the remainder of the season; while in the following autumn, I was asked down for the shooting by several wealthy *parvenus*, with a secret hope, unless I am greatly mistaken, that the ghost might conceive the idea of remaining with them permanently, thereby imparting to their brand-new palaces the necessary flavour of legend and mystery; but of course it never did.

To tell the truth, whatever novelty there was about it soon wore off – too soon, in fact, for, fickle as society is, I have no hesitation in asserting that we ought to have lasted it at least a second season, if only Barnjum's ghost had not persisted in making itself so ridiculously cheap that, in little more than a fortnight, society was as sick of it as I was myself.

And then the inconveniences which attached to my situation began to assert themselves more and more emphatically.

I began to stay at home sometimes in the evening, when I observed that the phantom had an unpleasant trick of illuminating itself at the approach of darkness with a bilious green light, which, as it was not nearly strong enough to enable me to dispense with a reading lamp, merely served to depress me.

And then it began to absent itself occasionally for days together, and though at first I was rather glad not to see so much of it, I grew uneasy at last. I was always fancying that the Psychical Society, who are credited with understanding the proper treatment of spectres in health and disease, from the tomb upwards, might have got hold of it and be teaching it to talk and compromise me. I heard afterwards that one of their most prominent members did happen to come across it, but, with a scepticism which I cannot but think was somewhat wanting in discernment, rejected it as a palpable imposition.

I had to leave the rooms where I had been so comfortable, for my landlady complained that the street was blocked up by a mob of the lowest description from seven till twelve every evening, and she really could not put up with it any longer.

On inquiry I found that this was owing to Barnjum's ghost getting out upon the roof almost every night after dark, and playing the fool among the chimney-pots, causing me, as its apparent owner, to be indicted five times for committing a common nuisance by obstructing the thoroughfare, and once for collecting an unlawful assembly: I spent all my spare cash in fines.

I believe there were portraits of us both in the "Illustrated Police News," but the distinction implied in this was more than outweighed by the fact that Barnjum's wraith was slowly but surely undermining both my fortune and my reputation.

It followed me one day to one of the underground railway stations, and *would* get into a compartment with me, which led to a lawsuit that made a nine days' sensation in the legal world. I need only mention the celebrated case of "The Metropolitan District Railway *v.* Bunting," in which the important principle was once for all laid down that a railway company by the terms of its contract is entitled to refuse to carry ghosts, spectres, or any other supernatural baggage, and can moreover exact a heavy penalty from passengers who infringe its bye-laws in this respect.

This was, of course, a decision against me, and carried heavy costs, which my private fortune was just sufficient to meet.

But Barnjum's ghost was bent upon alienating me from society also, for at one of the best dances of the season, at a house where I had with infinite pains just succeeded in establishing a precarious footing, that miserable phantom disgraced me for ever by executing a shadowy but decidedly objectionable species of *cancan* between the dances!

Feeling indirectly responsible for its behaviour, I apologised profusely to my hostess, but the affair found its way into the society journals, and she never either forgave or recognised me again.

Shortly after that, the committee of my club (one of the most exclusive in London) invited me to resign, intimating that, by introducing an acquaintance of questionable antecedents and disreputable exterior into the smoking-room, I had abused the privileges of membership.

I had been afraid of this when I saw it following me into the building, arrayed in Highland costume and a tall hat; but I was quite unable to drive it away.

Up to that time I had been at the bar, where I was doing pretty well, but now no respectable firm of solicitors would employ a man who had such an unprofessional thing as a phantom about his chambers. I threw up my practice, and had no sooner changed my last sovereign than I was summoned for keeping a ghost without a licence!

Some men, no doubt, would have given up there and then in despair – but I am made of sterner stuff, and, besides, an idea had already occurred to me of turning the table upon my shadowy persecutor.

Barnjum's ghost had ruined me: why should I not endeavour to turn an honest penny out of Barnjum's ghost? It was genuine – as I well knew; it was, in some respects, original; it was eminently calculated to delight the young and instruct the old; there was even a moral or two to be got out of it, and though it had long failed to attract in town, I saw no reason why it should not make a great hit in the provinces.

I borrowed the necessary funds and had soon made all preliminary arrangements for running the wraith of Barnjum on a short tour in the provinces, deciding to open at Tenby, in South Wales.

I took every precaution, travelling by night and keeping within doors all day, lest the shade (which was deplorably destitute of the commonest professional pride) should get about and exhibit itself beforehand for nothing; and so successful was I, that when it first burst upon a Welsh audience, from the platform of the Assembly Rooms, Tenby, no ghost could have wished for a more enthusiastic reception, and – for the first and last time – I felt positively proud of it!

But the applause gradually subsided, and was succeeded by an awkward pause. It had not struck me till that moment that it would be necessary to do or say anything in particular during the exhibition, beyond showing the spectators round the phantom, and making the customary assurance that there was no deception and no concealed machinery, which I could do with a clear conscience. But a terrible conviction struck me as I stood there bowing repeatedly, that the audience had come prepared for a comic duologue, with incidental music and dances.

This was quite out of the question, even supposing that Barnjum's ghost would have helped me to entertain them, which, perhaps, I could scarcely expect. As it was, it did nothing at all, except grimace at the audience and make an idiotic fool of itself and me – an exhibition of which they soon wearied. I am perfectly certain that an ordinary magic lantern would have made a far deeper impression upon them.

Whether the wraith managed in some covert way, when my attention was diverted, to insult the national prejudices of that sensitive and hot-blooded nation, I cannot say. All I know is, that after sitting still for some time they suddenly rose as one man; chairs were hurled at me through the ghost, and the stage was completely wrecked before the audience could be induced to go away.

It was all over. I was hopelessly ruined now! My weak fancy that even a spectre would have some remnants of common decency and good-feeling hanging about it, had put the finishing touch to my misfortunes!

I paid for the smashed platform and windows with the money that had been taken at the doors, and then I travelled back to London, third class, that night, with the feeling that everything was against me.

It was Christmas, and I was sitting gloomily in my shabby Bloomsbury lodgings, watching with a miserable, apathetic interest Barnjum's wraith as, clad in a Roman toga, topboots, and a turban, it flitted about the horsehair furniture.

I was wondering if they would admit me into any workhouse while the spectre continued my attendant; I was utterly and completely wretched, and now, for the first time, I really repented my conduct in having parted with Barnjum so abruptly by the bleak cliff side, that bright June morning.

I had heard no more of him – I knew he must have reached the bottom after his fall, because I heard the splash he made – but no tidings had come of the discovery of his body; the lake kept its dark secret well.

If I could only hope that this insidious shade, now that it had hounded me down to poverty, would consider this as a sufficient expiation of my error and go away and leave me in peace! But I felt, only too keenly, that it was one of those one-idea'd apparitions, which never know when they have had enough of a good thing – it would be sure to stay and see the very last of me!

All at once there came a sharp tap at my door, and another figure strode solemnly in. This, too, wore the semblance of Barnjum, but was cast in a more substantial mould, and possessed the power of speech, as I gathered from its addressing me instantly as a cowardly villain.

I started back, and stood behind an arm-chair, facing those two forms, the shadow and the solid, with a feeling of sick despair.

"Listen to me," I said, "both of you: so long as your – your original proprietor was content with a single wraith, I put up with it; I did not enjoy myself – but I endured it. But a *brace* of apparitions is really carrying the thing too far; it's more than any one man's fair allowance, and I won't stand it. I defy the pair of you. I will find means to escape you. I will leave the world! Other people can be ghosts as well as you – it's not a monopoly! If you don't go directly, I shall blow my brains out!"

There was no firearm of any description in the house, but I was too excited for perfect accuracy.

"Blow your brains out by all means!" said the solid figure; "I don't know what all this nonsense you're talking is about. I'm not a ghost that I'm aware of; I'm alive (no thanks to you); and, to come back to the point – scoundrel!"

"Barnjum – and alive!" I cried, almost with relief. "If that is so," I added, feeling that I had been imposed upon in a very unworthy and ungentlemanly manner, "will you have the goodness to tell me what right you have to this ridiculous apparition here?"

He did not seem to have noticed it particularly till then. "Hullo!" he said, looking at it with some curiosity, "what d'ye call *that* thing?"

"I call it a beastly nuisance!" I said. "Ever since – since I last saw you, it's been following me about everywhere in a – in a very annoying manner!"

Will it be believed that the unfeeling brute only chuckled at this? "*I* don't know anything about it," he said, "but all I can say is that it serves you jolly well right, and I hope it will go on annoying you."

"This is ungenerous," I said, determined to appeal to any better feelings he might have; "we did not part on – on the best of terms perhaps – "

"Considering that you kicked me over a precipice when I wasn't looking," he retorted brutally, "we may take that as admitted."

"But, at all events," I argued, "it is ridiculous to cherish an old grudge all this time; you must see the absurdity of it yourself."

"No, I don't," he said.

I determined to make a last effort to move him. "It is Christmas Eve, Barnjum," I said earnestly, "Christmas Eve. Think of it. At this hour, thousands of throbbing human hearts are speeding the cheap but genial Christmas card to such of their relations as they consider at all likely to respond with a turkey. The costermonger, imaginative for the nonce, is investing damaged evergreens with a purely fictitious value, and the cheery publican is sending the member of his village goose-club back to his cottage home, rich in the possession of a shot-distended bird and a bottle of poisonous port. Hear my appeal. If I was hasty with you, I have been punished. That detestable thing on the hearth-rug there has dogged my path to misery and ruin; you cannot be without *some* responsibility for its conduct. I ask you now, as a man – nay, as an individual – to call it off. You can do it well enough if you only choose; you know you can."

But Barnjum wouldn't; he only looked at his own wraith with a grim satisfaction as it capered in an imbecile fashion upon the rug.

"Do," I implored him; "I would do it for *you*, Barnjum. I've had it about me for six months, and I *am* so sick of it."

Still he hesitated. Some waits outside were playing one of those pathetic American melodies – I forget now whether it was "Silver Threads among the Gold," or "In the Sweet By-and-By" – but, at all events, they struck some sympathetic chord in Barnjum's rough bosom, for his face began to twitch, and presently he burst unexpectedly into tears.

"You don't deserve it," he said between his sobs, "but be it so"; then, turning to the ghost, he added: "Here, you, what's your name? avaunt! D'ye hear hook it!"

It wavered for an instant, and then, to my joy, it suddenly "gave" all over, and, shrivelling up into a sort of cobweb, was drawn by the draught into the fire-place, and carried up the chimney, and I never saw it again.

Barnjum's escape was very simple; he had fallen upon one of the herring-boats in the lake, and the heap of freshly-caught fish lying on the deck had merely broken his fall instead of his neck. As soon as he had recovered from the effects, he was called away from this country upon urgent business, and found himself unable to return for months.

But to this day the appearance of the wraith is a mystery to me. If Barnjum had been the kind of man to be an "esoteric Buddhist," it might be accounted for as an "astral shape"; but esoteric Buddhism requires an exemplary character and years of abstract meditation – both of which conditions were far beyond Barnjum's attainment.

The shape may have been one of those subtle emanations which we are told some people are constantly shedding, like the coats of an onion, and which certain conditions of the atmosphere, and the extreme activity of Barnjum's mind under sudden excitement, possibly contributed to materialise in this particular instance.

Or, perhaps, it was merely a caprice of one of those vagrant *Poltergeists*, or supernatural buffoons, which took upon itself, very officiously, the duty of avenging my behaviour to Barnjum.

Upon one point I am clear: the whole of this system of deliberate persecution being undertaken directly on Barnjum's account, he is morally and legally bound to reimburse me for the heavy expense and damage which have resulted therefrom.

Hitherto I have been unable to impress Barnjum with this principle, and so my wrongs are still without redress.

I may be asked why I do not make them the basis of an action at law; but persons of any refinement will understand my reluctance to resort to legal proceedings against one with whom I have at least lived on a footing of friendship. I would fain persuade, and shrink from appealing to force; and, besides, I have not succeeded as yet in persuading any solicitor – even a shady one – to take up my case.

1906

THE WOOD OF THE DEAD

Algernon Blackwood

Regarded as one of the masters of supernatural fiction, Algernon Blackwood (1869–1951) lived a long and remarkable life. He was born in England, but spent time as a dairy farmer in Canada, a journalist in New York and even had spells as an artist's model and violin teacher. When Blackwood moved back to England in his thirties, he devoted himself to writing, becoming a successful author of weird tales. He would publish a number of respected collections, beginning with *The Empty House and Other Ghost Stories*, from which "The Wood of the Dead" is drawn.

Blackwood was fascinated by occult knowledge – he was a member of the Hermetic Order of the Golden Dawn and immersed himself in topics such as Rosicrucianism and Theosophy. These mystical tendencies were coupled with a love of the outdoors; like many of his protagonists, he enjoyed skiing, hiking and climbing. Indeed, an intense connection with the natural world is evident in many of Blackwood's stories, with nature having the potential for agency in ways that usually spell trouble for his characters. Stories such as "The Willows", "Ancient Lights" and "The Man Whom the Trees Loved" are particularly focused on the weirdness of woodlands, and it is perhaps unsurprising that the strange, dreamlike events of this early story are associated with such a place.

One summer, in my wanderings with a knapsack, I was at luncheon in the room of a wayside inn in the western country, when the door opened and there entered an old rustic, who crossed close to my end of the table and sat himself down very quietly in the seat by the bow window. We exchanged glances, or, properly speaking, nods, for at the moment I did not actually raise my eyes to his face, so concerned was I with the important business of satisfying an appetite gained by tramping twelve miles over a difficult country.

The fine warm rain of seven o'clock, which had since risen in a kind of luminous mist about the tree tops, now floated far overhead in a deep blue sky, and the day was settling down into a blaze of golden light. It was one of those days peculiar to Somerset and North Devon, when the orchards shine and the meadows seem to add a radiance of their own, so brilliantly soft are the colourings of grass and foliage.

The inn-keeper's daughter, a little maiden with a simple country loveliness, presently entered with a foaming pewter mug, inquired after my welfare, and went out again. Apparently she had not noticed the old man sitting in the settle by the bow window, nor had he, for his part, so much as once turned his head in our direction.

Under ordinary circumstances I should probably have given no thought to this other occupant of the room; but the fact that it was supposed to be reserved for my private use, and the singular thing that he sat looking aimlessly out of the window, with no attempt to engage me in conversation, drew my eyes more than once somewhat curiously upon him, and I soon caught myself wondering why he sat there so silently, and always with averted head.

He was, I saw, a rather bent old man in rustic dress, and the skin of his face was wrinkled like that of an apple; corduroy trousers were caught up with a string below the knee, and he wore a sort of brown fustian jacket that was very much faded. His thin hand rested upon a stoutish stick. He wore no hat and carried none, and I noticed that his head, covered with silvery hair, was finely shaped and gave the impression of something noble.

Though rather piqued by his studied disregard of my presence, I came to the conclusion that he probably had something to do with the little hostel and had a perfect right to use this room with freedom, and I finished my luncheon without breaking the silence and then took the settle opposite to smoke a pipe before going on my way.

Through the open window came the scents of the blossoming fruit trees; the orchard was drenched in sunshine and the branches danced lazily in the breeze; the grass below fairly shone with white and yellow daisies, and the red roses climbing in profusion over the casement mingled their perfume with the sweetly penetrating odour of the sea.

It was a place to dawdle in, to lie and dream away a whole afternoon, watching the sleepy butterflies and listening to the chorus of birds which seemed to fill every corner of the sky. Indeed, I was already debating in my mind whether to linger and enjoy it all instead of taking the strenuous pathway over the hills, when the old rustic in the settle opposite suddenly turned his face towards me for the first time and began to speak.

His voice had a quiet dreamy note in it that was quite in harmony with the day and the scene, but it sounded far away, I thought, almost as though it came to me from outside where the shadows were weaving their eternal tissue of dreams upon the garden floor. Moreover, there was no trace in it of the rough quality one might naturally have expected, and, now that I saw the full face of the speaker for the first time, I noted with something like a start that the deep, gentle eyes seemed far more in keeping with the timbre of the voice than with the rough and very countrified appearance of the clothes and manner. His voice set pleasant waves of sound in motion towards me, and the actual words, if I remember rightly, were –

"You are a stranger in these parts?" or "Is not this part of the country strange to you?"

There was no "sir," nor any outward and visible sign of the deference usually paid by real country folk to the town-bred visitor, but in its place a gentleness, almost a sweetness, of polite sympathy that was far more of a compliment than either.

I answered that I was wandering on foot through a part of the country that was wholly new to me, and that I was surprised not to find a place of such idyllic loveliness marked upon my map.

"I have lived here all my life," he said, with a sigh, "and am never tired of coming back to it again."

"Then you no longer live in the immediate neighbourhood?"

"I have moved," he answered briefly, adding after a pause in which his eyes seemed to wander wistfully to the wealth of blossoms beyond the window; "but I am almost sorry, for nowhere else have I found the sunshine lie so warmly, the flowers smell so sweetly, or the winds and streams make such tender music..."

His voice died away into a thin stream of sound that lost itself in the rustle of the rose-leaves climbing in at the window, for he turned his head away from me as he spoke and looked out into the garden. But it was impossible to conceal my surprise, and I raised my eyes in frank astonishment on hearing so poetic an utterance from such a figure of a man, though at the same time realising that it was not in the least inappropriate, and that, in fact, no other sort of expression could have properly been expected from him.

"I am sure you are right," I answered at length, when it was clear he had ceased speaking; "for there is something of enchantment here – of real fairy-like enchantment – that makes me think of the visions of childhood days, before one knew anything of – of – "

I had been oddly drawn into his vein of speech, some inner force compelling me. But here the spell passed and I could not catch the thoughts that had a moment before opened a long vista before my inner vision.

"To tell you the truth," I concluded lamely, "the place fascinates me and I am in two minds about going further – "

Even at this stage I remember thinking it odd that I should be talking like this with a stranger whom I met in a country inn, for it has always been one of my failings that to strangers my manner is brief to surliness. It was as though we were figures meeting in a dream, speaking without sound, obeying laws not operative in the everyday working world, and about to play with a new scale of space and time perhaps. But my astonishment passed quickly into an entirely different feeling when I became aware that the old man opposite had turned his head from the window again, and was regarding me with eyes so bright they seemed almost to shine with an inner flame. His gaze was fixed upon my face with an intense ardour, and his whole manner had suddenly become alert and concentrated. There was something about him I now felt for the first time that made little thrills of excitement run up and down my back. I met his look squarely, but with an inward tremor.

"Stay, then, a little while longer," he said in a much lower and deeper voice than before; "stay, and I will teach you something of the purpose of my coming."

He stopped abruptly. I was conscious of a decided shiver.

"You have a special purpose then – in coming back?" I asked, hardly knowing what I was saying.

"To call away someone," he went on in the same thrilling voice, "someone who is not quite ready to come, but who is needed elsewhere for a worthier purpose." There was a sadness in his manner that mystified me more than ever.

"You mean – ?" I began, with an unaccountable access of trembling.

"I have come for someone who must soon move, even as I have moved."

He looked me through and through with a dreadfully piercing gaze, but I met his eyes with a full straight stare, trembling though I was, and I was aware that something stirred within me that had never stirred before, though for the life of me I could not have put a name to it, or have analysed its nature. Something lifted and rolled away. For one single second I understood clearly that the past and the future exist actually side by side in one immense Present; that it was *I* who moved to and fro among shifting, protean appearances.

The old man dropped his eyes from my face, and the momentary glimpse of a mightier universe passed utterly away. Reason regained its sway over a dull, limited kingdom.

"Come tonight," I heard the old man say, "come to me tonight into the Wood of the Dead. Come at midnight – "

Involuntarily I clutched the arm of the settle for support, for I then felt that I was speaking with someone who knew more of the real things that are and will be, than I could ever know while in the body, working through the ordinary channels of sense – and this curious half-promise of a partial lifting of the veil had its undeniable effect upon me.

The breeze from the sea had died away outside, and the blossoms were still. A yellow butterfly floated lazily past the window. The song of the birds hushed – I smelt the sea – I smelt the perfume of heated summer air rising from fields and flowers, the ineffable scents of June and of the long days of the year – and with it, from countless green meadows beyond, came the hum of myriad summer life, children's voices, sweet pipings, and the sound of water falling.

I knew myself to be on the threshold of a new order of experience – of an ecstasy. Something drew me forth with a sense of inexpressible yearning towards the being of this strange old man in the window seat, and for a moment I knew what it was to taste a mighty and wonderful sensation, and to touch the highest pinnacle of joy I have ever known. It lasted for less than a second, and was gone; but in that brief instant of time the same terrible lucidity came to me that had already shown me how the past and future exist in the present, and I realised and understood that pleasure and pain are one and the same force, for the joy I had just experienced included also all the pain I ever had felt, or ever could feel...

The sunshine grew to dazzling radiance, faded, passed away. The shadows paused in their dance upon the grass, deepened a moment, and then melted into air. The flowers of the fruit trees laughed with their little silvery laughter as the wind sighed over their radiant eyes the old, old tale of its impersonal love. Once or twice a voice called my name. A wonderful sensation of lightness and power began to steal over me.

Suddenly the door opened and the inn-keeper's daughter came in. By all ordinary standards, her's was a charming country loveliness, born of the stars and wild-flowers, of moonlight shining through autumn mists upon the river and the fields; yet, by contrast with the higher order of beauty I had just momentarily been in touch with, she seemed almost ugly. How dull her eyes, how thin her voice, how vapid her smile, and insipid her whole presentment.

For a moment she stood between me and the occupant of the window seat while I counted out the small change for my meal and for her services; but when, an instant later, she moved aside, I saw that the settle was empty and that there was no longer anyone in the room but our two selves.

This discovery was no shock to me; indeed, I had almost expected it, and the man had gone just as a figure goes out of a dream, causing no surprise and leaving me as part and parcel of the same dream without breaking of continuity. But, as soon as I had paid my bill and thus resumed in very practical fashion the thread of my normal consciousness, I turned to the girl and asked her if she knew the old man who had been sitting in the window seat, and what he had meant by the Wood of the Dead.

The maiden started visibly, glancing quickly round the empty room, but answering simply that she had seen no one. I described him in great detail, and then, as the description grew clearer, she turned a little pale under her pretty sunburn and said very gravely that it must have been the ghost.

"Ghost! What ghost?"

"Oh, the village ghost," she said quietly, coming closer to my chair with a little nervous movement of genuine alarm, and adding in a lower voice, "He comes before a death, they say!"

It was not difficult to induce the girl to talk, and the story she told me, shorn of the superstition that had obviously gathered with the years round the memory of a strangely picturesque figure, was an interesting and peculiar one.

The inn, she said, was originally a farmhouse, occupied by a yeoman farmer, evidently of a superior, if rather eccentric, character, who had been very poor until he reached old age, when a son died suddenly in the Colonies and left him an unexpected amount of money, almost a fortune.

The old man thereupon altered no whit his simple manner of living, but devoted his income entirely to the improvement of the village and to the assistance of its inhabitants; he did this quite regardless of his personal likes and dislikes, as if one and all were absolutely alike to him, objects of a genuine and impersonal benevolence. People had always been a little afraid of the man, not understanding his eccentricities, but the simple force of this love for humanity changed all that in a very short space of time; and before he died he came to be known as the Father of the Village and was held in great love and veneration by all.

A short time before his end, however, he began to act queerly. He spent his money just as usefully and wisely, but the shock of sudden wealth after a life of poverty, people said, had unsettled his mind. He claimed to see things that others did not see, to hear voices, and to have visions. Evidently, he was not of the harmless, foolish, visionary order, but a man of character and of great personal force, for the people became divided in their opinions, and the vicar, good man, regarded and treated him as a "special case." For many, his name and atmosphere became charged almost with a spiritual influence that was not of the best. People quoted texts about him; kept when possible out of his way, and avoided his house after dark. None understood him, but though the majority loved him, an element of dread and mystery became associated with his name, chiefly owing to the ignorant gossip of the few.

A grove of pine trees behind the farm – the girl pointed them out to me on the slope of the hill – he said was the Wood of the Dead, because just before anyone died in the village he saw them walk into that wood, singing. None who went in ever came out again. He often mentioned the names to his wife, who usually published them to all the inhabitants within an hour of her husband's confidence; and it was found that the people he had seen enter the wood – died. On warm summer nights he would sometimes take an old stick and wander out, hatless, under the pines, for he loved this wood, and used to say he met all his old friends there, and would one day walk in there never to return. His wife tried to break him gently of this habit, but he always had his own way; and once, when she followed and found him standing under a great pine in the thickest portion of the grove, talking earnestly to someone she could not see, he turned and rebuked her very gently, but in such a way that she never repeated the experiment, saying –

"You should never interrupt me, Mary, when I am talking with the others; for they teach me, remember, wonderful things, and I must learn all I can before I go to join them."

This story went like wild-fire through the village, increasing with every repetition, until at length everyone was able to give an accurate description of the great veiled figures the woman declared she had seen moving among the trees where her husband stood. The innocent pine-grove now became positively haunted, and the title of "Wood of the Dead" clung naturally as if it had been applied to it in the ordinary course of events by the compilers of the Ordnance Survey.

On the evening of his ninetieth birthday the old man went up to his wife and kissed her. His manner was loving, and very gentle, and there was something about him besides, she declared afterwards, that made her slightly in awe of him and feel that he was almost more of a spirit than a man.

He kissed her tenderly on both cheeks, but his eyes seemed to look right through her as he spoke.

"Dearest wife," he said, "I am saying good-bye to you, for I am now going into the Wood of the Dead, and I shall not return. Do not follow me, or send to search, but be ready soon to come upon the same journey yourself."

The good woman burst into tears and tried to hold him, but he easily slipped from her hands, and she was afraid to follow him. Slowly she saw him cross the field in the sunshine, and then enter the cool shadows of the grove, where he disappeared from her sight.

That same night, much later, she woke to find him lying peacefully by her side in bed, with one arm stretched out towards her, *dead.* Her story was half believed, half doubted at the time, but in a very few years afterwards it evidently came to be accepted by all the countryside. A funeral service was held to which the people flocked in great numbers, and everyone approved of the sentiment which led the widow to add the words, "The Father of the Village," after the usual texts which appeared upon the stone over his grave.

This, then, was the story I pieced together of the village ghost as the little inn-keeper's daughter told it to me that afternoon in the parlour of the inn.

"But you're not the first to say you've seen him," the girl concluded; "and your description is just what we've always heard, and that window, they say, was just where he used to sit and think, and think, when he was alive, and sometimes, they say, to cry for hours together."

"And would you feel afraid if you had seen him?" I asked, for the girl seemed strangely moved and interested in the whole story.

"I think so," she answered timidly. "Surely, if he spoke to me. He did speak to *you*, didn't he, sir?" she asked after a slight pause.

"He said he had come for someone."

"Come for someone," she repeated. "Did he say – " she went on falteringly.

"No, he did not say for whom," I said quickly, noticing the sudden shadow on her face and the tremulous voice.

"Are you really sure, sir?"

"Oh, quite sure," I answered cheerfully. "I did not even ask him." The girl looked at me steadily for nearly a whole minute as though there were many things she wished to tell me or to ask. But she said nothing, and presently picked up her tray from the table and walked slowly out of the room.

Instead of keeping to my original purpose and pushing on to the next village over the hills, I ordered a room to be prepared for me at the inn, and that afternoon I spent wandering about the fields and lying under the fruit trees, watching the white clouds sailing out over the sea. The Wood of the Dead I surveyed from a distance, but in the village I visited the stone erected to the memory of the "Father of the Village" – who was thus, evidently, no mythical personage – and saw also the monuments of his fine unselfish spirit: the schoolhouse he built, the library, the home for the aged poor, and the tiny hospital.

That night, as the clock in the church tower was striking half-past eleven, I stealthily left the inn and crept through the dark orchard and over the hayfield in the direction of the hill whose southern slope was clothed with the Wood of the Dead. A genuine interest impelled me to the adventure, but I also was obliged to confess to a certain sinking in my heart as I stumbled along over the field in the darkness, for I was approaching what might prove to be the birth-place of a real country myth, and a spot already lifted by the imaginative thoughts of a considerable number of people into the region of the haunted and ill-omened.

The inn lay below me, and all round it the village clustered in a soft black shadow unrelieved by a single light. The night was moonless, yet distinctly luminous, for the stars crowded the sky. The silence of deep slumber was everywhere; so still, indeed, that every time my foot kicked against a stone I thought the sound must be heard below in the village and waken the sleepers.

I climbed the hill slowly, thinking chiefly of the strange story of the noble old man who had seized the opportunity to do good to his fellows the moment it came his way, and wondering why the causes that operate ceaselessly behind human life did not always select such admirable instruments. Once or twice a night-bird circled swiftly over my head, but the bats had long since gone to rest, and there was no other sign of life stirring.

Then, suddenly, with a singular thrill of emotion, I saw the first trees of the Wood of the Dead rise in front of me in a high black wall. Their crests stood up like giant spears against the starry sky; and though there was no perceptible movement of the air on my cheek I heard a faint, rushing sound among their branches as the night breeze passed to and fro over their countless little needles. A remote, hushed murmur rose overhead and died away again almost immediately; for in these trees the wind seems to be never absolutely at rest, and on the calmest day there is always a sort of whispering music among their branches.

For a moment I hesitated on the edge of this dark wood, and listened intently. Delicate perfumes of earth and bark stole out to meet me. Impenetrable darkness faced me. Only the consciousness that I was obeying an order, strangely given, and including a mighty privilege, enabled me to find the courage to go forward and step in boldly under the trees.

Instantly the shadows closed in upon me and "something" came forward to meet me from the centre of the darkness. It would be easy enough to meet my imagination half-way with fact, and say that a cold hand grasped my own and led me by invisible paths into the unknown depths of the grove; but at any rate, without stumbling, and always with the positive knowledge that I was going straight towards the desired object, I pressed on confidently and securely into the wood. So dark was it that, at first, not a single star-beam pierced the roof of branches overhead; and, as we moved forward side by side, the trees shifted silently past us in long lines, row upon row, squadron upon squadron, like the units of a vast, soundless army.

And, at length, we came to a comparatively open space where the trees halted upon us for a while, and, looking up, I saw the white river of the sky beginning to yield to the influence of a new light that now seemed spreading swiftly across the heavens.

"It is the dawn coming," said the voice at my side that I certainly recognised, but which seemed almost like a whispering from the trees, "and we are now in the heart of the Wood of the Dead."

We seated ourselves on a moss-covered boulder and waited the coming of the sun. With marvellous swiftness, it seemed to me, the light in the east passed into the radiance of early morning, and when the wind awoke and began to whisper in the tree tops, the first rays of the risen sun fell between the trunks and rested in a circle of gold at our feet.

"Now, come with me," whispered my companion in the same deep voice, "for time has no existence here, and that which I would show you is already *there*!"

We trod gently and silently over the soft pine needles. Already the sun was high over our heads, and the shadows of the trees coiled closely about their feet. The wood became denser again, but occasionally we passed through little open bits where we could smell the hot sunshine and the dry, baked pine needles. Then, presently, we came to the edge of the grove, and I saw a hayfield lying in the blaze of day, and two horses basking lazily with switching tails in the shafts of a laden hay-waggon.

So complete and vivid was the sense of reality, that I remember the grateful realisation of the cool shade where we sat and looked out upon the hot world beyond.

The last pitchfork had tossed up its fragrant burden, and the great horses were already straining in the shafts after the driver, as he walked slowly in front with one hand upon their bridles. He was a stalwart fellow, with sunburned neck and hands. Then, for the first time, I noticed, perched aloft upon the trembling throne of hay, the figure of a slim young girl. I could not see her face, but her brown hair escaped in disorder from a white sun-bonnet, and her still browner hands held a well-worn hay rake. She was laughing and talking with the driver, and he, from time to time, cast up at her ardent glances of admiration – glances that won instant smiles and soft blushes in response.

The cart presently turned into the roadway that skirted the edge of the wood where we were sitting. I watched the scene with intense interest, and became so much absorbed in it that I quite forgot the manifold, strange steps by which I was permitted to become a spectator.

"Come down and walk with me," cried the young fellow, stopping a moment in front of the horses and opening wide his arms. "Jump! and I'll catch you!"

"Oh, oh," she laughed, and her voice sounded to me as the happiest, merriest laughter I had ever heard from a girl's throat. "Oh, oh! that's all very well. But remember I'm Queen of the Hay, and I must ride!"

"Then I must come and ride beside you," he cried, and began at once to climb up by way of the driver's seat. But, with a peal of silvery laughter, she slipped down easily over the back of the hay to escape him, and ran a little way along the road. I could see her quite clearly, and noticed the charming, natural grace of her movements, and the loving expression in her eyes as she looked over her shoulder to make sure he was following. Evidently, she did not wish to escape for long, certainly not for ever.

In two strides the big, brown swain was after her, leaving the horses to do as they pleased. Another second and his arms would have caught the slender waist and pressed the little body to his heart. But, just at that instant, the old man beside me uttered a peculiar cry. It was low and thrilling, and it went through me like a sharp sword.

HE had called her by her own name – and she had heard.

For a second she halted, glancing back with frightened eyes. Then, with a brief cry of despair, the girl swerved aside and dived in swiftly among the shadows of the trees.

But the young man saw the sudden movement and cried out to her passionately –

"Not that way, my love! Not that way! It's the Wood of the Dead!"

She threw a laughing glance over her shoulder at him, and the wind caught her hair and drew it out in a brown cloud under the sun. But the next minute she was close beside me, lying on the breast of my companion, and I was certain I heard the words repeatedly uttered with many sighs: "Father, you called, and I have come. And I come willingly, for I am very, very tired."

At any rate, so the words sounded to me, and mingled with them I seemed to catch the answer in that deep, thrilling whisper I already knew: "And you shall sleep, my child, sleep for a long, long time, until it is time for you to begin the journey again."

In that brief second of time I had recognised the face and voice of the inn-keeper's daughter but the next minute a dreadful wail broke from the lips of the young man, and the sky grew suddenly as dark as night, the wind rose and began to toss the branches about us, and the whole scene was swallowed up in a wave of utter blackness.

Again the chill fingers seemed to seize my hand, and I was guided by the way I had come to the edge of the wood, and crossing the hayfield still slumbering in the starlight, I crept back to the inn and went to bed.

A year later I happened to be in the same part of the country, and the memory of the strange summer vision returned to me with the added softness of distance. I went to the old village and had tea under the same orchard trees at the same inn.

But the little maid of the inn did not show her face, and I took occasion to inquire of her father as to her welfare and her whereabouts.

"Married, no doubt," I laughed, but with a strange feeling that clutched at my heart.

"No, sir," replied the innkeeper sadly, "not married – though she was just going to be – but dead. She got a sunstroke in the hayfields, just a few days after you were here, if I remember rightly, and she was gone from us in less than a week."

1924

THE FACE

E. F. Benson

Edward Frederic Benson (1867–1940) was a remarkably prolific author, whose output ranged across history, biography, memoir and fiction. His series of satirical novels, *Mapp and Lucia*, was a great hit – Benson was an expert observer of the dynamics of upper-middle class social intrigue. While the popularity of *Mapp and Lucia* endures, Benson is increasingly read for his inventive ghost stories, or, as he termed them, "spook stories". His uncanny work is incredibly varied, running from humorous takes on Spiritualism ("Spinach"), to gruesome creature pieces ("Caterpillars") and atmospheric Gothic tales ("The Room in the Tower"). "The Face", first published in *Hutchinson's Magazine* in February 1924, certainly fits into the latter category. It's one of Benson's strongest stories, building its forbidding mood brilliantly.

Benson was a regular holiday visitor to East Anglia, and probably had in mind the Suffolk village of Dunwich when he wrote "The Face" (he uses the village more explicitly in another story, "The Dust Cloud"). In the thirteenth century, Dunwich was a thriving port with thousands of residents, at least six churches and all the amenities of a prosperous medieval town. However, the settlement was gradually claimed by the sea: a series of terrible storms exacerbated the slow drip of erosion, resulting in three quarters of the town having been lost by 1602.

Emblematic of Dunwich's demise was the lingering collapse of All Saints, the last of the town's original churches. All Saints fell into disrepair in the eighteenth century, and began gradually tumbling over the cliffs as the land fell away, until, by the early twentieth century, little was left. Relevant to Benson's tale are the graves from the churchyard that also succumbed to the encroaching tides. Today, one grave remains, the headstone of Jacob Forster, who died in 1796, when All Saints' fate was already sealed.

Hester Ward, sitting by the open window on this hot afternoon in June, began seriously to argue with herself about the cloud of foreboding and depression which had encompassed her all day, and, very sensibly, she enumerated to herself the manifold causes for happiness in the fortunate circumstances of her life. She was young, she was extremely good-looking, she was well-off, she enjoyed excellent health, and above all, she had an adorable husband and two small, adorable children. There was no break, indeed, anywhere in the circle of prosperity which surrounded her, and had the wishing-cap been handed to her that moment by some beneficent fairy, she would have hesitated to put it on her head, for there was positively nothing that she could think of which would have been worthy of such solemnity. Moreover, she could not accuse herself of a want of appreciation of her blessings; she appreciated enormously, she enjoyed enormously, and she thoroughly wanted all those who so munificently contributed to her happiness to share in it.

She made a very deliberate review of these things, for she was really anxious, more anxious, indeed, than she admitted to herself, to find anything tangible which could possibly warrant this ominous feeling of approaching disaster. Then there was the weather to consider; for the last week London had been stiflingly hot, but if that was the cause, why had she not felt it before? Perhaps the effect of these broiling, airless days had been cumulative. That was an idea, but, frankly, it did not seem a very good one, for, as a matter of fact, she loved the heat; Dick, who hated it, said that it was odd he should have fallen in love with a salamander.

She shifted her position, sitting up straight in this low window-seat, for she was intending to make a call on her courage. She had known from the moment she awoke this morning what it was that lay so heavy on her, and now, having done her best to shift the reason of her depression on to anything else, and having completely failed, she meant to look the thing in the face. She was ashamed of doing so, for the cause of this leaden mood of fear which held her in its grip, was so trivial, so fantastic, so excessively silly.

"Yes, there never was anything so silly," she said to herself. "I must look at it straight, and convince myself how silly it is." She paused a moment, clenching her hands.

"Now for it," she said.

She had had a dream the previous night, which, years ago, used to be familiar to her, for again and again when she was a child she had dreamed it. In itself the dream was nothing, but in those childish days, whenever she had this dream which had visited her last night, it was followed on the next night by another which contained the source and the core of the horror, and she would awake screaming and struggling in the grip of overwhelming nightmare. For some ten years now she had not experienced it, and would have said that, though she remembered it, it had become dim and distant to her. But last night she had had that warning dream, which used to herald the visitation of the nightmare, and now that whole storehouse of memory crammed as it was with bright things and beautiful contained nothing so vivid.

The warning dream, the curtain that was drawn up on the succeeding night, and disclosed the vision she dreaded, was simple and harmless enough in itself. She seemed to be walking on a high sandy cliff covered with short down-grass; twenty yards to the left came the edge of this cliff, which sloped steeply down to the sea that lay at its foot. The path she followed led through fields bounded by low hedges, and mounted gradually upwards. She went through some half-dozen of these, climbing over the wooden stiles that gave communication; sheep grazed there, but she never saw another human being, and always it was dusk, as if evening was falling, and she had to hurry on, because someone (she knew not whom) was waiting for her, and had been waiting not a few minutes only, but for many years. Presently, as she mounted this slope, she saw in front of her a copse of stunted trees, growing crookedly under the continual pressure of the wind that blew from the sea, and when she saw those she knew her journey was nearly done, and that the nameless one, who had been waiting for her so long was somewhere close at hand. The path she followed was cut through this wood, and the slanting boughs of the trees on the seaward side almost roofed it in; it was like walking through a tunnel. Soon the trees in front began to grow thin, and she saw through them the grey tower of a lonely church. It stood in a graveyard, apparently long disused, and the body of the church, which lay between the tower and the edge of the cliff, was in ruins, roofless, and with gaping windows, round which ivy grew thickly.

At that point this prefatory dream always stopped. It was a troubled, uneasy dream, for there was over it the sense of dusk and of the man who had been waiting for her so long, but it was not of the order of nightmare. Many times in childhood had she experienced it, and perhaps it was the subconscious knowledge of the night that so surely followed it, which gave it its disquiet. And now last night it had come again, identical in every particular but one. For last night it seemed to her that in the course of these ten years which had intervened since last it had visited her, the glimpse of the church and churchyard was changed. The edge of the cliff had come nearer to the tower, so that it now was within a yard or two of it, and the ruined body of the church, but for one broken arch that remained, had vanished. The sea had encroached, and for ten years had been busily eating at the cliff.

Hester knew well that it was this dream and this alone which had darkened the day for her, by reason of the nightmares that used to follow it, and, like a sensible woman, having looked it once in the face, she refused to admit into her mind any conscious calling-up of the sequel. If she let herself contemplate that, as likely or not the very thinking about it would be sufficient to ensure its return, and of one thing she was very certain, namely, that she didn't at all want it to do so. It was not like the confused jumble and jangle of ordinary nightmare, it was very simple, and she felt it concerned the nameless one who waited for her... But she must not think of it; her whole will and intention was set on not thinking of it, and to aid her resolution, there was the rattle of Dick's latchkey in the front-door, and his voice calling her.

She went out into the little square front hall; there he was, strong and large, and wonderfully undreamlike.

"This heat's a scandal, it's an outrage, it's an abomination of desolation," he cried, vigorously mopping. "What have we done that Providence should place us in this frying-pan? Let us thwart him, Hester! Let us drive out of this inferno and have our dinner at – I'll whisper it so that he shan't overhear – at Hampton Court!"

She laughed: this plan suited her excellently. They would return late, after the distraction of a fresh scene; and dining out at night was both delicious and stupefying.

"The very thing," she said, "and I'm sure Providence didn't hear. Let's start now!"

"Rather. Any letters for me?"

He walked to the table where there were a few rather uninteresting-looking envelopes with halfpenny stamps.

"Ah, receipted bill," he said. "Just a reminder of one's folly in paying it. Circular... unasked advice to invest in German marks... Circular begging letter, beginning 'Dear Sir or Madam.' Such impertinence to ask one to subscribe to something without ascertaining one's sex... Private view, portraits at the Walton Gallery... Can't go: business meetings all day. You might like to have a look in, Hester. Some one told me there were some fine Vandycks. That's all: let's be off."

Hester spent a thoroughly reassuring evening, and though she thought of telling Dick about the dream that had so deeply imprinted itself on her consciousness all day, in order to hear the great laugh he would have given her for being such a goose, she refrained from doing so, since nothing that he could say would be so tonic to these fantastic fears as his general robustness. Besides, she would have to account for its disturbing effect, tell him that it was once familiar to her, and recount the sequel of the nightmares that followed. She would neither think of them, nor mention them: it was wiser by far just to soak herself in his extraordinary sanity, and wrap herself in his affection... They dined out-of-doors at a riverside restaurant and strolled about afterwards, and it was very nearly midnight when, soothed with coolness and fresh air, and the vigour of his strong companionship, she let herself into the house, while he took the car back to the garage. And now she marvelled at the mood which had beset her all day, so distant and unreal had it become. She felt as if she had dreamed of shipwreck, and had awoke to find herself in some secure and sheltered garden where no tempest raged nor waves beat. But was there, ever so remotely, ever so dimly, the noise of far-off breakers somewhere?

He slept in the dressing-room which communicated with her bedroom, the door of which was left open for the sake of air and coolness, and she fell asleep almost as soon as her light was out, and while his was still burning. And immediately she began to dream.

She was standing on the sea-shore; the tide was out, for level sands strewn with stranded jetsam glimmered in a dusk that was deepening into night. Though she had never seen the place it was awfully familiar to her. At the head of the beach there was a steep cliff of sand, and perched on the edge of it was a grey church tower. The sea must have encroached and undermined the body of the church, for tumbled blocks of masonry lay close to her at the bottom of the cliff, and there were gravestones there, while others still in place were silhouetted whitely against the sky. To the right of the church tower there was a wood of stunted trees, combed sideways by the prevalent sea-wind, and she knew that along the top of the cliff a few yards inland there lay a path through fields, with wooden stiles to climb, which led through a tunnel of trees and so out into the churchyard. All this she saw in a glance, and waited, looking at the sand-cliff crowned by the church tower, for the terror that was going to reveal itself. Already she knew what it was, and, as so many times before, she tried to run away. But the catalepsy of nightmare was already on her; frantically she strove to move, but her utmost endeavour could not raise a foot from the sand. Frantically she tried to look away from the sand-cliffs close in front of her, where in a moment now the horror would be manifested...

It came. There formed a pale oval light, the size of a man's face, dimly luminous in front of her and a few inches above the level of her eyes. It outlined itself, short reddish hair grew low on the forehead, below were two grey eyes, set very close together, which steadily and fixedly regarded her. On each side the ears stood noticeably away from the head, and the lines of the jaw met in a short pointed chin. The nose was straight and rather long, below it came a hairless lip, and last of all the mouth took shape and colour, and there lay the crowning terror. One side of it, soft-curved and beautiful, trembled into a smile, the other side, thick and gathered together as by some physical deformity, sneered and lusted.

The whole face, dim at first, gradually focused itself into clear outline: it was pale and rather lean, the face of a young man. And then the lower lip dropped a little, showing the glint of teeth, and there was the sound of speech. "I shall soon come for you now," it said, and on the words it drew a little nearer to her, and the smile broadened. At that the full hot blast of nightmare poured in upon her. Again she tried to run, again she tried to scream, and now she could feel the breath of that terrible mouth upon her. Then with a crash and a rending like the tearing asunder of soul and body she broke the spell, and heard her own voice yelling, and felt with her fingers for the switch of her light. And then she saw that the room was not dark, for Dick's door was open, and the next moment, not yet undressed, he was with her.

"My darling, what is it?" he said. "What's the matter?"

She clung desperately to him, still distraught with terror.

"Ah, he has been here again," she cried. "He says he will soon come to me. Keep him away, Dick."

For one moment her fear infected him, and he found himself glancing round the room.

"But what do you mean?" he said. "No one has been here."

She raised her head from his shoulder.

"No, it was just a dream," she said. "But it was the old dream, and I was terrified. Why, you've not undressed yet. What time is it?"

"You haven't been in bed ten minutes, dear," he said. "You had hardly put out your light when I heard you screaming."

She shuddered.

"Ah, it's awful," she said. "And he will come again..."

He sat down by her.

"Now tell me all about it," he said.

She shook her head.

"No, it will never do to talk about it," she said, "it will only make it more real. I suppose the children are all right, are they?"

"Of course they are. I looked in on my way upstairs."

"That's good. But I'm better now, Dick. A dream hasn't anything real about it, has it? It doesn't mean anything?"

He was quite reassuring on this point, and soon she quieted down. Before he went to bed he looked in again on her, and she was asleep.

Hester had a stern interview with herself when Dick had gone down to his office next morning. She told herself that what she was afraid of was nothing more than her own fear. How many times had that ill-omened face come to her in dreams, and what significance had it ever proved to possess? Absolutely none at all, except to make her afraid. She was afraid where no fear was: she was guarded, sheltered, prosperous, and what if a nightmare of childhood returned? It had no more meaning now than it had then, and all those visitations of her childhood had passed away without trace... And then, despite herself, she began thinking over that vision again. It was grimly identical with all its previous occurrences, except... And then, with a sudden shrinking of the heart, she remembered that in earlier years those terrible lips had said: "I shall come for you when you are older," and last night they had said: "I shall soon come for you now." She remembered, too, that in the warning dream the sea had encroached, and it had now demolished the body of the church. There was an awful consistency about these two changes in the otherwise identical visions. The years had brought their change to them, for in the one the encroaching sea had brought down the body of the church, in the other the time was now near...

It was no use to scold or reprimand herself, for to bring her mind to the contemplation of the vision meant merely that the grip of terror closed on her again; it was far wiser to occupy herself, and starve her fear out by refusing to bring it the sustenance of thought. So she went about her household duties, she took the children out for their airing in the park, and then, determined to leave no moment unoccupied, set off with the card of invitation to see the pictures in the private view at the Walton Gallery. After that her day was full enough, she was lunching out, and going on to a matinée, and by the time she got home Dick would have returned, and they would drive down to his little house at Rye for the weekend. All Saturday and Sunday she would be playing golf, and she felt that fresh air and physical fatigue would exorcise the dread of these dreaming fantasies.

The gallery was crowded when she got there; there were friends among the sightseers, and the inspection of the pictures was diversified by cheerful conversation. There were two or three fine Raeburns, a couple of Sir Joshuas, but the gems, so she gathered, were three Vandycks that hung in a small room by themselves. Presently she strolled in there, looking at her catalogue. The first of them, she saw, was a portrait of Sir Roger Wyburn. Still chatting to her friend she raised her eye and saw it...

Her heart hammered in her throat, and then seemed to stand still altogether. A qualm, as of some mental sickness of the soul overcame her, for there in front of her was he who would soon come for her. There was the reddish hair, the projecting ears, the greedy eyes set close together, and the mouth smiling on one side, and on the other gathered up into the sneering menace that she knew so well. It might have been her own nightmare rather than a living model which had sat to the painter for that face.

"Ah, what a portrait, and what a brute!" said her companion. "Look, Hester, isn't that marvellous?"

She recovered herself with an effort. To give way to this ever-mastering dread would have been to allow nightmare to invade her waking life, and there, for sure, madness lay. She forced herself to look at it again, but there were the steady and eager eyes regarding her; she could almost fancy the mouth began to move. All round her the crowd bustled and chattered, but to her own sense she was alone there with Roger Wyburn.

And yet, so she reasoned with herself, this picture of him – for it was he and no other – should have reassured her. Roger Wyburn, to have been painted by Vandyck, must have been dead near on two hundred years; how could he be a menace to her? Had she seen that portrait by some chance as a child; had it made some dreadful impression on her, since overscored by other memories, but still alive in the mysterious subconsciousness, which flows eternally, like some dark underground river, beneath the surface of human life? Psychologists taught that these early impressions fester or poison the mind like some hidden abscess. That might account for this dread of one, nameless no longer, who waited for her.

That night down at Rye there came again to her the prefatory dream, followed by the nightmare, and clinging to her husband as the terror began to subside, she told him what she had resolved to keep to herself. Just to tell it brought a measure of comfort, for it was so outrageously fantastic, and his robust common sense upheld her. But when on their return to London there was a recurrence of these visions, he made short work of her demur and took her straight to her doctor.

"Tell him all, darling," he said. "Unless you promise to do that, I will. I can't have you worried like this. It's all nonsense, you know, and doctors are wonderful people for curing nonsense."

She turned to him.

"Dick, you're frightened," she said quietly.

He laughed.

"I'm nothing of the kind," he said, "but I don't like being awakened by your screaming. Not my idea of a peaceful night. Here we are."

The medical report was decisive and peremptory. There was nothing whatever to be alarmed about; in brain and body she was perfectly healthy, but she was run down. These disturbing dreams were, as likely as not, an effect, a symptom of her condition, rather than the cause of it, and Dr Baring unhesitatingly recommended a complete change to some bracing place. The wise thing would be to send her out of this stuffy furnace to some quiet place to where she had never been. Complete change; quite so. For the same reason her husband had better not go with her; he must pack her off to, let us say, the East coast. Sea-air and coolness and complete idleness. No long walks; no long bathings; a dip, and a deck-chair on the sands. A lazy, soporific life. How about Rushton? He had no doubt that Rushton would set her up again. After a week or so, perhaps, her husband might go down and see her. Plenty of sleep – never mind the nightmares – plenty of fresh air.

Hester, rather to her husband's surprise, fell in with this suggestion at once, and the following evening saw her installed in solitude and tranquillity. The little hotel was still almost empty, for the rush of summer tourists had not yet begun, and all day she sat out on the beach with the sense of a struggle over. She need not fight the terror any more; dimly it seemed to her that its malignancy had been relaxed. Had she in some way yielded to it and done its secret bidding? At any rate no return of its nightly visitations had occurred, and she slept long and dreamlessly, and woke to another day of quiet. Every morning there was a line for her from Dick, with good news of himself and the children, but he and they alike seemed somehow remote, like memories of a very distant time. Something had driven in between her and them, and she saw them as if through glass. But equally did the memory of the face of Roger Wyburn, as seen on the master's canvas or hanging close in front of her against the crumbling sand-cliff, become blurred and indistinct, and no return of her nightly terrors visited her. This truce from all emotion reacted not on her mind alone, lulling her with a sense of soothed security, but on her body also, and she began to weary of this day-long inactivity.

The village lay on the lip of a stretch of land reclaimed from the sea. To the north the level marsh, now beginning to glow with the pale bloom of the sea-lavender, stretched away featureless till it lost itself in distance, but to the south a spur of hill came down to the shore ending in a wooded promontory. Gradually, as her physical health increased, she began to wonder what lay beyond this ridge which cut short the view, and one afternoon she walked across the intervening level and strolled up its wooded slopes. The day was close and windless, the invigorating sea-breeze which till now had spiced the heat with freshness had died, and she looked forward to finding a current of air stirring when she had topped the hill. To the south a mass of dark cloud lay along the horizon, but there was no imminent threat of storm. The slope was easily surmounted, and presently she stood at the top and found herself on the edge of a tableland of wooded pasture, and following the path, which ran not far from the edge of the cliff, she came out into more open country. Empty fields, where a few sheep were grazing, mounted gradually upwards. Wooden stiles made a communication in the hedges that bounded them. And there, not a mile in front of her, she saw a wood, with trees growing slantingly away from the push of the prevalent sea winds, crowning the upward slope, and over the top of it peered a grey church tower.

For the moment, as the awful and familiar scene identified itself, Hester's heart stood still: the next a wave of courage and resolution poured in upon her. Here, at last was the scene of that prefatory dream, and here was she presented with the opportunity of fathoming and dispelling it. Instantly her mind was made up, and under the strange twilight of the shrouded sky, she walked swiftly on through the fields she had so often traversed in sleep, and up to the wood, beyond which he was waiting for her. She closed her ears against the clanging bell of terror, which now she could silence for ever, and unfalteringly entered that dark tunnel of wood. Soon in front of her the trees began to thin, and through them, now close at hand, she saw the church tower. In a few yards farther she came out of the belt of trees, and round her were the monuments of a graveyard long disused. The cliff was broken off close to the church tower: between it and the edge there was no more of the body of the church than a broken arch, thick hung with ivy. Round this she passed and saw below the ruin of fallen masonry, and the level sands strewn with headstones and disjected rubble, and at the edge of the cliff were graves already cracked and toppling. But there was no one here, none waited for her, and the churchyard where she had so often pictured him was as empty as the fields she had just traversed.

A huge elation filled her; her courage had been rewarded, and all the terrors of the past became to her meaningless phantoms. But there was no time to linger, for now the storm threatened, and on the horizon a blink of lightning was followed by a crackling peal. Just as she turned to go her eye fell on a tombstone that was balanced on the very edge of the cliff, and she read on it that here lay the body of Roger Wyburn.

Fear, the catalepsy of nightmare, rooted her for the moment to the spot; she stared in stricken amazement at the moss-grown letters; almost she expected to see that fell terror of a face rise and hover over his resting-place. Then the fear which had frozen her lent her wings, and with hurrying feet she sped through the arched pathway in the wood and out into the fields. Not one backward glance did she give till she had come to the edge of the ridge above the village, and, turning, saw the pastures she had traversed empty of any living presence. None had followed; but the sheep, apprehensive of the coming storm, had ceased to feed, and were huddling under shelter of the stunted hedges.

Her first idea, in the panic of her mind, was to leave the place at once, but the last train for London had left an hour before, and besides, where was the use of flight if it was the spirit of a man long dead from which she fled? The distance from the place where his bones lay did not afford her safety; that must be sought for within. But she longed for Dick's sheltering and confident presence; he was arriving in any case tomorrow, but there were long dark hours before tomorrow, and who could say what the perils and dangers of the coming night might be? If he started this evening instead of tomorrow morning, he could motor down here in four hours, and would be with her by ten o'clock or eleven. She wrote an urgent telegram: "Come at once," she said. "Don't delay."

The storm which had flickered on the south now came quickly up, and soon after it burst in appalling violence. For preface there were but a few large drops that splashed and dried on the roadway as she came back from the post-office, and just as she reached the hotel again the roar of the approaching rain sounded, and the sluices of heaven were opened. Through the deluge flared the fire of the lightning, the thunder crashed and echoed overhead, and presently the street of the village was a torrent of sandy turbulent water, and sitting there in the dark one picture leapt floating before her eyes, that of the tombstone of Roger Wyburn, already tottering to its fall at the edge of the cliff of the church tower. In such rains as these, acres of the cliffs were loosened; she seemed to hear the whisper of the sliding sand that would precipitate those perished sepulchres and what lay within to the beach below.

By eight o'clock the storm was subsiding, and as she dined she was handed a telegram from Dick, saying that he had already started and sent this off *en route*. By half-past ten, therefore, if all was well, he would be here, and somehow he would stand between her and her fear. Strange how a few days ago both it and the thought of him had become distant and dim to her; now the one was as vivid as the other, and she counted the minutes to his arrival. Soon the rain ceased altogether, and looking out of the curtained window of her sitting-room where she sat watching the slow circle of the hands of the clock, she saw a tawny moon rising over the sea. Before it had climbed to the zenith, before her clock had twice told the hour again, Dick would be with her.

It had just struck ten when there came a knock at her door, and the page-boy entered with the message that a gentleman had come for her. Her heart leaped at the news; she had not expected Dick for half an hour yet, and now the lonely vigil was over. She ran downstairs, and there was the figure standing on the step outside. His face was turned away from her; no doubt he was giving some order to his chauffeur. He was outlined against the white moonlight, and in contrast with that, the gas-jet in the entrance just above his head gave his hair a warm, reddish tinge.

She ran across the hall to him.

"Ah, my darling, you've come," she said. "It was good of you. How quick you've been!" Just as she laid her hand on his shoulder he turned. His arm was thrown out round her, and she looked into a face with eyes close set, and a mouth smiling on one side, the other, thick and gathered together as by some physical deformity, sneered and lusted.

The nightmare was on her; she could neither run nor scream, and supporting her dragging steps, he went forth with her into the night.

Half an hour later Dick arrived. To his amazement he heard that a man had called for his wife not long before, and that she had gone out with him. He seemed to be a stranger here, for the boy who had taken his message to her had never seen him before, and presently surprise began to deepen into alarm; enquiries were made outside the hotel, and it appeared that a witness or two had seen the lady whom they knew to be staying there walking, hatless, along the top of the beach with a man whose arm was linked in hers. Neither of them knew him, but one had seen his face and could describe it.

The direction of the search thus became narrowed down, and though with a lantern to supplement the moonlight they came upon footprints which might have been hers, there were no marks of any who walked beside her. But they followed these until they came to an end, a mile away, in a great landslide of sand, which had fallen from the old churchyard on the cliff, and had brought down with it half the tower and a gravestone, with the body that had lain below.

The gravestone was that of Roger Wyburn, and his body lay by it, untouched by corruption or decay, though two hundred years had elapsed since it was interred there. For a week afterwards the work of searching the landslide went on, assisted by the high tides that gradually washed it away. But no further discovery was made.

1926

ALL HALLOWS

Walter de la Mare

Often remembered for his poetry and stories for children, Walter de la Mare (1873–1956) was also a master of the supernatural tale. As such, he was one of H. P. Lovecraft's favourite writers, and "All Hallows" certainly contains something of Lovecraft's unknowable, numinous dread.

After a long day on a coastal path, a rambler arrives at his intended destination, an immense, ancient cathedral close to the sea. He is keen to be off the dusty trail and out of the heat of a late summer's afternoon. However, the traveller soon discovers that there is something distinctly unsettling about this remote church. "All Hallows" is a masterpiece of suggestion, de la Mare carefully building a sense of a place besieged by sinister forces, a place where, as the old verger states, "there are devilish agencies at work".

De la Mare was apparently inspired to write "All Hallows" when he came across a striking description of St David's Cathedral in Pembrokeshire, on Wales' western edge. In Theresa Whistler's biography of de la Mare, *Imagination of the Heart,* she explains that the story "sprang from a sentence in a guide book describing the siting of St David's Cathedral, by the sea. From this phrase or two, he had spun a richly decorative tale, in which the Cathedral is the central character." The real church is not directly on the coast, but the Wales Coast Path runs close to St David's, and many fine walks can be plotted in the area around the UK's smallest cathedral city.

"And because time in itself... can receive no alteration, the hallowing... must consist in the shape or countenance which we put upon the affaires that are incident in these days."

RICHARD HOOKER.

It was about half-past three on an August afternoon when I found myself for the first time looking down upon All Hallows, And at first glimpse of it, every vestige of fatigue and vexation passed away. I stood "at gaze," as the old phrase goes – like the two children of Israel sent in to spy out the Promised Land. How often the imagined transcends the real. Not so All Hallows. Having at last reached the end of my journey – flies, dust, heat, wind – having at last come limping out upon the green sea-bluff beneath which lay its walls – I confess the actuality excelled my feeble dreams of it.

What most astonished me, perhaps, was the sense not so much of its age, its austerity, or even its solitude, but its air of abandonment. It lay couched there as if in its narrow sea-bay. Not a sound was in the air; not a jackdaw clapped its wings among its turrets. No other roof, not even a chimney, was in sight; only the dark-blue arch of the sky; the narrow snowline of the ebbing tide; and that gaunt coast fading away into the haze of a West over which were already gathering the veils of sunset.

We had met then, at an appropriate hour and season. And yet – I wonder. For it was certainly not the "beauty" of All Hallows, lulled as if into a dream in this serenity of air and heavens, which was to leave the sharpest impression upon me. And what kind of first showing would it have made, I speculated, if an autumnal gale had been shrilling and trumpeting across its narrow bay – clots of wind-borne spume floating among its dusky pinnacles – and the roar of the sea echoing against its walls! Imagine it frozen stark in winter, icy hoar-frost edging its every boss, moulding, finial, crocket, cusp!

Indeed, are there not works of man, legacies of a half-forgotten past, scattered across this human world of ours from China to Peru which seem to daunt the imagination with their incomprehensibility? Incomprehensible, I mean, in the sense that the passion that inspired and conceived them is incomprehensible. Viewed in the light of the passing day, they might be the monuments of a race of demi-gods. And yet, if we could but free ourselves from our timidities, realise, that even we ourselves have an obligation to leave behind us similar memorials – testaments to the creative and faithful genius not so much of the individual as of Humanity itself.

However that may be, it was my own personal fortune to see All Hallows for the first time in the heat of the Dog Days, after a journey which could hardly be justified except by its end. At this moment of the afternoon the great church almost cheated one into the belief that it was possessed of a life of its own. It lay, as I say, couched in its natural hollow, basking under the dark dome of the heavens like some half-fossilised monster that might at any moment stir and awaken out of the swoon to which the wand of the enchanter had committed it. And with every inch of the sun's descending journey it changed its appearance.

That is the charm of such things. Man himself, says the philosopher, is the sport of change. His life and the life around him are but the flotsam of a perpetual flux. Yet, haunted by ideals, egged on by impossibilities, he builds his vision of the changeless; and time diversifies it with its colours and its "effects" at leisure. It was drawing near to harvest now; the summer was nearly over; the corn would soon be in stook; the season of silence had come, not even the robins had yet begun to practise their autumnal lament. I should have come earlier.

The distance was of little account. But nine flinty hills in seven miles is certainly hard commons. To plod (the occupant of a cloud of dust) up one steep incline and so see another; to plod up that and so see a third; to surmount that and, half-choked, half-roasted, to see (as if in unbelievable mirage) a fourth – and always stone walls, discoloured grass, no flower but ragged ragwort, whited fleabane, moody nettle, and the exquisite stubborn bindweed with its almond-burdened censers, and always the glitter and dazzle of the sun – well, the experience grows irksome. And then that endless flint erection with which some jealous Lord of the Manor had barricaded his verdurous estate! A fly-infested mile of the company of that wall was tantamount to making one's way into the infernal regions – with Tantalus for fellow-pilgrim. And when a solitary and empty dung-wagon had lumbered by, lifting the dumb dust out of the road in swirling clouds into the heat-quivering air, I had all but wept aloud.

No, I shall not easily forget that walk – or the conclusion of it – when footsore, all but dead beat – dust all over me, cheeks, lips, eyelids, in my hair, dust in drifts even between my naked body and my clothes – I stretched my aching limbs on the turf under the straggle of trees which crowned the bluff of that last hill still blessedly green and verdant, and feasted my eyes on the cathedral beneath me. How odd Memory is – in her sorting arrangements. How perverse her pigeon-holes.

It had reminded me of a drizzling evening many years ago. I had stayed a moment to listen to an old Salvation Army officer preaching at a street corner. The sopped and squalid houses echoed with his harangue. His penitents' drum resembled the block of an executioner. His goatish beard wagged at every word he uttered. "My brothers and sisters," he was saying, "the very instant our fleshly bodies are born they begin to perish; the moment the Lord has put them together, time begins to take them to pieces again. *Now* at this very instant if you listen close, you can hear the nibblings and frettings of the moth and rust within – the worm that never dies. It's the same with human causes and creeds and institutions – just the same. O then for that Strand of Beauty where all that is mortal shall be shed away and we shall appear in the likeness and verisimilitude of what in sober and awful truth we are."

The light striking out of an oil and colourman's shop at the street corner lay across his cheek and beard and glassed his eye. The soaked circle of humanity in which he was gesticulating stood staring and motionless – the lassies, the probationers, the melancholy idlers. I had had enough. I went away. But it is odd that so utterly inappropriate a recollection should have edged back into my mind at this moment. There was, as I have said, not a living soul in sight. Only a few sea-birds – oyster catchers maybe – were jangling on the distant beach.

It was now a quarter to four by my watch, and the usual pensive "lin-lan-lone" from the belfry beneath me would soon no doubt be ringing to evensong. But if at that moment a triple bob-major had suddenly clanged its alarm over sea and shore, I couldn't have stirred a finger's breadth. Scanty though the shade afforded by the wind-shorn tuft of trees under which I lay might be – I was ineffably at peace.

No bell, as a matter of fact, loosed its tongue that stagnant half-hour. Unless then the walls beneath me already concealed a few such chance visitors as myself, All Hallows would be empty. A cathedral not only without a close but without a congregation – yet another romantic charm. The Deanery and the residences of its clergy, my old guidebook had long since informed me, were a full mile or more away. I determined in due time, first to make sure of an entry, and then having quenched my thirst, to bathe.

How inhuman any extremity – hunger, fatigue, pain, desire – makes us poor humans. Thirst and drought so haunted my mind that again and again as I glanced towards it I supped up at one long draught that complete blue sea. But meanwhile, too, my eyes had been steadily exploring and searching out this monument of the bygone centuries beneath me.

The headland faced approximately due west. The windows of the Lady Chapel therefore lay immediately beneath me, their fourteenth-century glass showing flatly dark amid their traceries. Above it, the shallow V-shaped, leaden-ribbed roof of the chancel converged towards the unfinished tower, then broke away at right angles – for the cathedral was cruciform. Walls so ancient and so sparsely adorned and decorated could not but be inhospitable in effect. Their stone was of a bleached bone-grey; a grey that none the less seemed to be as immaterial as flame – or incandescent ash. They were substantial enough, however, to cast a marvellously lucent shadow, of a blue no less vivid but paler than that of the sea, on the shelving sward beneath them. And that shadow was steadily shifting as I watched. But even if the complete edifice had vanished into the void, the scene would still have been of an incredible loveliness. The colours in air and sky on this dangerous coast seemed to shed a peculiar unreality even on the rocks of its own outworks.

So, from my vantage place on the hill that dominates it, I continued for a while to watch All Hallows; to spy upon it; and no less intently than a sentry who, not quite trusting his own eyes, has seen a dubious shape approaching him in the dusk. It may sound absurd, but I felt that at any moment I too might surprise All Hallows in the act of revealing what in very truth it looked like – and *was,* when no human witness was there to share its solitude.

Those gigantic statues, for example, which flanked the base of the unfinished tower – an intense bluish-white in the sunlight and a bluish-purple in shadow – images of angels and of saints, as I had learned of old from my guidebook. Only six of them at most could be visible, of course, from where I sat. And yet I found myself counting them again and yet again, as if doubting my own arithmetic. For my first impression had been that seven were in view – though the figure furthest from me at the western angle showed little more than a jutting fragment of stone which might perhaps be only part and parcel of the fabric itself.

But then the lights even of day may be deceitful, and fantasy plays strange tricks with one's eyes. With exercise, none the less, the mind is enabled to detect minute details which the unaided eye is incapable of particularising. Given the imagination, man himself indeed may some day be able to distinguish what shapes are walking during our own terrestrial midnight amid the black shadows of the craters in the noonday of the moon. At any rate, I could trace at last frets of carving, minute weather marks, crookednesses, incrustations, repairings, that had before passed unnoticed. These walls, indeed, like human faces, were maps and charts of their own long past.

In the midst of this prolonged scrutiny, the hypnotic air, the heat, must suddenly have overcome me. I fell asleep up there in my grove's scanty shade; and remained asleep, too, long enough (as time is measured by the clocks of sleep), to dream an immense panoramic dream. On waking, I could recall only the faintest vestiges of it, and found that the hand of my watch had crept on but a few minutes in the interval. It was eight minutes past four.

I scrambled up – numbed and inert – with that peculiar sense of panic which sometimes follows an uneasy sleep. What folly to have been frittering time away within sight of my goal at an hour when no doubt the cathedral would soon be closed to visitors, and abandoned for the night to its own secret ruminations. I hastened down the steep rounded incline of the hill, and having skirted under the sunlit expanse of the walls, came presently to the south door, only to discover that my forebodings had been justified, and that it was already barred and bolted. The discovery seemed to increase my fatigue fourfold. How foolish it is to obey mere caprices. What a straw is a man!

I glanced up into the beautiful shell of masonry above my head. Shapes and figures in stone it showed in plenty – symbols of an imagination that had flamed and faded, leaving this signature for sole witness – but not a living bird or butterfly. There was but one faint chance left of making an entry. Hunted now, rather than the hunter, I hastened out again into the full blazing flood of sunshine – and once more came within sight of the sea; a sea so near at last that I could hear its enormous sallies and murmurings. Indeed I had not realised until that moment how closely the great western doors of the cathedral abutted on the beach.

It was as if its hospitality had been deliberately designed, not for a people to whom the faith of which it was the shrine had become a weariness and a commonplace, but for the solace of pilgrims from over the ocean. I could see them tumbling into their cockle-boats out of their great hollow ships – sails idle, anchors down; see them leaping ashore and straggling up across the sands to these all-welcoming portals – "Parthians and Medes and Elamites; dwellers in Mesopotamia and in the parts of Egypt about Cyrene; strangers of Rome, Jews and Proselytes – we do hear them speak in our own tongue the wonderful works of God."

And so at last I found my way into All Hallows – entering by a rounded dwarfish side-door with zigzag mouldings. There hung for corbel to its dripstone a curious leering face, with its forked tongue out, to give me welcome. And an appropriate one, too, for the figure I made!

But once beneath that prodigious roof-tree, I forgot myself and everything that was mine. The hush, the coolness, the unfathomable twilight drifted in on my small human consciousness. Not even the ocean itself is able so completely to receive one into its solacing bosom. Except for the windows over my head, filtering with their stained glass the last western radiance of the sun, there was but little visible colour in those great spaces, and a severe economy of decoration. The stone piers carried their round arches with an almost intimidating impassivity.

By deliberate design, too, or by some illusion of perspective, the whole floor of the building appeared steadily to ascend towards the east, where a dark wooden multitudinously-figured rood-screen shut off the choir and the high altar from the nave. I seemed to have exchanged one universal actuality for another: the burning world of nature, for this oasis of quiet. Here, the wings of the imagination need never rest in their flight out of the wilderness into the unknown.

Thus resting, I must again have fallen asleep. And so swiftly can even the merest freshet of sleep affect the mind, that when my eyes opened, I was completely at a loss.

Where was I? What demon of what romantic chasm had swept my poor drowsy body into this immense haunt? The din and clamour of an horrific dream whose fainting rumour was still in my ear, became suddenly stilled. Then at one and the same moment, a sense of utter dismay at earthly surroundings no longer serene and peaceful, but grim and forbidding, flooded my mind, and I became aware that I was no longer alone. Twenty or thirty paces away, and a little this side of the rood-screen, an old man was standing.

To judge from the black and purple velvet and tassel-tagged gown he wore, he was a verger. He had not yet realised, it seemed, that a visitor shared his solitude. And yet he was listening. His head was craned forward and leaned sideways on his rusty shoulders. As I steadily watched him, he raised his eyes, and with a peculiar stealthy deliberation scanned the complete upper regions of the northern transept. Not the faintest rumour of any sound that may have attracted his attention reached me where I sat. Maybe a wild bird had made its entry through a broken pane of glass and with its cry had at the same moment awakened me and caught his attention. Or maybe the old man was waiting for some fellow-occupant to join him from above.

I continued to watch him. Even at this distance, the silvery twilight cast by the clerestory windows was sufficient to show me, though vaguely, his face: the high sloping nose, the lean cheekbones and protruding chin. He continued so long in the same position that I at last determined to break in on his reverie.

At sound of my footsteps his head sunk cautiously back upon his shoulders; and he turned; and then motionlessly surveyed me as I drew near. He resembled one of those old men whom Rembrandt delighted in drawing: the knotted hands, the blank drooping eyebrows, the wide thin-lipped ecclesiastical mouth, the intent cavernous dark eyes beneath the heavy folds of their lids. White as a miller with dust, hot and draggled, I was hardly the kind of visitor that any self-respecting custodian would warmly welcome, but he greeted me none the less with every mark of courtesy.

I apologised for the lateness of my arrival, and explained it as best I could. "Until I caught sight of you," I concluded lamely, "I hadn't ventured very far in: otherwise I might have found myself a prisoner for the night. It must be dark in here when there is no moon."

The old man smiled – but wryly. "As a matter of fact, sir," he replied, "the cathedral is closed to visitors at four – at such times, that is, when there is no afternoon service. Services are not as frequent as they were. But visitors are rare too. In winter, in particular, you notice the gloom – as you say, sir. Not that I ever spend the night here: though I am usually last to leave. There's the risk of fire to be thought of and... I think I should have detected your presence here, sir. One becomes accustomed after many years."

There was the usual trace of official pedantry in his voice, but it was more pleasing than otherwise. Nor did he show any wish to be rid of me. He continued his survey, although his eye was a little absent and his attention seemed to be divided.

"I thought perhaps I might be able to find a room for the night and really explore the cathedral tomorrow morning. It has been a tiring journey; I come from B——"

"Ah, from B——; it *is* a fatiguing journey, sir, taken on foot. I used to walk in there to see a sick daughter of mine. Carriage parties occasionally make their way here, but not so much as once. We are too far out of the hurly-burly to be much intruded on. Not that them who come to make their worship here are intruders. Far from it. But most that come are mere sightseers. And the fewer of them, I say, in the circumstances, the better."

Something in what I had said or in my appearance seemed to have reassured him. "Well, I cannot claim to be a regular churchgoer," I said. "I am myself a mere sightseer. And yet – even to sit here for a few minutes is to be reconciled."

"Ah, reconciled, sir," the old man repeated, turning away. "I can well imagine it after that journey on such a day as this. But to live here is another matter."

"I was thinking of that," I replied in a foolish attempt to retrieve the position. "It must, as you say, be desolate enough in the winter – for two-thirds of the year, indeed."

"We have our storms, sir – the bad with the good," he agreed, "and our position is specially prolific of what they call sea-fog. It comes driving in from the sea for days and nights together – gale and mist, so that you can scarcely see your open hand in front of your eyes even in broad daylight. And the noise of it, sir, sweeping across overhead in that wooliness of mist, if you take me, is most peculiar. It's shocking to a stranger. No, sir, we are left pretty much to ourselves when the fine weather birds are flown... You'd be astonished at the power of the winds here. There was a mason – a local man too – not above two or three years ago was blown clean off the roof from under the tower – tossed up in the air like an empty sack. But" – and the old man at last allowed his eyes to stray upwards to the roof again – "but there's not much doing now." He seemed to be pondering. "Nothing open."

"I mustn't detain you," I said, "but you were saying that services are infrequent now. Why is that? When one thinks of – " But tact restrained me.

"Pray don't think of keeping me, sir. It's a part of my duties. But from a remark you let fall I was supposing you may have seen something that appeared, I understand, not many months ago in the newspapers. We lost our Dean – Dean Pomfrey – last November. To all intents and purposes, I mean; and his office has not yet been filled. Between you and me, sir, there's a hitch – though I should wish it to go no further. They are greedy monsters – those newspapers: no respect, no discretion, no decency, in my view. And they copy each other like cats in a chorus.

"We have never wanted to be a notoriety here, sir: and not of late things of all times. We must face our own troubles. You'd be astonished how callous the mere sightseer can be. And not only them from over the water whom our particular troubles cannot concern – but far worse – parties as English as you or me. They ask you questions you wouldn't believe possible in a civilised country. Not that they care what becomes of us – not one iota, sir. We talk of them masked-up Inquisitors in olden times, but there's many a human being in our own would enjoy seeing a fellow-creature on the rack if he could get the opportunity. It's a heartless age, sir."

This was queerish talk in the circumstances: and after all I myself was of the glorious company of the sightseers. I held my peace. And the old man, as if to make amends, asked me if I would care to see any particular part of the building. "The light is smalling," he explained, "but still if we keep to the ground level there'll be a few minutes to spare; and we shall not be interrupted if we go quietly on our way."

For the moment the reference eluded me: I could only thank him for the suggestion and once more beg him not to put himself to any inconvenience. I explained, too, that though I had no personal acquaintance with Dr Pomfrey, I had read of his illness in the newspapers. "Isn't he," I added a little dubiously, "the author of *The Church and the Folk*? If so, he must be an exceedingly learned and delightful man."

"Ay, sir." The old verger put up a hand towards me; "you may well say it: a saint, if ever there was one. But it's worse than illness, sir – it's oblivion. And, thank God, the newspapers didn't get hold of more than a bare outline."

He dropped his voice. "This way, if you please;" and he led me off gently down the aisle, once more coming to a standstill beneath the roof of the tower. "What I mean, sir, is that there's very few left in this world who have any place in their minds for a sacred confidence – no reverence, sir. They would as lief All Hallows and all it stands for were swept away tomorrow, demolished to the dust. And that gives me the greatest caution with whom I speak. But sharing one's troubles is sometimes a relief. If it weren't so, why do those Cartholics have their wooden boxes all built for the purpose? What else, I ask you, is the meaning of their fasts and penances?

"You see, sir, I am myself, and have been for upwards of twelve years now, the Dean's verger. In the sight of no respecter of persons – of offices and dignities, that is I take it – I might claim to be even an elder brother. And our Dean, sir, was a man who was all things to all men. No pride of place, no vauntingness, none of your apron-and-gaiter high-and-mightiness whatsoever, sir. And then that! And to come on us without warning; or at least without warning as could be taken as *such*." I followed his eyes into the darkening stony spaces above us; a light like tarnished silver lay over the soundless vaultings. But so, of course, dusk, either of evening or day-break, would affect the ancient stones. Nothing moved there.

"You must understand, sir," the old man was continuing, "the procession for divine service proceeds from the vestry over yonder out through those wrought-iron gates and so under the rood-screen and into the chancel there. Visitors are admitted on showing a card or a word to the verger in charge: but not otherwise. If you stand a pace or two to the right, you will catch a glimpse of the altar-screen – fourteenth-century work, Bishop Robert de Beaufort – and a unique example of the age. But what I was saying is that when we proceed for the services *out* of here *into* there, it has always been our custom to keep pretty close together; more seemly and decent, sir, than straggling in like so many sheep.

"Besides, sir, aren't we at such times in the manner of an *array*; 'marching as to war,' if you take me: it's a lesson in objects. The third verger leading: then the choristers, boys and men, though sadly depleted; then the minor canons; then any other dignitaries who may happen to be present, with the canon in residence; then myself, sir, followed by the Dean.

"There hadn't been much amiss up to then, and on that afternoon, I can vouch – and I've repeated it *ad naushum* – there was not a single stranger out in this beyond here, sir – nave or transepts. Not within view, that is: one can't be expected to see through four feet of Norman stone. Well, sir, we had gone on our way, and I had actually turned about as usual to bow Dr Pomfrey into his stall, when I found to my consternation, to my consternation, I say, he wasn't there! It alarmed me, sir, and as you might well believe if you knew the full circumstances.

"Not that I lost my presence of mind. My first duty was to see all things to be in order and nothing unseemly to occur. My feelings were another matter. The old gentleman had left the vestry with us: that I knew: I had myself robed 'im as usual, and he in his own manner, smiling with his 'Well, Jones, another day gone; another day gone.' He was always an anxious gentleman for *time,* sir. How we spend it and all.

"As I say, then, he was behind me when we swept out of the gates. I saw him coming on out of the tail of my eye – we grow accustomed to it, to see with the whole of the eye, I mean. And then – not a vestige; and me – well sir, nonplussed, as you may imagine. I gave a look and sign at Canon Ockham, and the service proceeded as usual while I hurried back to the vestry thinking the poor gentleman must have been taken suddenly ill. And yet, sir, I was not surprised to find the vestry vacant, and him not there. I had been expecting matters to come to what you might call a head.

"As best I could I held my tongue, and a fortunate thing it was that Canon Ockham was then in residence, and not Canon Leigh Shougar, though perhaps I am not the one to say it. No, sir, our beloved Dean – as pious and harmless a gentleman as ever graced the Church – was gone for ever. He was not to appear in our midst again. He had been" – and the old man with elevated eyebrows and long lean mouth nearly whispered the words into my ear – "he had been absconded – abducted, sir."

"Abducted!" I murmured.

The old man closed his eyes, and with trembling lids added, "He was found, sir, late that night up there in what they call the Trophy Room – sitting in a corner there, weeping. A child. Not a word of what had persuaded him to go or misled him there, not a word of sorrow or sadness, thank God. He didn't know us, sir – didn't know *me.* Just simple; harmless; memory all gone. Simple, sir."

It was foolish to be whispering together like this beneath these enormous spaces with not so much as a clothes-moth for sign of life within view. But I even lowered my voice still further:

"Were there no premonitory symptoms? Had he been failing for long?"

The spectacle of grief in any human face is afflicting, but in a face as aged and resigned as this old man's – I turned away in remorse the moment the question was out of my lips; emotion of any kind is a human solvent and a sort of friendliness had sprung up between us.

"If you will just follow me," he whispered, "there's a little place where I make my ablutions that might be of service, sir. We could converse there in better comfort. I am sometimes reminded of those words in Ecclesiastes: 'And a bird of the air shall tell of the matter.' There is not much in our poor human affairs, sir, that was not known to the writer of that book."

He turned and led the way with surprising celerity, gliding along in his thin-soled, square-toed, clerical springside boots and came to a pause outside a nail-studded door. He opened it with a huge key, and admitted me into a recess under the central tower. We mounted a spiral stone staircase and passed along a corridor hardly more than two feet wide and so dark that now and again I thrust out my fingertips in search of his black velveted gown to make sure of my guide.

This corridor at length conducted us into a little room whose only illumination I gathered was that of the ebbing dusk from within the cathedral. The old man with trembling rheumatic fingers lit a candle, and thrusting its stick into the middle of an old oak table, pushed open yet another thick oaken door. "You will find a basin and a towel in there, sir, if you will be so kind."

I entered. A print of the Crucifixion was tin-tacked to the panelled wall, and beneath it stood a tin basin and jug on a stand. Never was water sweeter. I laved my face and hands, and drank deep; my throat like a parched river-course after a drought. What appeared to be a tarnished censer lay in one corner of the room; a pair of seven-branched candlesticks shared a recess with a mousetrap and a book. My eyes passed wearily yet gratefully from one to another of these mute discarded objects while I stood drying my hands.

When I returned, the old man was standing motionless before the spike-barred grill of the window, peering out and down.

"You asked me, sir," he said, turning his lank waxen face into the feeble rays of the candle, "you asked me, sir, a question which, if I understood you aright was this: Was there anything that had occurred *previous* that would explain what I have been telling you? Well, sir, it's a long story, and one best restricted to them perhaps that have the goodwill of things at heart. All Hallows, I might say, sir, is my second home. I have been here, boy and man, for close on fifty-five years – have seen four bishops pass away and have served under no less than five several deans, Dr Pomfrey, poor gentleman, being the last of the five.

"If such a word could be excused, sir, it's no exaggeration to say that Canon Leigh Shougar is a greenhorn by comparison: which may in part be why he has never quite hit it off, as they say, with Canon Ockham. Or even with Archdeacon Trafford, though he's another kind of gentleman altogether. And *he* is at present abroad. He had what they call a breakdown in health, sir.

"Now in my humble opinion, what was required was not only wisdom and knowledge but simple common sense. In the circumstances I am about to mention, it serves no purpose for any of us to be talking too much; to be for ever sitting at a table with shut doors and finger on lip, and discussing what to most intents and purposes would hardly be called evidence at all, sir. What is the use of argufying, splitting hairs, objurgating about trifles, when matters are sweeping rapidly on from bad to worse. I say it with all due respect and not, I hope, thrusting myself into what doesn't concern me: Dr Pomfrey might be with us now in his own self and reason if only common caution had been observed.

"But now that the poor gentleman is gone beyond all that, there is no hope of action or agreement left, none whatsoever. They meet and they meet, and they have now one expert now another down from London, and even from the continent. And I don't say they are not knowledgable gentlemen either, nor a pride to their profession. But why not tell *all?* Why keep back the very secret of what we know? That's what I am asking. And, what's the answer? Why simply that what they don't want to believe, what runs counter to their hopes and wishes and credibilities – and comfort – in this world, that's what they keep out of sight as long as decency permits.

"Canon Leigh Shougar *knows,* sir, what *I* know. And how, I ask, is he going to get to grips with it at this late day if he refuses to acknowledge that such things are what every fragment of evidence goes to prove that they are. It's *we,* sir, and not the rest of the heedless world outside, who in the long and the short of it are responsible. And what I say is: no power or principality here or hereunder can take possession of a place while those inside have faith enough to keep them out. But once let that falter – the seas are in. And when I say no power, sir, *I* mean – with all deference – even Satan himself." The lean lank face had set at the word like a wax mask. The black eyes beneath the heavy lids were fixed on mine with an acute intensity and – though more inscrutable things haunted them – with an unfaltering courage. So dense a hush hung about us that the very stones of the walls seemed to be of silence solidified. It is curious what a refreshment of spirit a mere tin basinful of water may be. I stood leaning against the edge of the table so that the candlelight still rested on my companion.

"What is *wrong* here?" I asked him baldly.

He seemed not to have expected so direct an enquiry. "Wrong, sir? Why, if I might make so bold," he replied with a wan, far-away smile and gently drawing his hand down one of the velvet lapels of his gown, "if I might make so bold, sir, I take it that you have come as a direct answer to prayer."

His voice faltered. "I am an old man now, and nearly at the end of my tether. You must realise, if you please, that I can't get any help that I can understand. I am not doubting that the gentlemen I have mentioned have only the salvation of the cathedral at heart – the cause, sir; and a graver responsibility yet. But they refuse to see how close to the edge of things we are: and how we are drifting.

"Take mere situation. So far as my knowledge tells me, there is no sacred edifice in the whole kingdom – of a piece, that is, with All Hallows not only in mere size and age but in what I might call sanctity and tradition – that is so open – open, I mean, sir, to attack of this peculiar and terrifying nature."

"Terrifying?"

"*Terrifying,* sir; though I hold fast to what wits my Maker has bestowed on me. Where else, may I ask, would you expect the powers of darkness to congregate in open besiegement than in this narrow valley? First, the sea out there. Are you aware, sir, that ever since living remembrance flood-tide has been gnawing and mumbling its way into this bay to the extent of three or four feet *per annum?* Forty inches, and forty inches, and forty inches corroding on and on: Watch it, sir, man and boy as I have these sixty years past and then make a century of it.

"And now, think a moment of the floods and gales that fall upon us autumn and winter through and even in spring, when this valley is liker paradise to young eyes than any place on earth. They make the roads from the nearest towns wellnigh impassable; which means that for seven months of the year we are to all intents and purposes clean cut off from the rest of the world – as the Schindels out there are from the mainland. Are you aware, sir, I continue, that as we stand now we are above a mile from traces of the nearest human habitation, and them merely the relics of a burnt-out old farmstead? I warrant that if (and which God forbid) you had been shut up here during the coming night, and it was a near thing but what you weren't – I warrant you might have shouted yourself dumb out of the nearest window if window you could reach – and not a human soul to heed or help you."

I shifted my hands on the table. It was tedious to be asking questions that received only such vague and evasive replies: and it is always a little disconcerting in the presence of a stranger to be spoken to so close, and with such positiveness.

"Well," I smiled, "I hope I should not have disgraced my nerves to such an extreme as that. As a small boy, one of my particular fancies was to spend a night in a pulpit. There's a cushion, you know!"

The old man's solemn glance never swerved from my eyes. "But I take it, sir," he said, "if you had ventured to give out a text up there in the dark hours, your innocent young mind would not have been prepared for any kind of a congregation?"

"You mean," I said a little sharply, "that the place is haunted?" The absurd notion had flitted across my mind of some wandering tribe of gipsies chancing on a refuge so ample and isolated as this, and taking up its quarters in its secret parts. The old church must be honeycombed with corridors and passages and chambers pretty much like the one in which we were now concealed: and what does "cartholic" imply but an infinite hospitality within prescribed limits? But the old man had taken me at my word.

"I mean, sir," he said firmly, shutting his eyes, "that there are devilish agencies at work here." He raised his hand. "Don't, I entreat you, dismiss what I am saying as the wanderings of a foolish old man." He drew a little nearer. "I have heard them with these ears; I have seen them with these eyes; though whether they have any positive substance, sir, is beyond my small knowledge to declare. But what indeed might we expect their substance to *be?* First: I 'take it,' says the Book, 'to be such as no man can by learning define, nor by wisdom search out.' Is that so? Then I go by the Book. And next: what does the same Word or very near it (I speak of the Apochrypha) say of their *purpose?* It says – and correct me if I go astray – 'Devils are creatures made by God, and *that for vengeance.*'

"So far, so good, sir. We stop when we can go no further. Vengeance. But of their power, of what they can *do,* I can give you definite evidences. It would be a byword if once the rumour was spread abroad. And if it is *not* so, why, I ask, does every expert that comes here leave us in haste and in dismay? They go off with their tails between their legs. They see, they grope in, but they don't believe. They *invent* reasons. And they *hasten* to leave us!" His face shook with the emphasis he laid upon the word. "Why? Why, because the experience is beyond their knowledge, sir." He drew back breathless and, as I could see, profoundly moved.

"But surely," I said, "every old building is bound in time to show symptoms of decay. Half the cathedrals in England, half its churches, even, of any age, have been 'restored' – and in many cases with ghastly results. This new grouting and so on. Why, only the other day... All I mean is, why should you suppose mere wear and tear should be caused by any other agency than – "

The old man turned away. "I must apologise," he interrupted me with his inimitable admixture of modesty and dignity, "I am a poor mouth at explanations, sir. Decay – stress – strain – settling – dissolution: I have heard those words bandied from lip to lip like a game at cup and ball. They fill me with nausea. Why, I am speaking not of dissolution, sir, but of *repairs, restorations.* Not decay, *strengthening.* Not a corroding loss, an awful *progress.* I could show you places – and chiefly obscured from direct view and difficult of a close examination, sir, where stones lately as rotten as pumice and as fretted as a sponge have been replaced by others fresh-quarried – and nothing of their kind within twenty miles.

"There are spots where massive blocks a yard or more square have been *pushed* into place by sheer force. All Hallows is safer at this moment than it has been for three hundred years. They meant well – them who came to see, full of talk and fine language, and went dumb away. I grant you they meant well. I allow that. They hummed and they hawed. They smirked this and they shrugged that. But at heart, sir, they were cowed – horrified: all at a loss. Their very faces showed it. But if you ask me for what purpose such doings are afoot – I have no answer; none.

"But now, supposing you yourself, sir, were one of them, with *your* repute at stake, and you were called in to look at a house which the owners of it and them who had it in trust were disturbed by its being re-edificated and restored by some agency unknown to them. Supposing that! *Why*," and he rapped with his knuckles on the table, "being human *and not one of us* mightn't you be going away too with mouth shut, because you didn't want to get talked about to your disadvantage? And wouldn't you at last dismiss the whole thing as a foolish delusion, in the belief that living in out-of-the-way parts like these cuts a man off from the world, breeds maggots in the mind?

"I assure you, sir, they don't – not even Canon Ockham himself to the full – they don't believe even me. And yet, when they have their meetings of the Chapter, they talk and wrangle round and round about nothing else. I can bear the other without a murmur. What God sends, I say, we humans deserve. We have laid ourselves open to it. But when you buttress up blindness and wickedness with downright folly, why then, sir, I sometimes fear for my own reason."

He set his shoulders as square as his aged frame would permit, and with fingers clutching the lapels beneath his chin, he stood gazing out into the darkness through that narrow inward window.

"Ah, sir," he began again, "I have not spent sixty years in this solitary place without paying heed to my own small wandering thoughts and instincts. Look at your newspapers, sir. What they call the Great War is over – and he'd be a brave man who would take an oath before heaven that *that* was only of human designing – and yet what do we see around us? Nothing but strife and juggleries and hatred and contempt and discord wherever you look. I am no scholar, sir, but so far as my knowledge and experience carry me, we human beings are living today what ought to have been done yesterday, and yet are at a loss to know what's to be done tomorrow.

"And the Church, sir. God forbid I should push my way into what does not concern me; and if you had told me half an hour gone by that you were a regular churchman, I shouldn't be pouring out all this to you now. It wouldn't be seemly. But being not so gives me confidence. By merely listening you can help me, sir; though you can't help *us*. Centuries ago – and in my humble judgment, rightly – we broke away from the parent stem and rooted ourselves in our own soil. But, right or wrong, doesn't that of itself, I ask you, make us all the more open to attack from him who never wearies in going to and fro in the world seeking whom he may devour?

"I am not wishing you to take sides. But a gentleman doesn't scoff; you don't find him jeering at what he doesn't rightly understand. He keeps his own counsel, sir. And that's where, as I say, Canon Leigh Shougar sets me doubting. He refuses to make allowances; though up there in London things may look different. He gets his company there; and then for him the whole kallyidoscope changes, if you take me."

The old man scanned me an instant as if enquiring within himself whether, after all, I too might not be one of the outcasts. "You see, sir," he went on dejectedly, "I can bear what may be to come. I can, if need be, live on through what few years may yet remain to me and keep going, as they say. But only if I can be assured that my own inmost senses are not cheating and misleading me. Tell me the worst, and you will have done an old man a service he can never repay. Tell me, on the other hand, that I am merely groping along in a network of devilish *delusion,* sir – well, in that case I hope to be with my master, with Dr Pomfrey, as soon as possible. We were all children once; and now there's nothing worse in this world for him to come into, in a manner of speaking.

"Oh, sir, I sometimes wonder if what we call childhood and growing up isn't a copy of the fate of our ancient forefathers. In the beginning of time there were Fallen Angels, we are told; but even if it weren't there in Holy Writ, we might have learnt it of our own fears and misgivings. I sometimes find myself looking at a young child with little short of awe, sir, knowing that within its mind is a scene of peace and paradise of which we older folk have no notion, and which will fade away out of it, as life wears in, like the mere tabernacling of a dream."

There was no trace of unction in his speech, though the phraseology might suggest it, and he smiled at me as if in reassurance. "You see, sir – if I have any true notion of the matter – then I say, heaven is dealing very gently with Dr Pomfrey. He has gone back, and, I take it, his soul is elsewhere and at rest."

He had come a pace or two nearer, and the candlelight now cast grotesque shadows in the hollows of his brows and cheekbones, silvering his long scanty hair. The eyes, dimming with age, were fixed on mine as if in incommunicable entreaty. I was at a loss to answer him.

He dropped his hands to his sides. "The fact is," he looked cautiously about him, "what I am now being so bold as to suggest, though it's a familiar enough experience to me, may put you in actual physical danger. But then, duty's duty, and a deed of kindness from stranger to stranger quite another matter. You seem to have come, if I may say so, in the nick of time: that was all. On the other hand we can leave the building at once if you are so minded. In any case we must be gone well before dark sets in; even mere human beings are best not disturbed at any night work they may be after. The dark brings recklessness: conscience cannot see as clear in the dark. Besides, I once delayed too long myself. There is not much of day left even now, though I see by the almanac there should be a slip of moon tonight – unless the sky is overclouded. All that I'm meaning is that our all-in-all, so to speak, is the calm untrammelled evidence of the outer senses, sir. And there comes a time when – well when one hesitates to trust one's own."

I have read somewhere that it is only its setting – the shape, the line, the fold, the angle of the lid and so on – that gives its finer shades of meaning and significance to the human eye. Looking into his, even in that narrow and melancholy illumination, was like pondering over a grey, salt, desolate pool – such as sometimes neighbours the sea on a flat and dangerous coast.

Perhaps if I had been a little less credulous, or less exhausted, I should by now have begun to doubt this old creature's sanity. And yet, surely, at even the faintest contact with the insane, a sentinel in the mind sends up flares and warnings; the very landscape changes; there is a sense of insecurity. If, too, the characters inscribed by age and experience on a man's face can be evidence of goodness and simplicity, then my companion was safe enough. To trust in his sagacity was another matter.

But then, there was All Hallows itself to take into account. That first glimpse from my green headland of its louring yet lovely walls had been strangely moving. There are buildings (almost as though they were once copies of originals now half-forgotten in the human mind) that have a singular influence on the imagination. Even now in this remote candlelit room, immured between its massive stones, the vast edifice seemed to be gently and furtively fretting its impression on my mind.

I glanced again at the old man: he had turned aside as if to leave me, unbiased, to my own decision. How would a lifetime spent between these sombre walls have affected *me,* I wondered? Surely it would be an act of mere decency to indulge their worn-out hermit! He had appealed to me. If I were ten times more reluctant to follow him, I could hardly refuse. Not at any rate without risking a retreat as humiliating as that of the architectural experts he had referred to – with my tail between my legs.

"I only wish I could hope to be of any real help."

He turned about; his expression changed, as if at the coming of a light. "Why, then, sir, let us be gone at once. You are with me, sir: that was all I hoped and asked. And now there's no time to waste."

He tilted his head to listen a moment – with that large, flat, shell-like ear of his which age alone seems to produce. "Matches and candle, sir," he had lowered his voice to a whisper, "but – though we mustn't lose each other; you and me, I mean – *not,* I think, a naked light. What I would suggest, if you have no objection, is your kindly grasping my gown. There is a kind of streamer here, you see – as if made for the purpose. There will be a good deal of up-and-downing, but I know the building blindfold and as you might say inch by inch. And now that the bell-ringers have given up ringing it is more in my charge than ever."

He stood back and looked at me with folded hands, a whimsical childlike smile on his aged face. "I sometimes think to myself I'm like the sentry, sir, in that play of William Shakespeare's. I saw it, sir, years ago, on my only visit to London – when I was a boy. If ever there was a villain for all his fine talk and all, commend me to that ghost. I see him yet."

Whisper though it was, a sort of chirrup had come into his voice, like that of a cricket in a baker's shop. I took tight hold of the velveted tag of his gown. He opened the door, pressed the box of safety matches into my hand, himself grasped the candlestick, and then blew out the light. We were instantly marooned in an impenetrable darkness. "Now, sir, if you would kindly remove your walking shoes," he muttered close in my ear, "we should proceed with less noise. I shan't hurry you. And please to tug at the streamer if you need attention. In a few minutes the blackness will be less intense."

As I stooped down to loose my shoe-laces I heard my heart thumping merrily away. It had been listening to our conversation apparently! I slung my shoes round my neck – as I had often done as a boy when going paddling – and we set out on our expedition.

I have endured too often the nightmare of being lost and abandoned in the stony bowels of some strange and prodigious building to take such an adventure lightly. I clung, I confess, desperately tight to my lifeline, and we groped steadily onward – my guide ever and again turning back to mutter warning or encouragement in my ear.

Now I found myself steadily ascending; and then in a while, feeling my way down flights of hollowly worn stone steps, and anon brushing along a gallery or cork-screwing up a newel staircase so narrow that my shoulders all but touched the walls on either side. In spite of the sepulchral cold in these bowels of the cathedral, I was soon suffocatingly hot, and the effort to see became intolerably fatiguing. Once, to recover our breath, we paused opposite a slit in the thickness of the masonry, at which to breathe the tepid sweetness of the outer air. It was faint with the scent of wild flowers and cool of the sea. And presently after, at a barred window, high overhead, I caught a glimpse of the night's first stars.

We then turned inward once more, ascending yet another spiral staircase. And now the intense darkness thinned a little, the groined roof above us becoming faintly discernible. A fresher air softly fanned my cheek; and then trembling fingers groped over my breast, and, cold and bony, clutched my own.

"Dead still here, sir, if you please." So close sounded the whispered syllables the voice might have been a messenger's within my own consciousness. "Dead still, here. There's a drop of some sixty or seventy feet a few paces on."

I peered out across the abyss, conscious, as it seemed, of the huge superincumbent weight of the noble fretted roof only a small space now immediately above our heads. As we approached the edge of this stony precipice, the gloom paled a little, and I guessed that we must be standing in some coign of the southern transept, for what light the evening skies now afforded was clearer towards the right. On the other hand, it seemed the northern windows opposite us were most of them boarded up, or obscured in some fashion. Gazing out, I could detect scaffolding poles – like knitting needles – thrust out from the walls and a balloon-like spread of canvas above them. For the moment my ear was haunted by what appeared to be the droning of an immense insect. But this presently ceased. I fancy it was internal only.

"You will understand, sir," breathed the old man close beside me – and we still stood, grotesquely enough, hand in hand – "the scaffolding over there has been in position a good many months now. It was put up when the last gentleman came down from London to inspect the fabric. And there it's been left ever since. Now, sir! – though I implore you to be cautious."

I hardly needed the warning. With one hand clutching my box of matches, the fingers of the other interlaced with my companion's, I strained every sense. And yet I could detect not the faintest stir or murmur under that wide-spreading roof. Only a hush as profound as that which must reign in the Royal Chamber of the pyramid of Cheops faintly swirled in the labyrinths of my ear.

How long we stayed in this position I cannot say; but minutes sometimes seem like hours. And then, without the slightest warning, I became aware of a peculiar and incessant vibration. It is impossible to give a name to it. It suggested the remote whirring of an enormous millstone, or that – though without definite pulsation – of revolving wings, or even the spinning of an immense top.

In spite of his age, my companion apparently had ears as acute as mine. He had clutched me tighter a full ten seconds before I myself became aware of this disturbance of the air. He pressed closer. "Do you see that, sir?"

I gazed and gazed, and saw nothing. Indeed even in what I had seemed to hear I might have been deceived. Nothing is more treacherous in certain circumstances – except possibly the eye – than the ear. It magnifies, distorts, and may even invent. As instantaneously as I had become aware of it, the murmur had ceased. And then – though I cannot be certain – it seemed the dingy and voluminous spread of canvas over there had perceptibly trembled, as if a huge cautious hand had been thrust out to draw it aside. No time was given me to make sure. The old man had hastily withdrawn me into the opening of the wall through which we had issued; and we made no pause in our retreat until we had come again to the narrow slit of window which I have spoken of and could refresh ourselves with a less stagnant air. We stood here resting awhile.

"Well, sir?" he enquired at last, in the same flat muffled tones.

"Do you ever pass along here alone?" I whispered.

"Oh, yes, sir. I make it a habit to be the last to leave – and often the first to come; but I am usually gone by this hour."

I looked close at the dim face in profile against that narrow oblong of night. "It is so difficult to be sure of oneself," I said. "Have you ever actually *encountered* anything – near at hand, I mean?"

"I keep a sharp look-out, sir. Maybe they don't think me of enough importance to molest – the last rat, as they say."

"But *have* you?" – I might myself have been communicating with the phantasmal *genius loci* of All Hallows – our muffled voices; this intense caution and secret listening; the slight breathlessness, as if at any instant one's heart were ready for flight: "But *have* you?"

"Well yes, sir," he said. "And in this very gallery. They nearly had me, sir. But by good fortune there's a recess a little further on – stored up with some old fragments of carving, from the original building, sixth-century, so it's said: stone-capitals, heads and hands, and such like. I had had my warning, and managed to leap in there and conceal myself. But only just in time. Indeed, sir, I confess I was in such a condition of terror and horror I turned my back."

"You mean you heard, but didn't look? And – something came?"

"Yes, sir, I seemed to be reduced to no bigger than a child, huddled up there in that corner. There was a sound like clanging metal – but I don't think it was metal. It drew near at a furious speed, then passed me, making a filthy gust of wind. For some instants I couldn't breathe; the air was gone."

"And no other sound?"

"No other, sir, except out of the distance a noise like the sounding of a stupendous kind of gibberish. A calling; or so it seemed – no human sound. The air shook with it. You see, sir, I myself wasn't of any consequence, I take it – unless a mere obstruction in the way. But – I have heard it said somewhere that the rarity of these happenings is only because it's a pain and torment and not any sort of pleasure for such beings, such apparitions, sir, good or bad, to visit our outward world. That's what I have heard said; though I can go no further.

"The time I'm telling you of was in the early winter – November. There was a dense sea-fog over the valley, I remember. It eddied through that opening there into the candlelight like flowing milk. I never light up now: and, if I may be forgiven the boast, sir, I seem to have almost forgotten how to be afraid. After all, in any walk of life a man can only do his best, and if there weren't such opposition and hindrances in high places, I should have nothing to complain of. What is anybody's life, sir (come past the gaiety of youth) but marking time... Did you hear anything *then*, sir?"

His gentle monotonous mumbling ceased and we listened together. But every ancient edifice has voices and soundings of its own: there was nothing audible that I could put a name to, only what seemed to be a faint perpetual stir or whirr of grinding such as (to one's over-stimulated senses) the stablest stones set one on top of the other with an ever slightly-varying weight and stress might be likely to make perceptible in a world of matter. A world which, after all, they say, is itself in unimaginably rapid rotation, and under the tyranny of time.

"No, I hear nothing," I answered: "but please don't think I am doubting what you say. Far from it. You must remember I am a stranger, and that therefore the influence of the place cannot but be less apparent to me. And you have no help in this now?"

"No sir. Not now. But even at the best of times we had small company hereabouts, and no money. Not for any substantial outlay, I mean. And not even the boldest suggests making what's called a public appeal. It's a strange thing to me, sir, but whenever the newspapers get hold of anything, they turn it into a byword and a sham. Yet how can they help themselves? – with no beliefs to guide them and nothing to stay their mouths except about what for sheer human decency's sake they daren't talk about. But then, who am I to complain? And now, sir," he continued with a sigh of utter weariness, "if you are sufficiently rested, would you perhaps follow me on to the roof? It is the last visit I make – though by rights perhaps I should take in what there is of the tower. But I'm too old now for that – clambering and climbing over naked beams; and the ladders are not so safe as they were."

We had not far to go. The old man drew open a squat heavily-ironed door at the head of a flight of wooden stairs. It was latched but not bolted, and admitted us at once to the leaden roof of the building and to the immense amphitheatre of evening. The last faint hues of sunset were fading in the west; and silver-bright Spica shared with the tilted crescent of the moon the serene lagoon-like expanse of sky above the sea. Even at this height, the air was audibly stirred with the low lullaby of the tide.

The staircase by which we had come out was surmounted *by* a flat penthouse roof about seven feet high. We edged softly along, then paused once more; to find ourselves now all but *tête-à-tête* with the gigantic figures that stood sentinel at the base of the buttresses to the unfinished tower.

The tower was so far unfinished, indeed, as to wear the appearance of the ruinous; besides which, what appeared to be scars and stains as if of fire were detectable on some of its stones, reminding me of the legend which years before I had chanced upon, that this stretch of coast had more than once been visited centuries ago by pillaging Norsemen.

The night was unfathomably clear and still. On our left rose the conical bluff of the headland crowned with the solitary grove of trees beneath which I had taken refuge from the blinding sunshine that very afternoon. Its grasses were now hoary with faintest moonlight. Far to the right stretched the flat cold plain of the Atlantic – that enormous darkened looking-glass of space; only a distant lightship ever and again stealthily signalling to us with a lean phosphoric finger from its outermost reaches.

The mere sense of that abysm of space – its waste powdered with the stars of the Milky Way; the mere presence of the stony leviathan on whose back we two humans now stood, dwarfed into insignificance beside these gesturing images of stone, were enough of themselves to excite the imagination. And – whether matter-of-fact or pure delusion – this old verger's insinuations that the cathedral was now menaced by some inconceivable danger and assault had set my nerves on edge. My feet were numb as the lead they stood upon; while the tips of my fingers tingled as if a powerful electric discharge were coursing through my body.

We moved gently on – the spare shape of the old man a few steps ahead, peering cautiously to right and left of him as we advanced. Once with a hasty gesture he drew me back and fixed his eyes for a full minute on a figure – at two removes – which was silhouetted at that moment against the starry emptiness: a forbidding thing enough, viewed in this vague luminosity, which seemed in spite of the unmoving stare that I fixed on it to be perceptibly stirring on its windworn pedestal.

But no; "All's well!" the old man had mutely signalled to me, and we pushed on. Slowly and cautiously; indeed I had time to notice in passing that this particular figure held stretched in its right hand a bent bow, and was crowned with a high weather-worn stone coronet. One and all were frigid company. At last we completed our circuit of the tower, had come back to the place we had set out from, and stood eyeing one another like two conspirators in the clear dusk. Maybe there was a tinge of incredulity on my face.

"No, sir," murmured the old man, "I expected no other. The night is uncommonly quiet. I've noticed that before. They seem to leave us at peace on nights of quiet. We must turn in again and be getting home."

Until that moment I had thought no more of where I was to sleep or to get food, nor had even realised how famished with hunger I was. Nevertheless, the notion of fumbling down again out of the open air into the narrow inward blackness of the walls from which we had just issued was singularly uninviting. Across these wide flat stretches of roof there was at least space for flight, and there were recesses for concealment. To gain a moment's respite, I enquired if I should have much difficulty in getting a bed in the village. And as I had hoped, the old man himself offered me hospitality.

I thanked him; but still hesitated to follow, for at that moment I was trying to discover what peculiar effect of dusk and darkness a moment before had deceived me into the belief that some small animal – a dog, a spaniel, I should have guessed – had suddenly and surreptitiously taken cover behind the stone buttress nearby. But that apparently had been a mere illusion. The creature, whatever it might be, was no barker at any rate. Nothing stirred now; and my companion seemed to have noticed nothing amiss.

"You were saying," I pressed him, "that when repairs – restorations – of the building were in contemplation, even the experts were perplexed by what they discovered? What did they actually say?"

"Say, sir!" Our voices sounded as small and meaningless up here as those of grasshoppers in a noonday meadow. "Examine that balustrade which you are leaning against at this minute. Look at that gnawing and fretting – that furrowing above the lead. All that is honest wear and tear – constant weathering of the mere elements, sir – rain and wind and snow and frost. That's honest *nature*-work, sir. But now compare it, if you please, with this St Mark here; and remember, sir, these images were intended to be part and parcel of the fabric as you might say, sentries on a castle – symbols, you understand."

I stooped close under the huge grey creature of stone until my eyes were scarcely more than six inches from its pedestal. And, unless the moon deceived me, I confess I could find not the slightest trace of fret or friction. Far from it. The stone had been grotesquely decorated in low relief with a gaping crocodile – a two-headed crocodile; and the angles, knubs and undulations of the creature were cut as sharp as with a knife in cheese. I drew back.

"Now cast your glance upwards, sir. Is that what you would call a saintly shape and gesture?"

What I took to represent an eagle was perched on the image's lifted wrist – but louring and vulture-like. The head of the figure was poised at an angle of defiance – the ears unnaturally high up on the skull; the lean right forearm extended with pointing forefinger as if in derision. Its stony gaze was fixed upon the stars; its whole aspect was undeniably sinister and intimidating. The faintest puff of milk-warm air from over the sea stirred on my cheek. I drew aside.

"Ay, sir, and so with one or two of the rest of them," the old man commented, as he watched me, "there are other wills than the Almighty's."

At this, the pent-up excitement within me broke bounds. This nebulous insinuatory talk! – I all but lost my temper. "I can't, for the life of me, understand what you are saying," I exclaimed in a voice that astonished me with its shrill volume of sound in that intense lofty quiet. "One doesn't *repair* in order to destroy."

The old man met me without flinching. "No, sir? Say you so? And why not? Are there not two kinds of change in this world? – a building-up and a breaking-down? To give strength and endurance for evil or misguided purposes, would that be time wasted, if such was your aim? Why sir, isn't that true even of the human mind and heart? We here are on the outskirts, I grant, but where would you expect the activity to show itself unless in the outer defences? An institution may be beyond dying, sir: it may be being restored for a worse destruction. And a hundred trumpeting voices would make no difference when the faith and life within is tottering to its fall."

Somehow, this muddle of metaphors reassured me. Obviously the old man's wits had worn a little thin: he was the victim of an intelligible but monstrous hallucination.

"And yet you are taking it for granted," I expostulated, "that, if what you say is true, a stranger could be of the slightest help. A visitor – mind you – who hasn't been inside the doors of a church, except in search of what is old and gone, for years."

The old man laid a trembling hand upon my sleeve. The folly of it – with my shoes hanging like ludicrous millstones round my neck!

"If you please, sir," he pleaded, "have a little patience with me. I'm preaching at nobody. I'm not even hinting that them outside the fold circumstantially speaking aren't of the flock. All in good time, sir; the Almighty's time. Maybe – with all due respect – it's from them within we have most to fear. And indeed, sir, believe an old man: I could never express the gratitude I feel. You have given me the occasion to unbosom myself, to make a clean breast, as they say. All Hallows is my earthly home, and – well, there, let us say no more. You couldn't *help me* – except only by your presence here. God alone knows who can!"

At that instant, a dull enormous rumble reverberated from within the building – as if a huge boulder or block of stone had been shifted or dislodged in the fabric; a peculiar grinding nerve-wracking sound. And for the fraction of a second the flags on which we stood seemed to tremble beneath our feet.

The fingers tightened on my arm. "Come, sir; keep close; we must be gone at once," the quavering old voice whispered; "we have stayed too long."

But we emerged into the night at last without mishap. The little western door, above which the grinning head had welcomed me on my arrival, admitted us to *terra firma* again, and we made our way up a deep sandy track, bordered by clumps of herb agrimony and fennel and hemlock, with viper's bugloss and sea-poppy blooming in the gentle dusk of night at our feet. We turned when we reached the summit of this sandy incline and looked back. All Hallows, vague and enormous, lay beneath us in its hollow, resembling some natural prehistoric outcrop of that sea-worn rock-bound coast; but strangely human and saturnine.

The air was mild as milk – a pool of faintest sweetnesses – gorse, bracken, heather; and not a rumour disturbed its calm, except only the furtive and stertorous sighings of the tide. But far out to sea and beneath the horizon summer lightnings were now in idle play – flickering into the sky like the unfolding of a signal, planet to planet – then gone. That alone, and perhaps too this feeble moonlight glinting on the ancient glass, may have accounted for the faint vitreous glare that seemed ever and again to glitter across the windows of the northern transept far beneath. And yet how easily deceived is the imagination. This old man's talk still echoing in my ear, I could have vowed this was no reflection but the glow of some light shining fitfully from within outwards.

The old man paused beside a flowering bush of fuchsia at the wicket gate leading into his small square of country garden. "You'll forgive me, sir, for mentioning it; but I make it a rule as far as possible to leave all my troubles and misgivings outside when I come home. My daughter is a widow, and not long in that sad condition, so I keep as happy a face as I can on things. And yet: well, sir, I wonder at times if – if a personal sacrifice isn't incumbent on them that have their object most at heart. I'd go out myself very willingly, sir, I can assure you, if there was any certainty in my mind that it would serve the cause. It would be little to me if – " He made no attempt to complete the sentence.

On my way to bed, that night, the old man led me in on tiptoe to show me his grandson. His daughter watched me intently as I stooped over the child's cot – with that bird-like solicitude which all mothers show in the presence of a stranger.

Her small son was of that fairness which almost suggests the unreal. He had flung back his bedclothes – as if innocence in this world needed no covering or defence – and lay at ease, the dews of sleep on lip, cheek, and forehead. He was breathing so quietly that not the least movement of shoulder or narrow breast was perceptible.

"The lovely thing!" I muttered, staring at him. "Where is he now, I wonder?" His mother lifted her face and smiled at me with a drowsy ecstatic happiness, then sighed.

And from out of the distance there came the first prolonged whisper of a wind from over the sea. It was eleven by my watch, the storm after the long heat of the day seemed to be drifting inland; but All Hallows, apparently, had forgotten to wind its clock.

1929

THE CAIRN

H. R. Wakefield

Like several noted writers of uncanny fiction, Herbert Russell Wakefield (1888–1964) was born into ecclesiastical circles. His father was a vicar who rose through the Anglican ranks to become the Bishop of Birmingham in 1911. Wakefield was educated at Marlborough College and University College, Oxford, and although not the most distinguished scholar, he played golf and cricket to a high level – passions that would inform later stories. After serving in the First World War, and a spell as his father's secretary, Wakefield turned to the world of publishing and writing, working as an editor at William Collins.

Today, Wakefield is remembered for his supernatural fiction, first collected in *They Return at Evening* in 1928. "The Cairn" appeared a year later in *Old Man's Beard: Fifteen Disturbing Tales*. Alongside the likes of Eleanor Scott, Wakefield was an occasional exponent of what would later be known as folk horror – in some of his strongest tales, ancient powers are unearthed and strange rites enacted in the British countryside. And although Wakefield's depictions of rural characters can betray 1920s stereotypes, in these stories it is often the worldly incomers, rather than the locals, who come unstuck.

"I'd like to go with you," said Welland, "but I think I had better nurse this heel if I'm to get through the rest of the trip."

"Yes, certainly," agreed Seebright, "you'd be a fool to attempt it. But I like the look of those silvery slopes above the wood. Ever since I was a kid I've loved high hills and virgin snow. I don't imagine it will take me more than four hours or so up and down. All the same it might be as well to get one of the locals to go with me – it's easy to miss the shortest way even on such a simple climb as old Brudon looks to be."

"Well, ring for our worthy host and see if he can arrange it."

Seebright pulled the bell-knob, and a moment later the landlord appeared, a tubby, rubicund Midlander, genial, of andante intelligence and consequently at perfect peace with the world.

"Oh, Mr Reddle," said Seebright, "I'm going to climb Brudon tomorrow. Mr Welland has a bad heel and I want a companion; would someone from the village go with me?"

"I don't believe they would, sir," replied the landlord.

"What on earth do you mean? Don't they like the look of me?"

Mr Reddle shifted about on his feet. "It isn't that, sir, but the chaps about here won't climb Brudon when snow's lying."

"Why the devil not?"

"Well, sir, it's just that way. They won't go beyond the wood on any account, and most of 'em don't like setting foot on the hill when snow's lying."

"But why? I can't imagine a simpler or easier climb. Is it because it's too much like work?"

"No, 'tain't that. I'm not a native of these parts, so I don't hear everything as a local chap would; but they've got some reason why they won't go above Dim Wood in the snow."

"Is that big spinney half-way up Dim Wood?" asked Welland.

"Yes, sir. The fact is they think there's something that wanders on the slopes above it when snow's there."

"And hides behind the cairn and pounces on the unsuspecting climber?" suggested Seebright, laughing.

"Yes," replied Mr Reddle, looking startled, "that's just what they does think."

"Well, I'm damned!" said Seebright. "Do they think they've seen it?"

"They're pretty close about it, sir. The chaps get sullen like and changes the subject if it's mentioned, but it seems as though they think they've seen some marks. I gather it's a very old story, a sort of village secret."

"A very typical piece of folk-funk," said Welland. "A few probably perfectly explainable marks in the snow, and, of course, the devil or some other undesirable is abroad. Away goes the snow, away go the marks and away goes the devil."

"Well, landlord," said Seebright, "you're above that sort of thing. Come with me tomorrow and help to lay what must be rather an inconvenient bogey."

"I don't believe I will, sir," said Mr Reddle.

"What!" cried Seebright, "you don't mean to say you believe this tripe?"

"I don't say I does, but I believes in being on the safe side in such things. I'd do the same if I was you, sir."

"Be damned to that! I'll climb Brudon if it snows ink!"

"As you please, sir, but in any case you wouldn't want a guide, the way is as easy to find as hard to miss. I'll show you, if you'll look through the telescope. You takes the third turn to the right in the village – Dim Lane – that takes you up to that big clump of oaks; then you follows the hedge till you comes to a gate, and then you goes straight up to the wood. There is a path through that and then it's all plain sailing to the cairn. And now I must go and see about your dinners, sir."

Pat Seebright and Leonard Welland differed in temperament as much as they differed in their command of this world's goods. Yet to have laid down his life for the other would have been considered a privilege by either of them. If the summons had come, neither of them would have hesitated for a moment. They had been the fastest, firmest friends for twenty years. Pat made an easy £10,000 a year in his father's stockbroker's firm. Leonard secured from the National Income a precarious £250 as an usher in a small school. Yet the overwhelming disparity between their income-tax returns had never in the slightest degree tarnished their friendship, and Pat had never lent Leonard a penny. All he had done was to persuade him to allow him occasionally to do a little marginal speculation on his behalf with a rather mythical £50. These occasional flutters came off in a most magical manner, and every year a most welcome little increment was paid into Leonard's bank. Intellectually, Pat was a child in comparison with Leonard, but in the practical affairs of life he was absolutely his master. Each envied and complemented the other. Pat was of an enterprising and inquiring type of mind, and Leonard stimulated and vitalised strata of his brain which would otherwise have perished of malnutrition.

Neither was ever quite happy when separated from the other, though an innate sense of the supreme obscenity of sentimentality would ever have prevented them from acknowledging the fact. Their affection for each other so far surpassed the love of woman that had they been forced to face the conventionally considered ultimate tie of friendship by falling in love with the same one, they would have left her to celibacy or a third person with absolute contentment, in the certain knowledge that such a competition would have been essentially discordant and disgusting. Each secretly dreaded the possible marriage of the other, though in the case of poor Leonard, who had to think twice about purchasing packets of cigarettes, and who met about three fresh females per annum, such a contingency was highly improbable. (As things turned out there was no need for either of them to worry.) They always spent their holidays together, and on this occasion were passing the Christmas vacation in tramping the Lake District. Their time was almost up, for in three days' time they were due to drive back to London in Pat's impressive car. Perhaps it was this which seemed to cast a shadow over their dinner together that night. Both felt it and confessed to it. Pat applied his usually infallible antidote to irrational gloom by ordering a bottle of Mr Reddle's champagne and two large glasses of his mediocre port. However, this medicine was not quite as successful as it should have been – the shadow remained.

"That's a curious yarn about Brudon and the snow," said Welland. "In other circumstances it would be easier to explain. This alleged bogey might be, let us say, the personified terror of avalanches, but I don't suppose an avalanche has sprayed down Brudon since the end of the Ice Age, and even the traditional memory of the good folk of Borthwaite cannot be as long as that. Still, even on Brudon a blizzard might not be too pleasant; are you sure you're wise to go alone?"

"Oh, perfectly," replied Seebright; "anyway I shan't start if the weather breaks. How's the glass, Mr Reddle?"

"Steady enough, sir. From the looks of the sky I'd say 'twill be fine but dullish tomorrow."

They went to bed early and Welland was asleep at once, but his rest was disturbed by the recurrence of a very idiotic little dream. It seemed to him that it was moonlight and that he was gazing through the telescope at the cairn, which was throwing a hard shadow on to the snow. And then this shadow began to move, and as it moved it changed its shape and became more like a crouching beast of some kind than any such shadow had a right to be. And were those flaming points red eyes? And each time, before he could make up his mind on this – for some reason or other – rather urgent question, he awoke. "Now I will not dream that again," he said to himself, but a moment later he was once more scrutinising with a growing anxiety and distaste this erratic and enigmatic shade. After this had happened five or six times he sat up in bed. Self-flatterers, he said to himself, would attribute this bother to nerves; honest men to alcohol. What should he do about it? Well, it occurred to him that if he crept very quietly downstairs and swung the telescope on to the cairn and proved to his full consciousness that nothing of the sort was abroad, then his subconscious – or whatever it was – would be convinced that no such wearisome phenomenon, such change of shape, was occurring at the crest of Brudon.

The moon was filtering vague rays through light clouds. So much of his dream *was* true. Well, here was the telescope and there was Brudon. He put his eye to the lens and swung the glass to the cairn. And then he put it down and rubbed his eyes, and then he took it up again, stared through it intently for a full twenty seconds and put it down again. And then he returned rather slowly and thoughtfully to bed.

"Of course I must be slightly tight," he said to himself. "That's why I can't sleep, that's why I see things through telescopes. No more double ports for me. All the same – " And for a moment he felt a powerful inclination to go down again and take up the telescope and make quite sure that – He looked at his watch – five o'clock – and he did not feel sleepy. He decided to read till it was time to get up; something which would mobilise his powers of concentration, *Essays on Truth and Reality*, for example. Once he found himself dozing off and there was just the vague, spectral outline of a cairn and a shadow beginning most exasperatingly to reappear. He pulled himself back to consciousness, and taking each sentence slowly etched it on his brain.

As Mr Reddle had prophesied, the morning was fine but overcast, and the glass remaining high, Seebright announced his intention of starting at 12.30. He would reach the wood about 2.0 and the summit about 3.30 – just as dusk was beginning to fall. There would be enough light to see him down to the wood and he would be back at the inn before 5.0.

"And you can follow my progress, Leonard, through the telescope," he said, "and mutter prayers for my safety. Now, Mr Reddle, are you sure you won't come with me?"

"No, thank 'ee, sir, and if you'd take my advice you'd change your mind. Why not have a try for some of them ducks on the marsh?"

"I'm going to climb the Haunted Hill," said Seebright with the utmost emphasis. "I am determined to convince the superstitious natives of these parts that climbing this measly hill with two inches of snow on it is not precisely the perilous ordeal they profess to consider it. I shall – if he appears – tweak the nose of the local bogey, and I am off to do this now."

"Very well, sir," replied the landlord, "and I wish you luck."

Seebright set forth punctually at 12.30 and Welland watched his strong, stocky figure striding away down the village street. As he reached the third turning on the right he turned back and waved.

Welland lunched at 1.0, and afterwards sat down by the telescope, and attempted once again to concentrate upon the profound yet racy speculations of Dr Bradley, but again without much success. His body seemed to protest against its immobility. It joined in a conspiracy with his nervous system to compel fidgets and fussiness and a sort of tingling unease, so that he repeatedly pulled out his watch and yawned and lit cigarettes and shifted his position, and these tendencies developed and became more insistent – they almost took charge of him – and the effort to resist them was exhausting in a small way.

Presently he gave up the attempt to read and took up the telescope. He searched very carefully the slopes between the wood and the cairn. If those weren't footmarks in the snow what were they? Very possibly the locals were in the habit of pulling Mr Reddle's – "the foreigner's" – leg. Certainly someone had travelled those slopes. Those marks were extraordinarily distinct. Would that be due to their size? He looked at his watch again – five minutes to two. Pat should be appearing at any moment now. Looking through a small telescope like this was a damned tiring business. Ah, there he was! As he came out from the wood Welland saw him pause – he is looking at those footprints – or whatever they are – he thought. Seebright remained peering down for half a minute or so and then began climbing steadily again. Welland found he could just follow him with the naked eye, so he put down the telescope. Mr Reddle came in just then. "How's he getting on?" he asked.

"He should be at the top in twenty minutes or so."

The landlord seemed not quite at his ease. "Getting a bit misty near the cairn, isn't it, sir?"

"Yes," replied Welland, "the clouds are coming down; looks like a change in the weather, I fancy."

"Well, sir, I shall be in the kitchen for a bit yet. Would you mind letting me know when Mr Seebright gets back to the wood again."

"All right," replied Welland, looking at him a shade sharply.

"It's just a fancy of mine, sir," said Mr Reddle, "if it's no bother," and he went out again.

Welland watched the little dark speck climbing steadily towards the cairn till it was but a hundred yards or so from it and then once again put the telescope to his eye. A few minutes later he saw Seebright reach the cairn, slap it with his hand and then turn and face towards the inn and wave his right arm above his head. And then he began rapidly to descend. Welland had started instinctively to wave back and then had smiled at his stupidity. He was just about to put the glass down again when he suddenly became tense and intent. He put the telescope down sharply and rubbed both lenses with his handkerchief, and then he put it to his eye again. For a moment he remained taut and rigid, and then he began to tremble, and then he dropped the telescope to the floor, and then he rushed from the room, out through the front door and down the village street. As it happened there was only one person who saw him pass, old Mrs Elm, who was beating a rug outside her cottage door. When she saw a hatless figure dash hobbling past, and that queer look on his face too, her mouth fell open and the rug dropped from her hands. A moment later she saw this figure turn up the lane and disappear, and then for several minutes she remained staring open-mouthed.

Now Mrs Elm's brain never exceeded largo in its tempo, and seldom reached it. At the same time she had a sense for the unusual. She went back to her kitchen and wrestled with the problem of what to do. So presently she put her shawl around her head and trotted up to the Hare and Form, where she found Mr Reddle squeezing the digestive apparatus from a chicken.

"Mr Reddle," she began, and fiddled with her shawl.

"Yes, what is it?" asked the landlord, pausing in the midst of his culinary business.

"Well," said Mrs Elm. "I sees one of those young chaps who's putting up here, and I sees him running by in his slippers and without his hat and he turned up Dim Lane. I thought I ought to tell you."

Mr Reddle stared at her for a moment; then he rushed past Mrs Elm and into the guest parlour, stood stock still for a moment gazing round the room, then noticed the end of the telescope sticking out from beneath the table. He picked it up, stared for a moment through it at the dusk-rimmed crest of Brudon, and then rushed through the front door and down the village street. By a lucky chance he met the local representative of Law and Order, Constable Lamb. Mr Reddle clutched his arm. "I think there's maybe something wrong on Brudon," he said, "maybe something's happened to those young chaps staying with me."

Mr Lamb started at him sharply, but something in Mr Reddle's face, and a rather disturbing memory which had often recurred to lubricate the somewhat sluggish machinery of his imagination, prevented him from asking some rather natural questions. All he said was, "We'd better see if the doctor's in."

They ran together down the street to where a brass plate announced that "R. Ford, M. D., Physician and Surgeon," had there his habitat. He was in and he *did* ask a few questions, but his natural scepticism was also diluted with a certain memory, and presently he picked up his bag, his hat and coat and an electric torch and started off with the other two. Soon they were climbing in panting silence through the dusk, the doctor's torch faintly revealing the way. They had just reached the last turn on the path through Dim Wood when the doctor stumbled over something...

"Just describe to us, constable, exactly how you found the deceased," said the coroner.

"Well," said Mr Lamb, "Mr Seebright was lying on his back, his arms thrown out like, and Mr Welland was about six yards away. *He* was lying on his face – more crouching than lying – but his face was in the snow. They'd both fallen hard."

"Did you examine the snow for tracks of a third person?"

"Yes, sir."

"Did you find anything?"

"No, sir."

"You saw tracks of Mr Seebright going up and coming down to the wood, but nothing else?"

"Nothing else, sir."

Dr Ford was the next witness.

"Dr Ford," said the coroner, "I take it you have performed an autopsy on the deceased."

"I have."

"Would you tell the Court what you learned from so doing?"

"Both were strong, healthy young men, organically flawless. They had sustained extensive superficial injuries, bruises and so forth, and Mr Welland had a broken arm. These injuries were consistent with the fact that they had been thrown down with great violence."

"Were these injuries sufficient to cause death?"

"No, emphatically not."

"Then can you suggest why these two young men died?"

"Frankly, I cannot. It is conceivable that some very violent shock, sudden terror for example, may have resulted in heart failure in each case. When I say conceivable I mean just possible, but I am at a loss for a convincing explanation of their deaths. I have known no parallel case."

"Is Mr Reddle still here?" asked the coroner.

Mr Reddle was, and returned to the box.

"Mr Reddle, as I understand it, Mr Welland had decided not to accompany Mr Seebright on this climb?"

"Yes, sir, he'd hurt his heel."

"Then the fact that he suddenly made up his mind to go to meet his friend was a complete surprise to you."

"Yes, 'twas, sir."

"Can you account for it?"

"No, but I think he'd been watching Mr Seebright through the telescope."

"Well, what's that got to do with it?"

Mr Reddle was silent for a moment, searching for words.

"I should say nothing, sir, like as not. I only mentioned it, sir."

The coroner drummed on the table but there was otherwise no sound. From outside there came the light crack of a whip and the slow rumble of wheels.

"Well," said the coroner at length, "this seems to me an extremely unsatisfactory affair. All I can do is to express my profound sympathy with the parents of these poor young men" – and here he bowed to four persons in deep mourning – "and to express my hope that further light will be eventually shed on this highly mysterious and tragic affair, but I see no object in adjourning the inquest." The verdict was open.

Mr Reddle followed P. C. Lamb out of the Court and suggested to him that he should come up to the Hare and Form and have some refreshment. The constable had no objection whatsoever. When they were seated in the parlour and furnished with some glossy old pewter, Mr Reddle said, "You didn't tell the whole truth and nothing but it at the inquest, did you, Mr Lamb?"

The constable put down his mug and looked suspiciously at the landlord. "How's that?" he said. "What makes you for to say that?"

"Because I was watching you through the glass when you climbed Brudon the morning after we found those poor young chaps."

The constable shifted uneasily in his chair.

"If I tell you what I see'd, will it go no further, will you keep your tongue quiet about it?" he said at length.

"I'll do that," replied Mr Reddle.

"Well," said Mr Lamb, "a year or two afore you came, there was a London chap found dead in the wood and that time I *did* tell all I'd see'd. And the Chief Constable sent for me to Rendle and asked me a lot of questions. And at the end of it he said, 'They brew strong ale in Borthwaite, don't they?'"

"What did you say to make him laugh?"

"I said I'd seen marks in the snow coming along behind the marks made by the London chap."

"What sort of marks?"

"I don't believe I'll be after saying what those marks was like. I don't somehow feel like doing it – not out loud that is, but I'll say this: it seemed to me that whatever made those marks some of the time made four and not two of 'em."

"Sort of crouched down like a time or two?"

"Maybe that," replied the constable.

"About those tracks," said the landlord, "you could make out the ones Mr Seebright made up and down."

"Yes, I could."

"Would you say he noticed anything? I mean anything that might have to do with them other marks?"

"Well," said Mr Lamb, "he went up steadily enough, but after he'd come down a couple of hundred yards I judge he'd stopped and looked round; well, you could tell that plain enough, and then he'd started to run."

"Started to run, did he!" exclaimed Mr Reddle.

"That was easy to read too; his stride got longer and he came down harder, and he kept up the running till he got to the top edge of the wood – where we found him. And just as he got there I take it this Mr Welland met him, and Mr Seebright stopped and the two of them faced up to whatever – well – to whatever there was to face up to."

"That's what they would have done," said Mr Reddle emphatically. "I guess that's the rights of it. They'd face up to it together."

And then there was a long silence in the Hare and Form.

"Snow's off Brudon now, I take it?" asked the constable at length.

"Yes," said Mr Reddle, "I looked through glass at it round about dinner-time and even that last big patch round cairn is melted."

1945

THE WHITE SACK

A. N. L. Munby

Alan Noel Latimer Munby (1913–1974) was a respected librarian and antiquarian book collector. Known as Tim, he studied at King's College, Cambridge before working in the rare book trade in the years leading up to the Second World War. As a member of the territorial army, he was commissioned when war broke out, and headed to Calais in 1940 as part of a bid to occupy Nazi forces while Allied troops were evacuated from Dunkirk. He was eventually captured and held for five years in German prisoner-of-war camps. It was at Oflag VII-B, a camp in Bavaria, that Munby first published "The White Sack" in *Touchstone*, a prisoners' magazine. The story was later collected in his book, *The Alabaster Hand*, in 1949. By this time, Munby was back at King's (fertile ground for ghost stories, of course), where he served as librarian for 27 years.

Munby's strange tale takes place around the Black Cuillin ridge on the Isle of Skye. The area has long been a hub for experienced mountaineers wishing to test themselves on the scree slopes, boulders and tight ridges en route to the Cuillin's peaks. The Black Cuillin contains the highest point in all the Scottish islands, Sgùrr Alasdair. (Now named after a Victorian climber, the peak's traditional name is Sgùrr Biorach – "Pointed Peak".) Although he mentions Sgùrr Alasdair, it is "the mighty bastion of Sron na Ciche" that really impresses Munby's Tony Marchand – "perhaps the most awesome mountain precipice in the British Isles, rising sheer from the floor of the glen to a height of over 2,500 feet."

If you prefer a good ramble to technical climbing, there's still plenty to enjoy in this part of Skye. Glen Brittle, where Marchand camps, has lots of route options, with epic views of the Cuillin giving you a sense of the dramatic escapades in Munby's tale.

I had no idea that Tony Marchand was in Town until I ran into him in Bond Street. He seemed to be at a loose end, and readily accepted my invitation to dinner. During the meal he seemed silent and preoccupied, and I began to regret having asked him. He had normally a fund of amusing gossip and small talk. After dinner, more for the sake of making conversation than for any other reason, I asked him whether he'd made his annual trip to Skye this year. He said that he had just returned – then he suddenly blurted out:

"Look here, you're interested in the supernatural. Do you mind if I tell you of something that happened to me there? I know you won't laugh at me, and I've been wanting to get it off my chest to someone."

Of course I agreed.

"As you know," he began, "I've always had a passion for mountains. I know nothing about rock climbing, but I love scrambling among high hills. Don't think that I treat mountains with the over-confident foolhardiness of the novice! Far from it. I'm fully alive to my limitations; and while mountains exercise strange fascination over me, they also frighten me. And since my recent experience in the Black Cuillin they've frightened me a great deal more.

"Late this September I was spending a fortnight in Skye in the company of a friend. We had pitched our tent in Glen Brittle. Behind us soared up the southern peaks of the great horseshoe-shaped range of the Cuillin. From the glen they presented a fantastic, jagged-shaped skyline, all too often shrouded in mist. My friend was a climber of some ability, but out of deference to my inexperience we had spent the first two days of our visit clambering about among the foothills. On the third morning, however, we set out on a whole day's expedition. Leaving at nine o'clock, we soon traversed the boggy grassland that separated our camp from the hills, and the ground became firm and rocky under our feet. The grass became sparser, and finally disappeared as we climbed the west ridge of Sgurr Dearg. Though this is one of the highest peaks, it is also perhaps the easiest to climb, and two hours' clambering found us at the top. Some of the upper stages provided stretches of stiff scrambling, where the use of hands as well as feet was necessary, and I was glad to relax when the summit was gained. The view out to sea was superb. The islands of Canna, Rhum and Eigg seemed quite close, whilst beyond them to the right we could see the Outer Hebrides, a low chain in an illimitable vista of ocean. We picked them out one by one on the map. Then moving to the other side of the ridge, we looked down into Loch Coruisk.

"Ever since the days of Sir Walter Scott descriptive writers have exhausted their superlatives on the scene that met our gaze, and I shan't try to compete with them. The grandeur of that mighty semicircular amphitheatre beggars description. The sheer rock walls ran right round to the sea at either end, and three thousand feet below lay the blue-black loch, a land-locked stretch of water unrivalled in its sinister beauty. Two and a half miles across the valley lay the great symmetrical shape of Blaven; on its left were the jagged teeth of Sgurr nan Gillean. In the immediate foreground was the Inaccessible Pinnacle and below it a thousand feet of sheer cliff.

"My friend and I were to part here. He was to spend the day on the ridge, while I was to descend on the far side and go down to the end of Loch Coruisk, where it runs over the falls into the sea at Loch Scavaig. On the previous afternoon I had been most carefully coached in my route. To the north of the peak on which we sat was a gully, well known to my friend and marked on the map as a safe walk for the tyro. My path having been described in the greatest detail, I set off along the ridge and duly found the place for my descent. For a thousand feet it was a straightforward scramble. At only one place did I encounter any difficulty, which a little care soon surmounted. The gully ended abruptly and I found myself at the top of a vast scree slope, stretching downwards for fifteen hundred feet. I always find walking on scree an exhilarating experience. One gets the illusion of cheating the laws of gravity; by rights the whole of the loose surface should begin to slide in an ever-increasing avalanche into the valley below – but in fact, of course, it slides a foot or two and then stops. The grinding, scrunching noise of my descent disturbed an eagle on the cliffs above, and I watched it wheel away over the range with slow strokes of its great wings. At the bottom of the scree was a shorter stretch of boulder-strewn hillside, and I soon found myself by the shore of the loch. This proved to be surprisingly difficult going. Great glacial slabs were everywhere, and they needed careful negotiation. I was hot and exhausted when I reached the waterfall. It was one o'clock, and the sun was now high in the sky. I unpacked my satchel and consumed the sandwiches I had brought with me, and as I ate I looked back at the great rock wall that I had surmounted. There was not a sign of life in that great bowl in the mountains. I scanned the ridge for some sign of my companion, but I could see nothing – nothing except the purple and grey gabbro cliffs and the dark waters of the loch. Any noise was drowned in the monotonous roar of the waterfall.

"I am not usually affected by solitude, but even in the bright sunlight I was not insensible to the sinister associations of the place. Queer unwelcome fancies began to obtrude themselves upon my imagination. I got the impression that in the dark shadows of those cliffs unseen watchers had me under observation, and I felt that their interest in me was the reverse of benevolent. I craved for company, and again I ran my eye along the mountain tops for some sign of my friend, but he was nowhere to be seen. With an effort of will power I turned my back upon Loch Coruisk and looked out to sea.

"I was surprisingly tired. I had come perhaps six miles, and my muscles were not yet accustomed to the demands of the hills. The sun was very hot, and before setting off on the return journey I lay down to rest on a stone slab.

"I must have slept; for I had a strange dream. It was a familiar nightmare of my childhood, but it must have been quite twenty years since I had last experienced it. I was back in the garden of our Gloucestershire home, peering through the boundary hedge at the old watermill which lay just beyond it. This mill had exercised an unholy fascination over my brother and myself as children, particularly as the miller was a bad-tempered, cross-grained old man, who detested children and never failed to chase us away with threats when we trespassed on his property. Consequently an air of mystery enveloped the place for us, and there was nothing so evil that we did not believe it of the miller. In my dream I scrambled through the hedge, and made my way along the river bank to the open doorway of the building. The mill was working, and I listened enthralled to the continuous rumble and splash of the great water-wheel, which served as an undertone for the clatter and squeaks of the wooden gear-wheels and the harsher grinding note of the millstones.

"I could see my arch enemy, the old miller, bending over his work, with his back towards me, and greatly daring, I tiptoed past him and concealed myself in the storeroom at the side of the building. The walls were lined with row upon row of full sacks, and I sat there in almost complete darkness, for the only light came through the door, which was slightly ajar. I must have been there for perhaps ten minutes, when in some mysterious way the miller divined my presence. He wheeled round suddenly and with a low laugh he hobbled across and slammed the door of my hiding-place. I was frightened and wondered what he would do next, but nothing happened. Then the vibrations that shook the whole building decreased in their tempo, and I realised that he was stopping the wheel. Gradually the rumbling and the clatter ceased, and was succeeded by comparative silence, broken only by the sound of the millstream. I sat there in the darkness, straining my ears. Suddenly my attention was distracted by a sound I detected in the storeroom itself. The great white sacks which lined the walls seemed to be moving, slowly but none the less surely, inwards. I could just see their dim outlines, strangely magnified in the gloom, and above the noise of the stream I could hear the steady scraping of the coarse fabric on the floor. Gradually the space in which I stood was contracted in its diameter: it decreased from twenty feet to ten – from ten to five. I tried to cry out, but found that I couldn't. And this, I think, is one of the most distressing features of a nightmare – to strain every nerve to call for help and to find that no sound will come. Then, as always happened in my childhood's dream, just as the circle of great sacks drew so close that they almost touched me, I somehow contrived to break the spell and I awoke.

"I sat up and shivered. Then I looked at my watch and saw that it was nearly six o'clock. The whole aspect of the place had changed. The sun had passed behind the barrier of the mountains and the whole landscape was in shadow. The cliffs which had been a friendly purple and grey were now black and forbidding, and the loch had assumed the hue of pitch. I lifted my eyes expecting to see the familiar jagged skyline in silhouette, but the sight that met my gaze made me catch my breath. For the peaks were shrouded in mist. Darkness would fall before I could repass that formidable frontier and regain the camp. The mist would probably grow thicker – and every tale of men lost in these hills came into my mind with horrid clarity. I knew, too, with what anxiety my companion would view my non-appearance, and I thought that he might be tempted to wait among those unfamiliar precipices and try to find me. To cross them alone in the misty darkness I felt to be quite beyond my power, and I hastily got out my map.

"I knew that, if I skirted the outer edge of the range on the seaward side, I could get back to Glen Brittle. But it was not quite so simple as that. It was, of course, much longer – probably ten or eleven miles. But between me and the glen lay two great spurs which ran out at right angles from the main range. The first was perhaps two miles in length, and consisted of a series of peaks gradually diminishing in height. To go round it would put at least three miles on to my journey, and I wanted above all things to get back before my friend took serious alarm and roused Glen Brittle Lodge on my behalf. I didn't want the humiliation of search parties going off into the mist to look for me. The map marked a route over the spur to the south of Sgurr nan Eag, and from where I sat I could see the saddle that I must cross. It was not very high, perhaps fifteen hundred feet. At present it was clear of mist, and I set off briskly round the edge of the range, about a hundred feet above the sea. A deep ravine in my path gave me some trouble, but I found a place higher up where I could cross it, and climbed steadily. The marshy heather of the coastal strip gave place to boulders, then the boulders became scree. I had lost sight of the spot where I must cross the ridge, and the scree above me ended in two gullies. I hesitated and took the left-hand one. After a quarter of an hour's hard scrambling it ended in a sheer rock face, and I had no alternative but to retrace my steps.

"The half-hour that I had wasted was an important one – for the mist had come down and I could no longer see the skyline. But there was nothing for it but to go on, and I climbed the other gully as fast as I could. Soon I was surrounded by the damp swirling cloud, which reduced visibility to a few feet and muffled the sound of my footsteps. It was cold, too, and damp. As often as I thought that the summit was reached, I found a fresh stretch of hillside looming out of the mist. At length, however, the ridge was passed without incident, and I started to descend. I was trying to hurry, and this was nearly my undoing, for, missing my footing, I stumbled forward and half fell, half slithered for perhaps thirty feet before I came to rest on some scree. I was considerably shaken, but it was with great relief that I found that I hadn't turned my ankle or done myself any serious harm. With greater caution I continued my descent, and I came down out of the mist once more. The going was easier; I paused to consider the next stretch of my route, and got out my map again.

"There was still another great spur between me and the camp, but it was very different from the one I had just surmounted. Instead of being a gently diminishing series of peaks with saddles between them, it ran out at right angles to the range and ended in the mighty bastion of Sron na Ciche, perhaps the most awesome mountain precipice in the British Isles, rising sheer from the floor of the glen to a height of over 2,500 feet. Between the gigantic cliff and Sgurr Alasdair on the main range there were two routes marked on my map as possible crossing-places without recourse to rock climbing, but I could not bring myself to try to find them.

"My experience in the mist had unnerved me, and I decided that, though it would make a considerable detour, I would skirt the spur and not take to the hills again.

"As I refolded my map, I turned and looked back up the hillside. The mist was slowly dropping down on to me. As I watched I saw its white tentacles writhing their way down through the gullies that I had just traversed. It was like some vast army advancing on me, and leading it were detached white patches and spirals which moved ahead of the main body. I was irresistibly reminded of my dream, and confirmed in my resolution to make my way home at a lower level.

"So I scrambled down the steep mountain-side, and soon found myself in what I thought was the lesser evil – the great peat bog that lies between the mountains and the sea.

"It was not a dangerous bog, if one picked one's way carefully. Frequent changes of direction were necessary to avoid bad patches, and I was soon covered to above the knees with the noisome black mud and slime that I floundered through in my path. I found also that it was almost unbelievably exhausting after the strenuous events of the day. I leaped from tussock to tussock of coarse grass and, as I landed on each, it settled slowly down into the ooze with a bubbling, squelching sound that drove me on to seek the next tuft. At last I found myself under the great rock walls of Sron na Ciche, and here the ground was firmer. I lay down full length for a few minutes and gathered my strength; the bog had taken more out of me than I thought. Then I skirted the cliffs which soared above my head until they were lost in the mist. By this time it was very nearly dark, as dark in fact as it would ever get in Skye at this time of the year. As I rounded the farthest extremity of the barrier, a sight met my eyes which made me almost shout aloud for joy. Across perhaps three miles of bog I could see the lights in the windows of Glen Brittle Lodge. My goal was in sight.

"I expect you'll think that that was the end of my adventure. I certainly thought so myself at the time. But the rest of my journey was not to be without event. It is not a subject on which I care to dwell, but I will do my best to give you a faithful account of what I saw and what I felt. Explanation I have none, except perhaps that my physical exhaustion was playing tricks with my mind.

"I set out again slowly across the bog. I knew now how tiring my passage would be, and I wanted to husband my strength. I'm afraid that any thought of alleviating my friend's anxiety by an early arrival had long ago disappeared. My sole concern was to arrive at all, early or late.

"I picked my way from tussock to tussock, keeping my eyes fixed on the light ahead. When I had gone about six hundred yards I turned and looked back. There was no ground mist at all; the clouds still lay at about a thousand feet, but as I looked I saw what I thought was a spiral of mist detach itself from the gloom of the vast black precipice I had left behind me. It drifted forward for a few yards and then stopped, hanging motionless in the air.

"It struck me as an odd phenomenon – nothing more: perhaps the forerunner of a bank of fog, as yet invisible, which might be coming up from the sea, and I turned my face again towards the light. After a further twenty minutes I rested again and turned my head. My heart missed a beat. The white pillar had moved, it was closer now, perhaps a quarter of a mile away. It seemed roughly oblong in shape and about five feet high. As I looked, it seemed to hesitate and stop too. I took a few steps forward and looked again, and I saw that it was moving in my direction once more. With a sudden access of terror I realised that I was being followed by something – something that could not see me, but could hear me as I squelched and floundered across the bog. I assure you that in that moment all the previous fears and anxieties of the day were as nothing. An icy shiver ran down my spine. I tried to move forward silently. At any other time the idea of a man trying to tiptoe across a bog would have been ludicrous. I assure you that there was no humour in it for me. Of course it was hopeless, and as the water oozed and bubbled round my feet I could see out of the corner of my eye the shape moving steadily on, always seeming to gain a little on me.

"My nerve broke. Never before or since have I given way to such blind panic as possessed me then. I started to run. My exhaustion was forgotten. I stumbled and floundered from tuft to tuft, and the still night seemed to resound with the awful sucking noise that my feet made and with the hammering of my heart. I no longer tried to pick my route; I ran straight towards the beckoning light of the house in the glen. A small pool lay across my path and before I knew what I was doing I was up to my waist in the ooze and slime of that accursed bog. Somehow I gained the comparatively firm clumps of reed and grass on the other side, and with much kicking and splashing I hauled myself out of the water.

"But this had taken time: and one apprehensive look over my shoulder told me that the thing was gaining on me fast. It couldn't have been more than fifty yards away, and I ran as I have never run before. I dimly realised that the worst of the bog was past and that the ground was getting firmer under my feet. I seemed to see another light ahead of me, moving as if to meet me. Suddenly I felt something clutch at my ankles, and I went down like a stone. As I fell I gave a great despairing cry, and then everything seemed to be blotted out. I got the impression of being enveloped in some coarse damp fabric; my face was pressed into the moist soft ground, and my nostrils were filled with the reek of rotting vegetation.

"I can remember nothing clearly after that. I have a hazy recollection of being half-dragged and half-carried back to the camp by my friend. The moving light I had seen had been his: he had heard my approach and hurried out to meet me. He laid me out on my bed and poured brandy down my throat. I was prostrate with terror and exhaustion. After a while the latter triumphed, and I fell into a deep sleep. It was sixteen solid hours before I opened my eyes again.

"I was terribly ashamed. In the clear light of the sun I realised what an appalling fool I had made of myself. I was abject in my apologies for causing so much anxiety by my fecklessness. I told my friend how I had slept by the waterfall and had decided to come home by the longer route; how I had fallen on the hillside and stumbled across the bog, and finally had given way to weariness and panic. But I couldn't bring myself to speak of the thing that had followed me, and he didn't mention having seen anything. It must have been a figment of my overwrought brain.

"But was it? I cannot believe that I imagined the whole episode. I was tired and worried, but surely that couldn't account for so vivid an apparition? After all, it didn't occur until the end of my journey was in sight and my anxieties on that score were at rest. What do you think about it?"

I was silent for a minute or two. Marchand's narrative had struck a chord in my memory. Then I rose and walked across to the bookshelves. I took down a recent volume of the publications of the Scottish Folklore Society. In it were printed certain Gaelic legends and stories collected in the last century by that great antiquary, John Francis Campbell of Islay. I found the passage I wanted and handed the open book across to Marchand. It read:

"The White Sack used to roll itself round men's feet, bringing them down, then, getting on top of them, it used to flatten them out and murder them."

1948

CWM GARON

L. T. C. Rolt

Known as Tom to his friends, Lionel Thomas Caswall Rolt (1910–1974) was a writer with a particular interest in industrial and transport history. His book *Narrow Boat* was a bestseller when it was first published in 1944. A romantic account of a canal tour on his boat, *Cressy*, it inspired a generation of canal-lovers, and led to Rolt co-founding the Inland Waterways Association with his friend and fellow writer of uncanny fiction, Robert Aickman. The two would later fall out over the direction their preservation efforts should take, and Rolt would move on to other projects, not least saving the Talyllyn steam railway in Wales. Although he would continue to write prolifically, the only collection of supernatural stories published in his lifetime remained the remarkable *Sleep No More* (1948), where "Cwm Garon" can be found.

It is wonderful and strange that two of the great campaigners for Britain's waterways should also have written such brilliant weird fiction. Rolt's stories can feel more traditionally Jamesian than Aickman's unique, disquieting pieces, but he maintains a distinct style, frequently drawing upon his knowledge of Britain's engineering heritage. "Cwm Garon" is a more decidedly rural tale, with Rolt steadily developing an unsettling atmosphere as the narrative of an ancient evil that has seeped into a Welsh valley unfolds.

The story takes place around Llangaron Abbey, which Rolt based on Llanthony Priory in the Black Mountains, a place he loved. "No building in Britain has so majestical a setting as Llanthony," he wrote in *Landscape with Machines*, the first part of his autobiography. The ruined priory sits in a stunning location below imposing slopes and does indeed have an inn adjoining it, providing the perfect spot for a post-hike pint. And if primeval powers do lurk in the hills around the priory ruins, we can only imagine, based on our own visits to this landscape, that they are distinctly benevolent.

After a long winter spent in the fog and grime of London, this Welsh Borderland was balm to the eye. Spring had only just touched the soot-blackened trees in the squares with the lightest film of green, but here she had already run riot, dressing the whole countryside in fresh splendour. So thought John Carfax as the labouring branch-line train bore him slowly over the last stage of his long journey to Wales. The map lay disregarded on his knees as he watched the moving panorama of hills stippled with April cloud shadows, of neat farms buried in the white mist of fruit orchards, and of rich meadows dotted with sheep or the red cattle of Herefordshire. He was in that mood of exhilaration and heightened perception which only a well-earned and long-awaited holiday in new surroundings can awaken, and he sniffed delightedly at the limpid air, crystalline as spring water yet somehow filled with unidentifiable sweetness, which blew in through the open window. He was alone in the compartment now, but it had evidently been market day in the town where he had left the London express, for the little train standing at the bay platform had been filled with country folk. Black-gaitered farmers and their plump, basket-laden wives, all had gone, but still he seemed to smell sheep-dip and carbolic, to hear the lilt of their Border speech, and to see the lithe Welsh sheep-dog which had sat between his master's legs, regarding him with wall-eyed suspicion.

The rhythm of wheels over rail joints slowed, and Carfax could tell from the labouring exhaust beats of the engine that they were climbing steeply. A chasm-like cutting hewn through the old red sandstone cut off the view and plunged the compartment into sudden twilight. As suddenly, the train emerged and, with a hollow reverberation, crossed a swift mountain torrent, before swinging round a curve so sharp that the wheel flanges grunted and squealed in protest. As it did so, the carriage window framed a picture which made Carfax start and catch his breath in wonder, so startling was it in its wild grandeur after looking so long on the smooth fields and hills of England. A towering mountain wall had suddenly arisen to enclose the whole western horizon, and to dominate and dwarf the familiar landscape of the foreground. Seen thus against the westering light of late afternoon, the shadowed face of this great massif presented so marked a contrast to the sunlit levels below as to seem unreal and as menacing as a thunder-cloud. So impenetrable was the shadow on the mountain that its contours were invisible, and the long, level line of the ridge, sharply etched across the sky's brightness, appeared to mark the lip of a precipice the height of which seemed monstrously magnified.

Reluctantly, John Carfax turned his attention from the window to the map. Then, as he felt the brakes applied, he got up and lifted his rucksack down from the luggage rack. This must be Pont Newydd; he would have to step out if he was to cross the mountain and reach the inn at Llangaron Abbey by nightfall. A good map-reader, he had no doubt of his ability to find his way through strange country by daylight, but to be overtaken by darkness on an open mountain was a very different matter. He welcomed the prospect of the long, hard walk after the inactivity of the train journey, and set off at a smart pace up the narrow road from the station. Behind him, he heard the train pant heavily out of earshot. It seemed to symbolise the last link between him and the civilisation he had so lately left, and as he turned to glance at the thin plume of steam fast vanishing into the distance he felt something of the sensation a voyager feels when, landed on some remote, far distant island, he sees the ship that has brought him fade over the horizon. He experienced momentarily a strange feeling of loneliness, realising that the train was an intruder from that world of elaborate artifice by means of which man had shut himself away from the eternal world of earth and sky as though fearful of their elemental mystery. It had ruffled a still pool of silence, but now the last ripples died away into stillness, until there remained no sounds but his own footfall, a distant rumour of birdsong and the sibilant voice of the little brook which ran beside the road.

He had been walking for the best part of an hour before he came in sight of the first of the landmarks he had previously noted on his map, a grey, ruined tower set upon a conical mound and surrounded by a ditch. He conjectured correctly that it was one of the border keeps erected by the Norman Lords Marcher in their efforts to subdue the Silurians of the mountains. Here, turning off the metalled road into a rutted, high-banked lane, he set his face towards the mountain wall which had hitherto marched on his left hand. Pressing on, he passed by two small whitewashed farms where sheep-dogs ran out to bark and sniff at his heels, but though the lane climbed continuously, the skyline of the ridge seemed to retreat elusively before him. At length, however, he emerged on to a level plateau, treeless except for a few stunted thorn bushes, and patterned by crumbling, dry stone walls which had proved powerless to resist the downward march of the bracken. Here he came within the mountain's shadow, so that his eyes could, for the first time, penetrate its darkness to discern the steep diagonal path which scaled the ridge. Following its upward course he could see, too, the shallow notch cut in the skyline of the ridge which marked the pass, if "pass" it could be called, for his map told him that the path climbed almost to the 2000 feet contour. The premature dusk of the shadow spurred him on, and he had soon passed through a rickety gate on to the open mountain and was tackling the steep ascent. Pausing on the break-neck path to regain his breath, he turned and saw that already the plateau, which had seemed so high and windswept, now looked insignificant, merging imperceptibly into a vast chequer-work of field and copse whose folds this height had now smoothed out. He plodded on, and had nearly reached the summit before he stopped and turned again to find that the familiar landscape had shrunk to a remote perspective, while the evening sunlight on the farther fields looked pallid and unreal as though seen through a veil. Glancing about him he saw the reason. A white wall of cloud was rolling along the ridge out of the north-west, and in the next instant the scene below was lost in swirling mist. No rain fell, but his rough tweed jacket was soon pearled with beads of moisture, while a chill wind blew about him.

The sudden coming of the mist brought with it a feeling of utter isolation, intensifying the loneliness he had felt when he left the station. It seemed to mark a further stage in some inexorable progress designed deliberately to cut him off from the familiar world of his fellow-men. Sole occupant of a minute island of mountain turf, heather and whinberry, that familiar world already seemed incredibly remote. Fortunately for him, the path was clearly defined, so that he was able to press on without pause or doubt. And as he did so, some curious trick of the silver light threw his shadow upon the white curtain before him so that it seemed that a figure, monstrous, yet tenuous as the mist itself, was leading him onward towards the summit of the pass. Watching it, he thought he could understand the stories he had heard of the creatures which were believed to haunt the mountain mists, and he felt he knew the terror that might come with this loneliness as terror comes with darkness to the child. His heart seemed to beat in his ears like a muffled drum, for the stillness was intense, even his footfall was muffled now by the resilient turf of the path. When, faint and far off, his ear caught the cry of a curlew, the sound brought no comforting sense of companionship, but by its plaintive wildness, seemed only to accentuate the silence and the loneliness. Suddenly, the path swung right-handed, levelled out, and he found himself passing through a narrow defile which he knew must mark the spine of the ridge. Immediately beyond the pass, the track skirted a mawne pit, a hole from which peats had once been dug, but which had now become a quagmire ringed by livid green moss and tufted cotton-grass. A luckless mountain pony had evidently floundered into it at some time and, unable to extricate itself, had perished miserably. Now that ravens, crows and mountain foxes had done their work, all that remained was a skeleton of whitened bones wrapped in the hide as in a winding-sheet. Carfax paused for a moment at this desolate sight, and as he did so the curlew cried again, nearer at hand this time, and the mist seemed to eddy more densely about him. He shivered involuntarily and went on, happy to find that the path was now leading him downwards as steeply as it had climbed. As he stumbled along, his feet pressing uncomfortably into the toes of his shoes, he noticed that the mist was now thinning, and that its whiteness was becoming suffused with golden light although the invisible depths into which he was descending still seemed dark. Not only was he walking out of the mists, but the cloud itself appeared to be lifting, sweeping up the steep flank of the mountain like steam out of a cauldron until, with breathtaking and dramatic suddenness, the veil which had imprisoned and blinded him lifted like a curtain to reveal the whole wild prospect clearly before him. "You'll find the valley enchanting" – he suddenly recalled the words of the friend who had first suggested his holiday, not in their original sense as a conventional overstatement, but with a new, and strangely literal significance.

He stood in the last stormy light of a sun that was just about to set behind the rim of yet another mountain ridge which marched parallel with that upon which he stood, and which appeared to be of equal, if not greater height. It could not be much more than a mile by crow-flight, he judged, from ridge to ridge, yet between them yawned Cwm Garon, a stupendous furrow which, in the course of unnumbered centuries, the Afon Garon had carved into the heart of the mountains. Already this valley was wrapped in the blue shades of a premature twilight, yet Carfax could sense rather than see the intense green of the meadows along the floor of the Cwm. Here and there, lights gleamed from farmhouse windows. Faintly there rose into the thin mountain air the resinous incense of pine-wood smoke, and the murmur of the swiftly flowing river. At one point the valley widened into a natural amphitheatre in the centre of which stood the grey shape of a building larger than a mountain farm. This Carfax took to be his destination, the ruined Abbey of Llangaron and its adjoining inn. After the cloud-blinded solitude of the mountain-top, the sight of his goal raised his spirits to high good humour, and he strode on down the steep path at a great pace, his mind occupied with the prospect of a blazing fire, a well-earned dinner and a foaming tankard.

Great anticipations are often the prelude to disillusionment, but in this instance John Carfax was not disappointed. The dinner was excellent, and he gave a sigh of contentment as he stirred his coffee and extended his slippered feet towards the friendly flame of the log fire. Its warmth was welcome for the spring nights were chilly in this valley which the sun so soon forsook. In the opposite chimney-corner, likewise toasting his toes, sat his only fellow-guest at the inn. He was busily writing in what appeared to Carfax to be a large journal or diary which he balanced on his knee, and the tireless scratching of his pen mingled with the comfortable crackling of the fire, and the occasional faint bubbling sound which Carfax's pipe made when he drew deeply. In London, he thought, it is never truly quiet, but here one becomes conscious of the slightest sound. He had exchanged generalities with his companion during their meal when they had sat together, but the latter had not been very forthcoming. He was much older than Carfax; in middle age he had obviously been a man of great strength, tall and broad in proportion. Now the wide shoulders stooped, and a suit of rough, grey tweed hung loosely about his gaunt frame. Yet it was obvious that he was still very active, nor had his presence lost its power of command. A fine head of white hair and a short, pointed beard meticulously trimmed made a fitting frame for the massive brow and the distinguished features. The most remarkable thing about these features, Carfax thought, were the eyes, bright blue eyes which had no need of glasses and whose keenness quite belied his age. When he had spoken he had regarded his fellow-guest with a penetrating, unblinking gaze that was almost hypnotic in its intensity and which, in a lesser man, would have seemed mere ill-mannered arrogance. Carfax found it disconcerting, for it gave him the impression that a keen intelligence, possessing a store of secret knowledge, was coolly taking the measure of his own mind while it remained itself inscrutable, permitting him no such liberty. He recalled with a slight feeling of resentment that whereas he had straightway introduced himself, the other had not responded similarly.

He yawned and must have dozed, for he suddenly became conscious that the fire had burned lower, and that the bole of his pipe was cold. He hoped that he had not snored, and glanced apprehensively at his companion. If he had, it would seem that his bad manners had passed unnoticed for the other's head was still bent over his book and his pen travelled imperturbably on. He glanced at his watch. The hour was not late, but the long journey, the keen air and the warmth of the fire had told upon him, and his eyelids were heavy with sleep. He rose to go to bed, but before doing so some chance impulse made him walk to the window, part the curtains and look out.

The night was clear, and a bright moon, near the full, rode above a wrack of clouds which was drifting like smoke from lip to lip of the defile. Yet despite the swiftly moving clouds overhead an absolute stillness held the valley, for the trees stood motionless. Only the unseen river, rushing over its rocky bed, sounded incessantly. The window looked directly up the roofless nave of the Abbey, and the great columns threw upon the moonlit grass, shadows so dense that the eye could scarcely distinguish image from substance. Beyond, above the site of the high altar, the great east window, devoid of tracery, framed the dark brooding shape of the mountain which Carfax had crossed that evening. The scene was so extravagant in its chiaroscuro, so humiliating in its grandeur, that he could not restrain a muttered exclamation –

"Oh who will tell me where
He found thee at that dead and silent hour?
What hallowed solitary ground did bear
So rare a flower
Within whose sacred leaves did lie
The fullness of the Deity?"

It was appropriate that these lines of the Silurist should have sprung to his mind, for it was not surprising, he reflected, that this country should have been the inspiration of Vaughan and Traherne. Here, truly, heaven seemed nearer earth...

"And hell, too, maybe."

Carfax started, not only because the voice sounded close at his elbow, but because he was not aware that he had spoken his thoughts aloud. He realised that his taciturn companion had moved silently from his chair and was gazing out into the night with those strange, unblinking eyes of his.

"Yes," he went on in a soft, ruminative tone, as though he were speaking more to himself than to Carfax, "it is certainly very beautiful, so beautiful that it distils some influence – call it magic if you like – which turns men's minds from material to spiritual things. Unless I am much mistaken, it set you thinking of the Dominicans who built their great church in this solitude, and of the Silurists, Traherne and Vaughan."

Carfax turned back into the room, letting the curtain fall across the window. The uncanny accuracy with which the other had read his thoughts disturbed him.

His expression must have revealed this disquiet, for the other chuckled. "I must really apologise," he went on, "if I startled you. I can assure you I am not really such an accomplished thought-reader.

Let me explain: I have visited this valley on numerous occasions spread over a period of years, and I know that on first acquaintance it always casts this same spell over visitors who, like yourself, are gifted with imagination. All I have done was to observe in you the familiar symptoms."

Carfax was somewhat mollified, though he still felt slightly irritated by the other's self-assurance, and by the way in which he talked of what had been to him a profound spiritual experience as though it were a cold in the head. Nevertheless, his companion's words had roused his curiosity.

"What exactly do you mean by saying 'on first acquaintance'?" he asked. "Are you suggesting that my present impression of Cwm Garon is likely to change? And what did you mean by your odd remark about hell?"

"Taking the first question first," replied the other, "if I have judged you correctly, then I think your impressions will change, but I don't propose to bias your mind by suggesting how that change may come, or what form it will take. Explore the valley for yourself tomorrow and then, if you should feel so disposed, I should be most interested to hear your views. As to your second question," he went on, "I regret the remark, and do not know what prompted me to make it. I would prefer not to explain myself further for the moment, except to suggest that a belief in heaven implies a corresponding belief in hell."

Despite renewed questioning, the older man refused to commit himself further, and it was a puzzled and thoughtful Carfax who eventually bid his fellow-guest good night, lit his candle, and made his way up the narrow, stone newel stair to his bed in the tower room.

He slept soundly, rose early and breakfasted alone. He was about to set out on his tour of exploration, in fact he was standing in the hall of the inn packing sandwiches into his haversack, when he noticed the visitors' book and remembered that he had not yet signed it. As he turned the pages to remedy this omission, he discovered the identity of his fellow-guest, for in the last occupied space was written "Charles Elphinstone, Oxford", in a fluent, scholarly hand. The name seemed familiar, but for the life of him he could not place it.

By the time he had reached the valley floor the previous night, darkness had prevented him from forming an adequate picture of his new surroundings, and now the weather conditions could scarcely have been less favourable. The portents of a stormy sunset and an ominously clear night had been fulfilled. The mountain walls upon either hand were hidden by a moving wrack of clouds whose tattered fringe had descended almost to the upper limit of the cultivated fields. A fine but deceptively penetrating rain was falling, and although occasional strong gusts of wind came eddying off the mountains, now from this direction, now from that, the air was humid and stifling. The swollen Garon and the innumerable small torrents cascading down the steep slopes filled the valley with the sound of falling water. Nevertheless, knowing how swiftly the mountain climate could change, Carfax was not unduly downcast and, buttoning up the collar of his mackintosh, he set off resolutely up the valley. The lane was narrow and high banked, and was never far away from the line of alder and hazel which overhung the shallow gorge through which the river flowed. He noticed that the small fields, both pasture and arable, looked clean and well tended, their hedges neatly laid and trimmed, but he saw no one at work in them. The small farms seemed equally deserted, and had he not scented wood-smoke as he passed them he would have thought that they were empty. No doubt the weather accounted for this suspension of activity. It struck him as ironical that the only fellow-mortal he encountered in the morning's solitude he passed by unawares. Only a chance glance over his shoulder had revealed the figure of a man sheltering beneath a tree which he had lately passed. The man stood so still, and the old brown overcoat, together with the sack which he had thrown over head and shoulders against the wet, blended so exactly with the colour of the tree bole at his back, that Carfax stopped for a moment to confirm his first glance. The man ignored his scrutiny, but when, at the bend of the road, he looked back again, he was no longer to be seen.

He had been walking for the best part of an hour when he saw on the left of the road what he took to be the ruins of a church. The valley was narrower here, and its walls more precipitous, for the clouds revealed glimpses of naked crags and desolate screes of shattered boulders. As though these features had not already made the site of the church sombre enough, a dense belt of pine-trees had been planted beside it. This must be Capel Cwm Garon, he reflected, recalling his study of the map during breakfast. He thought he had never seen so gloomy a place, it would seem dark even in sunlight, and, as the ruined church appeared to be of no architectural merit, he walked on. He conjectured that he must be nearing the head of the valley, for the lane grew rougher and commenced to climb steeply until he presently gained the open mountain. The rain had stopped, the sky looked brighter ahead, while the clouds showed signs of lifting. The rain, the lowering clouds and the oppressive humid warmth of the valley had between them damped his spirits, but now he stepped out cheerfully, a cooler and drier wind in his face which made him feel as one who passes into fresh night air out of some overheated room.

By the time he had reached the head of the pass and could look down on the great landscape of hill and vale spread out beneath him, there was blue sky overhead, and a moving pattern of sunlight and shadow was dappling the slopes of the mountains. Carfax felt very well content as he sat with his back against a sheltering boulder and munched his sandwiches. Not far away a little group of mountain ponies were grazing, while high overhead a buzzard soared on moth-like wings. A shepherd was gathering his sheep off the north face of the mountain; Carfax could see his tiny foreshortened figure on the plateau far below, and his shrill whistle as he worked his dogs was borne up to him on the wind. These things brought a sense of life and companionship, dispelling the feeling of loneliness that had been growing upon him since he left the train on the previous day. He took out his map and checked his position. He had reached the central massif of the range. From it, the long ridges stretched southward like the fingers of an outspread hand. Between them, and to the west, lay two valleys, the Llan Fawr and the Llan Fechan, running parallel with Cwm Garon. As the weather seemed to have set fair, and there was plenty of time, he decided he would walk back down the Llan Fawr valley, cross the intervening ridge at a point well below Llangaron, and so return to the inn from the opposite direction.

He found that the valley of Llan Fawr was physically very similar to that of Cwm Garon. If anything, it was even narrower, while the mountain walls were equally high. Yet somehow the atmosphere of the place seemed quite different; "more friendly" was the description which at once occurred to him. Obviously the improvement in the weather must be responsible, he decided; this mountain country was strangely temperamental. Owing to the more restricted area of cultivated land, the small farms were spaced farther apart than those in Cwm Garon, yet there seemed to be no lack of life and activity. A hedger at work beside the lane, and a swarthy individual leading a pair of jennets with pack-saddles, bid him a lilting good day as he passed. In one farmyard three small children paused from play to stare round-eyed as he went by, while in a nearby field, sown with oats, a farmer was working a two-horse roll. Finally, just before he turned off the road to climb back over the ridge, he met a woman driving three cows to the evening milking.

When he had finished the climb and begun the steep descent, the sun was still lighting the fields on the farther side of Cwm Garon, but he noticed that they looked just as deserted as they had done that morning. There still seemed to be neither sight nor sound of any activity. Silence seemed to well up from the valley like water from a spring, in fact the distant murmur of the Garon seemed to symbolise and accentuate it. He began to recall all the small workaday noises which he had heard but not remarked in Llan Fawr, and the lower he descended, the louder his footfalls seemed to sound. Despite the sunlight and the clear air he found the feeling of loneliness and of strange oppression inexplicably returning. There was a sense of menacing constriction about the towering walls which hemmed in this valley and cut him off from the outer world, and yet, after his experience in Llan Fawr, he knew that it could not merely be a case of claustrophobia.

He had not gone far along the road back to Llangaron when he came in sight of a small public-house, and decided that a glass of beer would help him over the last lap of the way. Probably, too, he would find company there which would dispel this curious illusion that the valley was deserted.

The dim, low-ceilinged room – there was no bar – was snug and spotless. The stone-flagged floor looked newly scrubbed, and the dark polished surfaces of table, settle and high-backed Welsh dresser caught the light of the cheerful fire which burned in the hob grate. But the room was empty and silent save for the small settling sounds of the fire and the measured ticking of the grandfather clock. Carfax coughed and scuffed his feet on the flags. A latch clicked in the back of the house, and as the unseen door opened he heard a deep rumble of male voices. A woman appeared, and when she had fetched his drink he made some trivial pleasantry, but she seemed either shy or taciturn, for she answered in monosyllables, and after standing awkwardly for a moment, retired again to what he imagined to be the kitchen. The indistinguishable murmur of male talk went on. Carfax took a deep and gratifying draught, and then stooped to knock out his pipe in the ash-tray. As he did so, he realised that the dottle already in the tray was warm, and that the cigarette stub beside it was still smouldering. Looking round the room curiously, he then saw that a man's cap lay in the chimney-corner of the settle, and that two knarled hazel sticks were propped against the wall near the door. At any other time and place, Carfax would not have observed such trivialities, and even if he had he would have attached no importance to them. But now they bred in him a disquieting suspicion which refused to be dispelled. It was that his approach had been discreetly observed by the late occupants of the room, and that for reasons best known to themselves they had retreated to the kitchen. The uncomfortable feeling of unwelcome intrusion which this suspicion prompted scarcely encouraged him to linger. The room seemed to have grown suddenly hostile, so much so that he did not even pause to refill his pipe, but drained his glass and set out once more upon his way.

The sunlight had now crept away from the fields, so that although the higher slopes of the eastern ridge were still suffused with golden light, the shadows in the valley were already thickening into twilight. His experience at the inn had exerted a curious influence over his mind, he discovered, for although the farms he passed seemed as still and deserted as those he had seen that morning, they no longer gave him the impression of being uninhabited. On the contrary, he imagined that every window concealed a watcher, that every house was the centre of some intense and secret life which, at his approach, was instantly suspended. The farther he went the more certain did he become that his every movement was the subject of furtive scrutiny, yet it was a certainty which his reason was powerless either to confirm or to disprove. Time and again he would stop and look back quickly, hoping to surprise the swaying of a curtain, the movement of a door, or to see in the shadows of tree or hedge some tangible shape. He looked in vain. Yet the feeling and the fear continued to grow upon him despite his senses' negative evidence. It was no longer confined to the houses he passed and to the people who might or might not lurk within them; it was a fear distilled by the valley itself. The brooding mountains, the still pines, even the heavy, windless air itself seemed to have suspended some secret activity to join in this silent and malign watch. As he walked resolutely on, fear stalked at his elbow, and he felt as if he was the focal point of some great burning-glass of hostile forces. Just as the first lightning flash and thunder-clap puts a welcome end to the breath-bating suspense that precedes the storm, Carfax found himself wishing that something, however fearful, might happen. But no material event took place, and he reached the inn at Llangaron in good time for dinner. In the cheerful light of the dining-room he felt inclined to dismiss the matter as so much hallucination, but he could not deny that, as his fellow-guest had prophesied, his first impression of the valley had undergone radical revision.

"Well," queried Elphinstone as they drew their chairs to the fire after dinner, "what's the verdict now?"

Carfax hesitated. Considered in retrospect, his fears seemed so intangible and groundless, that he felt foolish and doubted his ability to express them in so many words. With the other's encouragement, however, he presently gave as detailed and faithful an account of his day as he was able. During his narration Elphinstone nodded occasionally, but seemed to evince no surprise. When Carfax had finished speaking he remained silent for a few moments, pulling at a thin, black cheroot.

"Interesting," he said at length. "Very interesting, but not, I can assure you, a unique experience by any means. For years, I might safely say for centuries, strangers have been made aware, by some such means as you describe, that they were not welcome in this valley."

"But it's not just the people," put in Carfax. "It's as though the valley..."

"I know, I know," the older man cut him short. "It's not as simple as that, is it? 'An angel satyr walks these hills'," he quoted; "know who wrote that? Why Kilvert. 'Angel satyr' – a curious association of opposites – what do you suppose induced a mild little Victorian curate to use such a term?"

"I think I can understand now," Carfax admitted. "*And* yet," he went on, "I refuse to believe that this sense of evil is a natural emanation of the place itself. As a Christian, I hold that both good and evil are human concepts, and that they do not exist in nature."

"Well put," said the other, "and probably true, but if, as a Christian, you believe that there are spiritual as well as material powers, then don't you think it possible that man might abuse and pervert the former no less than the latter?"

Carfax nodded. "Yes," he agreed, thoughtfully, "I suppose such a thing is possible."

"I am sure of it," Elphinstone went on, "and what's more I consider that this valley can prove my contention."

"Go on," prompted Carfax.

"I believe," the other continued, "that some evil force dominates Cwm Garon. I think it is a natural force which man, in some remote time, released and harnessed to secret and perverted ends. For centuries this dark power has been, as it were, dammed up in this valley until it has soaked into the very stones of the place. That is why a more superficial mind than yours might imagine that it is a natural phenomenon. Outside interference has an effect upon it like that of a stone flung into a still pool. That's why Cwm Garon and its people have always implacably resisted intrusion." He paused.

"But is that really so?" queried Carfax. "What evidence have you?"

"Apart from many similar experiences to your own," the older man replied, "there is ample historical evidence. Take this Abbey, for instance." He made a sweeping gesture. "It did not survive until the Dissolution. What happened? The community dwindled. Its numbers could not be maintained. Finally, a new Abbey of Llangaron was built in the safe, flat lands beside the Wye, and the old was abandoned. It has been said that it was too solitary, too open to attack by wolves or raiding hillmen. Do you find that explanation convincing? Do you think that a Church which deliberately sought the solitudes, and which established flourishing communities at such places as Valle Crucis or Strata Florida would be defeated merely by the loneliness of Cwm Garon? No, I suggest that they went because they feared something more potent but less tangible than wolves or robbers.

"You say you saw the ruined church at Capel Cwm Garon; do you know the history of that? It was built by a nineteenth-century religious sect headed by a man who called himself Brother Jeremy. What happened? History repeated itself; the community dwindled; misfortune followed misfortune. The eventual result you have seen for yourself. It's not only the efforts of the Church that have failed," he went on. "On the slope of the mountain just behind here you'll find the ruins of a house. There's not much to see, but it is all that's left of the place that Alaric Stephenson the artist tried to build for himself. I say 'tried' because it was never finished. He apparently had some grandiose notion that he was going to make a sort of miniature paradise for himself here, but he soon found he was mistaken. Everything went wrong. No local contractors would work for him. What was done during the day was undone at night. Even the trees he tried to plant were uprooted. I could quote several other examples of the same kind of thing, but the repetition would be boring."

"But do these… these forces manifest themselves in any way?" questioned Carfax.

"That depends," was the answer. "Unless you deliberately seek them or try to interfere with them, I should say no; you might stay here a month without experiencing any more than the sense of hostility and surveillance which you felt today!"

Elphinstone rose to his feet and lit the candle on the side-table.

"What is this extraordinary influence, and how exactly does it affect the people who live in Cwm Garon?" Carfax persisted.

The other was standing in the doorway about to bid him good night. His keen eyes glittered in the flickering candle flame as he smiled and shook his head.

"I cannot answer that question," he replied. "At least, not yet. I think I have a shrewd idea, but one day – soon perhaps – I hope to know."

The conversation had filled Carfax's head with disturbing speculations, and despite his long day in the mountain air it was some time before he lost consciousness. Even so, it must have been a light doze instead of his usual sound sleep, for he presently awoke and, glancing at the luminous dial of his wrist-watch, saw that it was nearly midnight. He became aware of stealthy movement in the room overhead at the top of the tower, movement betrayed by sounds so slight that he could never have detected them but for the profound stillness. Then he heard the pad of stealthy feet descending the stone stairs. A thin pencil of light flickered momentarily beneath his door and was gone. Carfax climbed softly out of the bed and crossed to the open window. He was in time to see a tall, slightly stooping, figure which he recognised unmistakably as that of Charles Elphinstone, cross the grass below and disappear beyond the ruined wall of the cloister garth. As he watched, he suddenly recalled the association of the name which had eluded him all day – Professor Charles Elphinstone, probably the greatest authority on folklore and magic since Frazer. "One day – soon perhaps – I hope to know." He seemed to hear an echo of his last words. Though Carfax was by no means of a timid disposition, he felt a reluctant, even envious feeling of admiration for the intrepid old man. Admittedly, on the face of it, a midnight stroll in this quiet Welsh valley seemed to call for no particular display of courage. The night was clear and brightly moonlit, the scene the same as before, the same black shadows of the nave arches on the dew-laden grass, the same black grandeur of mountains framed in the gaping east window, the same stillness. Yet this time, Carfax had no thought of Vaughan or Traherne, for he knew the fear that lurked in this silence. Were those lights, moving and dancing along the slopes of the mountains, or was it merely a trick of moonlight shining upon stone? Somewhere near at hand an owl hooted mournfully, and there came into his mind a line from the thirteenth chapter of Isaiah: "Owls shall dwell there, and satyrs shall dance there." He shivered, and returned to the welcome warmth of the bed.

The Professor did not appear at breakfast. Doubtless he was making up for lost sleep thought Carfax, but the reflection could not dispel a vague sense of uneasiness which refused to be quieted. He deliberately loitered in the dining-room, hoping Elphinstone would come. When, at half-past ten, his place was still empty, Carfax determined to settle his fears. He climbed the tower stairs to the Professor's room. A can stood outside his door. It was full, and the water was quite cold. He knocked softly, then more loudly. There was no response. Turning the handle very gently he opened the door a few inches and looked in. The room was empty.

Some instinct prompted Carfax to set out on his search in the same direction as he had taken the previous day, towards the ruined church of Capel Cwm Garon. He was still trying to reassure himself that his fears were groundless. Though Elphinstone had not, it appeared, warned the inn of any intended absence, he might well have decided to stay out on such a fine morning, while even involuntary absence might be caused by no worse mishap than a sprained ankle. Yet the feeling of foreboding would not be appeased. He realised that the date was May the first, that last night, in fact, had been "Eve of May" of ancient celebration, and somehow this knowledge by no means allayed his concern. Meanwhile, his senses observed the same atmosphere of hostility and watchfulness, but now, preoccupied with fresh fears, he no longer turned to peer at vacant windows or into the shadows beneath the trees, knowing that to do so would be fruitless. So he strode on until he came in sight of the crags of Black Daren which towered above the ruined church. As his eyes roamed over the precipice, he thought he detected a movement among the boulders of the screes below. He fumbled for his binoculars, and focused them hurriedly. Two men appeared to be bending over something which lay behind a rock, invisible to him. "No doubt a sheep has fallen from the crags," whispered reason, but dread lent wings to his feet.

Professor Charles Elphinstone had obviously slipped and fallen from a great height in attempting to scale the crags, and his body lay against the rock in that attitude of macabre abandonment which betokens shattered bones. His hat had fallen off, and the luxuriant white hair was matted with congealed blood. Carfax, who was familiar with death in many forms, was not dismayed by these gruesome commonplaces of violent dissolution. What drained the blood from his face and impelled him quickly to replace the sack which covered the body, was the expression on the face. He would not have believed that the features he had lately seen so calm and self confident, could have been moulded by terror to such hideous contortion.

It may be thought that Carfax would have no desire ever to revisit the valley; he would certainly have subscribed to this view himself when he left Llangaron on the day following the tragic accident. Everything about Cwm Garon had become repulsive to him and, as many others, it seemed, had done before him, he retired defeated. Never did the mundane environment of the outside world seem so friendly and welcoming. When the train pulled in to the little station at Pont Newydd he could scarcely resist the impulse to run up to the footplate and shake the driver by the hand. Yet – and to those who have never visited Cwm Garon this will seem the most improbable part of this strange story – as the weeks went by after his return to London, fear turned to curiosity, and repulsion to an attraction which he found increasingly difficult to resist. It was almost as though some powerful influence was luring him back.

Be that as it may, Carfax did return to the valley, and a sultry night on the eve of August the first found him once again walking up the lane toward Capel Cwm Garon. The heat in the valley that day had been stifling. Everything had felt hot to the touch, and the outlines of the mountain ridges shimmered in a haze which mingled with the acrid smoke of a heather fire. Never had the atmosphere seemed so surcharged with still suspense. Even the interminable voice of the Garon had been muted by weeks of drought. Only occasionally, far away over the mountains toward Radnor, faint thunder growled and muttered. At evening a grey veil of cloud had spread slowly across the sky so that the night fell black and starless. Yet the heat was still insufferable and there was no breath of wind. Everything, from towering mountain to individual leaf or grass blade, seemed poised in tense expectancy as though awaiting some tremendous event.

I will not attempt to analyse Carfax's state of mind as he strode on through the dark of the high-banked lane. Though still beyond the reach of his five senses, his reason no longer questioned the reality of a malign, unsleeping watch. Yet still, "For lust of knowing what should not be known", he held on purposefully. Somewhere above the invisible crags of the Black Daren a heather fire was still burning, a livid wheal of flickering flame twisting snakelike across the face of the mountain. But Carfax also saw other lights in the darkness, moving points of light which no comfortable theory could explain. They appeared to move swiftly along and down the mountain walls, converging, it would seem, upon the church at Capel Cwm Garon. There must, he thought, be another fire just beyond the church, for the ruined walls were visible against its dull red glare. As he approached more closely, however, he saw, with a new fear stirring in his heart, that he was mistaken, and that the light was actually coming from within the church itself.

While fascination fought with terror within him he drew nearer, leaving the lane for the short turf of the field where his footfalls made no sound, until he reached a position from which he could see into the roofless nave. In the centre of the church stood a brazier which glowed redly and sent up swirling clouds of smoke whose pungent aromatic odour drifted across to where Carfax stood. Around and about the brazier moved a considerable company of men and women. They were naked, and as they moved, their bodies seemed to capture and reflect the ruddy glare of the fire as though they were lacquered. When he glimpsed them momentarily in the firelight, Carfax thought that the faces of a few of the taller ones seemed vaguely familiar, but the majority of the company appeared to be very short in stature, so short, in fact, that at the first instant of vision he thought they must be children. Their bodies, however, belied this impression, as did their faces, for their countenances were such that Carfax was grateful for the smoke which prevented him from seeing them clearly. Sometimes the company moved in slow and stately dance, sometimes the pace quickened to a frenzy accompanied by gesture and posture indescribably obscene. Naked feet moved silently and there was no sound of music, yet always they seemed obedient to the measure of some inaudible rhythm. Now and again the smoke whirled aside to reveal, in the shadows beyond the brazier, a horned figure seated upon some kind of throne. Carfax marked this inhuman shape with a renewed access of fear until he realised that it was a man clothed in skins and wearing a horned head-dress. He knew then that he was beholding the celebration of rites unbelievably ancient, and temporarily his interest overcame his revulsion and his fear. But only momentarily, for it dawned upon him that this spectacle, for all its diabolic depravity, was human, and that it inspired a purely physical emotion, whereas the malignant power which brooded over the valley itself was something more or less than human. These forms which writhed in the firelight might conjure or appease that power, but they were not the power itself; their monstrous celebration had not abated the tense expectancy of the stillness. The valley still awaited some greater event.

Suddenly, a blinding flash of lightning, followed immediately by a crash of thunder tore through the veil of darkness and silence. Reverberating like great drums, the mountains took up the roar of sound and flung it from wall to wall, echoing and re-echoing down Cwm Garon. The figures round the fire had ceased their dance and flung themselves prostrate on the ground. The fire itself burnt low. The thunder died away with a sound like the closing of some vast door, and with its passing there seized Carfax a terror of the soul so abject that it was as though the valley yawned like the mouth of hell. For there fell about him a silence that was like the soundless desolation of outer space, and a sightless darkness blacker than any midnight. Though his eyes were blinded and his ears heard no sound, he knew that there stalked through the valley something intangible, unearthly, monstrous and very terrible. Though no leaf moved, something stirred in his hair. It seemed to pass as a storm cloud passes, sweeping down Cwm Garon, and with that passage the spell which had bound senses and held limbs from motion lifted. Carfax screamed, and, slipping and stumbling, he ran towards the crags of Black Daren. At the sound of his voice, two squat figures left the circle round the fire. Their pale forms glimmered in the darkness as they followed lithely after, moving in swift silence over the screes.

1963

THE HOUSE OF BALFOTHER

William Croft Dickinson

William Croft Dickinson (1897–1963) was a historian of early modern Scotland and an author who penned fiction for both adults and children. Born in Leicester, Dickinson attended the University of St Andrews, but his degree was interrupted when he volunteered to fight in the First World War. He would earn the Military Cross for gallantry on the opening day of the Third Battle of Ypres in 1917, his citation noting that his "devotion saved his battalion heavy losses." After the war he returned to St Andrews, where he was awarded a first-class degree in History.

Dickinson remained in academia and in 1943 was made Sir William Fraser Professor of Scottish History and Palaeography at the University of Edinburgh. A deep understanding of Scotland's history and landscape informs many of the ghost stories he enjoyed writing away from his role at the university. First published in *Dark Encounters* in 1963, "The House of Balfother" is no exception. Here, Dickinson draws upon knowledge of James IV's reign to create his haunting tale, John Damian de Falcuis being a historical figure who practised alchemy at the behest of the Scottish king.

The area around Loch Rannoch in Perth and Kinross remains wild and beautiful rambling country. If hunting fog-shrouded tower-houses is not your bag, Rannoch Forest is perfect for a wander, and includes a remnant of the ancient Caledonian Forest, which goes by the enigmatic name of the Black Wood of Rannoch. For those prepared for a more challenging hike, the iconic cone-shaped peak of Schiehallion ("Fairy Hill of the Caledonians") is close by.

"I sometimes wonder about those traditional immortals who live in secret chambers, like Earl Beardie at Glamis. Do they grow older and older? Do the years weary them? Or do they live on and on at exactly the same age? That's the worst of legends," continued Drummond, addressing the company at large, "they leave too much to the imagination."

"Well, if Earl Beardie is growing older and older, his beard must be mighty long by now, after some four hundred years," put in Sharples, with mock gravity. "Unless at some point in time, or at some given length, a man's beard ceases to grow."

"I know nothing about legends. Scottish history is too full of them," said Petrie, critical as always. "But, if someone will give me a long drink, I will tell you of one 'immortal' who was certainly burdened by the years – so much so that he had declined into something worse than a second childhood. Yet from what I saw and experienced, I shudder to think what 'life' would have meant to him had he not suffered an unnatural and terrible end."

Someone got up to provide the drink.

"It will have to be a long one," Petrie added, quickly, "for I shall have to tell you how I came to the House of Balfother, before I try to describe what happened there. And, after that, you will still have to hear the end of the tale."

A very long drink was provided.

*

It all happened when I was a student at St Andrews – a "magistrand", in my final year. And when I was also a great walker: which meant something more than the traditional ten-mile walk of St Andrews men, "out by Cameron, and in by Grange". To me, walking in those days meant striding across the hills by map and compass – the road to be taken only in times of sheer necessity – and never doing less than twenty miles a day. I can still do my twenty miles, but, in my student days, my long walks also meant trusting to hospitality, and hoping that the lonely farm or shepherd's cottage, marked with a small dot on the map, would somehow or other provide me with shelter for the night. Youth hostels were still unknown. Yet I was seldom turned away – even though, upon occasion, I must have been taken in at great inconvenience. And when I knew that that had been the case, I always strove to show my gratitude by giving any services I could on the following morning before setting out again – for I knew that any offer of payment would certainly be refused.

After the night of my strange experience, however, I left long before the day broke. And I was glad to be gone.

It was the Easter vacation of my final year and, faced with my examinations at the end of the coming summer term, I had decided upon a noble walk. I would take with me a copy of *Kidnapped*, and I would retrace David Balfour's route – partly that of "the lad with the silver button", and partly that of David Balfour and Alan Breck when they "took to the heather" after the murder of the "Red Fox", Glenure. But I would do it in reverse, from North Queensferry to the Ross of Mull. Then back to Oban, and thence to St Andrews by train – to be at my books once more.

I had set out with high heart, and, blessed with fine clear days, I was well ahead of my schedule when I reached the few small houses of Kilchonan, on Loch Rannoch-side. From there I walked the mile or so to the Bridge of Ericht and then struck northwards towards Loch Ericht. It was hardly midday, so I planned to go up the valley of the stream, skirt the loch on its western side (for I would find no Cluny's "gillie" to row me across), and, with luck, find shelter for the night at Ben Alder Cottage. I knew I was giving myself something of a task, for, according to the map, it was ten miles and a bit, with no habitation of any kind between Kilchonan and the Cottage. But I was in fine fettle, the day was glorious, and I had every confidence.

And then, for the first time, I found myself in difficulties. The way by the fast-running stream soon proved to be more troublesome than I had expected, so I struck up to the higher ground on the west. There I was beginning to make better progress, with a track to help me, when, gradually, the sun paled and the afternoon grew colder. I knew well enough what that meant. I knew that before long I should be running the dangers of a mountain mist.

Wisely, I decided to turn back to Kilchonan. And then came the mist: thin at first, but soon, all too soon, thick and enveloping. I knew that all I had to do was to keep on due south. If I did that, I was bound to strike Loch Rannoch – and Kilchonan – again; or, if I had strayed too far west, I would strike the road that ran from the western end of the loch to Rannoch Station. After all, I had my compass – a fine prismatic one, with a luminous dial, a legacy of my father's service in the First World War. More than once I had had to rely upon it amid the hills, and more than once it had served me well. But, although I could keep on walking in the right direction, I could not see where I was going; and, almost immediately, I was reminded of a new danger. Stumbling badly on some rough ground, I twisted my foot. Fortunately I was wearing heavy boots, but there and then I pictured myself, with a sprained ankle, trying painfully to make my way back and perhaps not succeeding, perhaps not being found. I took greater care, but, trying to pick my way slowly in thick white mist, over ground that I could barely see ahead of me, meant that before long I was chilled to the bone.

I cannot say that I was alarmed or dispirited. To the best of my recollection, my first feeling was simply one of frustration – partly that I had had to abandon my plan of reaching Ben Alder Cottage that night, and partly at the enforced slowness of my return to Kilchonan. But, as the afternoon wore on, and still I had reached neither Loch Rannoch, nor the road, I began to feel worried. Also, I was tired out. My slow groping through the mist would have tired anyone. But why had I made such poor progress? I had kept steadily south. Where was I? By now, too, although the mist was beginning to lift, darkness was taking its place.

And then, in the strange light that was half mist and half darkness, a tall square-standing tower suddenly loomed up a few yards ahead of me. Here was luck, indeed. Here I could find shelter for the night. Then came a strange sense of puzzlement, perhaps even of disquiet. What was this tower-house? It was certainly not marked on the map. There was no house of this kind anywhere between Kilchonan and Loch Ericht. But there it stood: a solid pile, much like a Border tower. It was no figment of my imagination.

There was no surrounding wall of any kind, and I walked straight up to the door. Again I was puzzled. The door was of solid oak, studded with iron nails. Surely no house still boasted such a mediæval defence? I knocked as loudly as I could, but my knuckles seemed to make no sound that would carry through the thick oak. Wondering what to do, I kicked the door with my heavy boots, and knew that the noise I made was bound to be heard. Standing there, cold and shivering, I kicked again and again. And at last my demand was answered. I heard the drawing of bars, the door opened slowly, and a man stood in the narrow opening as though to contest any entry.

"For why are ye makand sic dunts on the door?" he asked.

"Could I have shelter for the night?" I replied.

"Na stranger enters Balfother. It's weel kent. The king's writ aye has it so," he answered, and would have closed the door.

But I was in no mood to be put off so easily, and, being young and impetuous, I thrust my foot into the gap.

"I'm sorry," I said firmly, "but you can't leave me out all night. I will be no trouble to you. I have food in my pack, and I can sleep on the kitchen floor, or in an outhouse if you have one. I want only that, and a fire to dry out my clothes."

He seemed to hesitate, and then said again, almost as though it were a set phrase, "Na stranger enters Balfother. The king's writ has it. It canna be."

"But it must be," I returned, and, pushing against the door, I edged myself in.

"Bide ye there, then," said the man, seeing that I had indeed entered Balfother, and apparently not wishing to dispute my entry. He shuffled away in the darkness of what I assumed to be some kind of entrance-passage, and left me standing there. A minute or two later, however, he reappeared, carrying a lighted tallow candle on a dish. Beckoning me to follow him, he led the way up a winding stone stairway, opened a door, and ushered me into a small room. There he set the candle upon a rough table, and, without a word, left me again.

I looked at my quarters for the night, and again I felt that strange sense of disquiet. The room was perhaps twelve feet square and completely empty save for the rough table on which the man had set my candle, and a bed that was even more roughly made and was completely devoid of bedclothes of any kind. The stone walls were cold and bare; as also was the stone floor. Only a small window, high up in one of the walls, and a crude fire-place in the wall opposite the bed, broke the forbidding monotony of stone. More than that, the whole room smelled dank and musty, as though the one window had never been opened, and the room had never been used, for countless years.

"A chilly reception, if ever there was one," I muttered resentfully. "Surely there's a fire in the house, somewhere."

But I did my reluctant host an injustice. I had barely muttered my resentment than he came into the room, bearing an armful of logs. Again without speaking he laid them in a neat pile in the fireplace and went out, returning a second time with a log that was still glowing from a fire elsewhere. He placed the glowing log in the centre of the pile, lay full length upon the floor and blew until the log broke into flames and began to set the other logs alight.

At any rate I shall have a fire, I thought, thankfully, as I watched him at his task. And then once more I was puzzled. What was this house with an ancient look about everything? Who was this man? And why did his coarse clothes seem so odd? Had he inherited them from a grandfather, or a great-grandfather?

As the man rose from his task, I thanked him sincerely for his attention to my wants. But he merely looked at me blankly and moved to the door. There, however, he turned before leaving.

"God keep ye through the night," he said, and, with that, he was gone.

"And what might that mean?" I wondered. Was it just a benison, or was it a warning? I had virtually commanded shelter for the night, but what sort of shelter had I taken? What sort of a night was I to have?

Dismissing various vague apprehensions which flitted through my mind, I opened my pack and took out the spare socks, shirt and underclothing which I always carried on my long walks. These I laid, like a hearth-rug, on the stone floor in front of the fire, and then stripped to the skin. Standing on my hearth-rug, I rubbed myself hard and long with my towel. Then I began to dry out my soaking clothes, first arranging them in small pyramids before the fire and then holding them up, one at a time, close to the flames. I knew I ran the risk of singeing them, but dry clothes I had to have if I was to sleep without blankets. For perhaps an hour I continued this task until all my clothes were dry. Then I dressed, ate some chocolate and plain biscuits, and felt completely refreshed.

I stress all this to show that I was fully alert and far from likely to "imagine" things. Sitting on the edge of the bed I was ready to accept the shelter I had demanded and to face whatever the night might bring. Again taking out my map, I looked for a house somewhere in the hills to the south of Loch Ericht. No house was marked. But surely a tower-house like this was bound to be marked. What was this House of Balfother? And what had my queer host meant about "na stranger", and "the king's writ"? Well, I was ready for anything.

The fire was now burning low, but there was still life in the tallow candle. And then, just as I was debating whether or not to trust myself to the bed, and its possible vermin, I saw the door slowly opening. I flatter myself I was not in the least afraid. If robbery was intended, I felt in just the right mood to put up a good fight for my few pounds and pence. But it was not my host who entered. I was being visited by a large dog.

The animal, yellowish-white, and strangely devoid of fur, crawled slowly into the room and made straight for the fire-place and the warmth of the glowing embers there. But, instead of lying down, it *sat* down, much as a human would sit on the floor in front of a fire. Startled, I looked more closely at that strange posture. With a sudden feeling of revulsion, I realised that I was looking, not at a dog, but at a man.

He was completely naked. His skin was yellow, loose, and wrinkled – much like a piece of faded paper that had been crumpled up and then roughly smoothed out again. Soon, as he sat there, warming himself before the fire, he began to make little noises, similar to those made by a baby before it first begins to talk. After a while, he stopped and, teetering to and fro, began to croon to himself: "Robbie Norrie, Robbie Norrie canna die. Robbie Norrie wilna die."

It is impossible to describe my feelings as I witnessed this complete degradation of humanity. And, as I wondered what to do, the man turned, and saw me sitting on the bed. With a gurgle of delight, he got up and crawled towards me. Never had I seen, never shall I see again such an old, old face. It looked as though it had aged through centuries. Now too, as he came close to me, I could smell his body – a horrible, indefinable smell of rank flesh.

"Robbie Norrie," he gibbered. "Robbie Norrie."

I strove to push him away, and his body yielded to my hands like a soft sponge.

"Robbie Norrie. Robbie Norrie," I heard in a kind of childish sing-song as I feverishly struggled to avoid an approach that sent shivers of horror through every nerve in my frame.

I have no idea how long I struggled with that degenerate lump of human flesh. I was contending with a creature (for that is the only appropriate name) that seemed to have risen in bodily form from an age-old grave; a creature that sought to nestle close to me and that I pushed away again and again.

"Robbie Norrie, Robbie Norrie." The childish repetition, as the foul creature constantly returned and strove to nestle against me, suddenly snapped my control. I seized him by the throat, and might well have strangled him, had not the door opened, just in time.

I let go my hold as I saw my host enter the room. The creature dropped on all fours at my feet; my host gave a sharp word of command; and the horrible thing, that once had been a man, sidled slowly out. My host, without a word, followed it.

I am not ashamed to say that I was in a state of complete collapse. I was a strong well-built youngster of twenty-two, and all I had had to do was to repulse a weak and decrepit creature, feeble alike in body and mind. Yet, somehow, I felt that I had been struggling with something so unwholesome that I myself had been in danger of corruption. Perhaps people in the middle ages felt like that about contact with a leper. I do not know.

As I gradually became myself again, I decided there was only one course to take. I had had enough of Balfother. I put my things into my pack and, creeping out of the room, felt my way about until I had discovered the stairway. I stole quietly down, found the door, drew back the wooden bars, and literally ran out into the night. It was still dark, but the mist had cleared. Again I struck south by compass, this time not caring whether I sprained an ankle or not. And, to my surprise, I had been walking for barely a quarter of an hour when I reached Loch Rannoch. There I stayed until dawn, resting my back against a tree, pondering over my strange adventure and regaining peace of mind.

My walk was over, save for the few miles to Rannoch Station. I caught a train there, changed at Crianlarich, and journeyed slowly, across country, back to St Andrews.

A week or so after my return, I received a note from John Barnet, my professor of Greek, inviting me to his house for tea. Term had not yet started, and the only other guest at tea was Duncan Mackinnon, the senior lecturer in History. I had told Barnet of my intention to walk from North Queensferry to the Ross of Mull, and naturally his first question was to ask me how I had fared. You can easily understand that my immediate response was to tell the whole story of my night at Balfother. But I was not prepared for what followed.

"Balfother?" interrupted Mackinnon, when I told of my arrival at the house.

"Robert Norrie?" he asked, excitedly, a little later.

But he let me finish.

"You know something about all this?" queried Barnet, turning to Mackinnon, when my tale had ended.

"Wait!" he answered. "I'll slip over to my house and bring back a document which goes some way towards an explanation – though even then the whole thing is incredible."

Mackinnon went out, leaving us to await his return impatiently – wondering what his document could be, and what explanation it could possibly give.

About ten minutes later he was back.

"As you know," he began, taking a folded paper from his pocket, "I have been working on the Fortingall Papers in the Scottish Record Office. And as soon as Petrie mentioned Balfother I remembered a queer letter under the Privy Seal which I found in the Fortingall Papers and which intrigued me so much that I transcribed it in full."

He unfolded his sheet of paper, and although I cannot give you the exact words – though I still have a copy of the document at home – what he read out to us ran roughly like this:

> A letter made to William Fowler of Balfother, his heirs and assigns, making mention that for the good, true and thankful service done and to be done by the said William, his heirs and assigns, in the keeping and maintaining of Robert Norrie, the man to whom the French leech Damian gave the quintessence in the time of our sovereign Lord's predecessor King James IV, whom God assoil, and the said Robert Norrie being still on life, therefore our sovereign Lord grants to the said William, his heirs and assigns, an annual rent of five hundred shillings to be uptaken yearly of the lands of Dall and Finnart. Providing always that the said William Fowler, his heirs and assigns, shall keep the said Robert Norrie close from all other persons whatsomever that he may be scatheless and harmless in his body, and that our sovereign Lord and, if God wills, our sovereign Lord's successors, may know to what age the said Robert shall live.

"Now you can understand my excitement," continued Mackinnon. "The date of that letter is 3rd April 1622. James IV died at Flodden in 1513. So already Robert Norrie had lived to at least the age of 109, and probably several years more – for the quintessence would hardly be given to him in his infancy. That had aroused my interest when I first read the extract; but, if Petrie saw the same Robert Norrie at Balfother, as he seems to have done, the man must now be more than 400 years old."

For a minute or so we digested this in silence.

"He *was* centuries old," I said. "I felt it at the time."

"And what's all this about the French leech Damian, and the quintessence?" asked Barnet.

"Oh, that part is straightforward enough," answered Mackinnon. "We know that James IV encouraged the experiments of a certain Damian who believed he could distil the 'quintessence' – not only to turn base metals into gold but also to yield an elixir that would prolong man's life indefinitely. James IV even made him abbot of Tongland; and, if you are interested, you can find the materials which he used in his experiments, and for which the King paid, in the *Accounts of the Lord High Treasurer* from about 1501 to 1513. My extract proves conclusively that Robert Norrie, who had been given the 'quintessence', lived to be at least 109. Is he still alive? At 400? What's more, when Petrie knocked at the door of Balfother he was told that no stranger could be admitted, and that the King's writ said so. Doesn't that mean that the same Robert Norrie is still being kept 'close'?"

"We'll go to Balfother ourselves," cried Barnet. "And we'll ask James Waters to come with us. He takes so much interest in his anatomical reconstructions from the skulls and bones of men who have been dead for centuries that he's sure to be interested in the anatomy of a man who is still alive at the age of at least 400. All that puzzles me is how the affair has been kept secret for so long. Food – and even tallow candles – must be bought; and people are always curious about any queer goings-on in their neighbourhood. Surely the good folk of Kilchonan must know of the strange 'creature' kept in Balfother. However, we'll see. I propose we ring up Waters and, if he's free, we'll drive to Kilchonan tomorrow."

Waters was free. And Barnet was a good driver. We arrived at Kilchonan about noon and, after a picnic lunch by the loch-side, the four of us retraced my steps up the high ground to the west of the stream that runs from Loch Ericht into Loch Rannoch. But we found no tower-house. Reaching the point where I thought I had turned back, we spread out, far wider than beaters on a grouse-moor, and walked southwards again. We met on the road by the Loch, and again we had failed to find Balfother.

"Are you sure you didn't fall asleep and dream it all?" asked Barnet, turning to me with a twinkle in his eye.

"I'm certain I didn't," I replied, firmly.

"It can't have been a dream," confirmed Mackinnon. "Petrie had never heard of Balfother and Robert Norrie. He knew nothing of a letter under the Privy Seal – a 'king's writ' – which banned the entry of strangers."

"Well," said the practical Waters, "I suggest we inquire at Kilchonan. Perhaps we should have done so first of all."

We inquired. But no one in Kilchonan had heard of a house called Balfother. One encouragement, however, did emerge from our inquiries. It was suggested that we should call on a Mr Alastair MacGregor, in Aberfeldy, who, we were told, was writing a local history, and who, of all people, was the most likely to be of help to us.

We drove to Aberfeldy, and we found Mr MacGregor.

"Balfother?" he repeated. "Yes, there was certainly a tower-house of that name. It belonged to the Fowlers; but it was destroyed long ago. A grim and tragic affair. Come in, and I'll tell you about it."

Alastair MacGregor did not live long enough to see his book in print. I can give you no reference to volume and page. But I am not likely to forget his account.

It appears that in 1649 there was a veritable epidemic of witch-huntings, witch-trials and witch-burnings throughout all Scotland from one end of the country to the other. And, in the August of that year, someone denounced William Fowler of Balfother, and Bessie Wilson, his wife, of keeping a "familiar". The "familiar" had been seen. It was in the form of an old and naked man, who could not be clothed, and who ran about on all fours like a dog.

A body of men, headed by a minister, went out to Balfother. Apparently they had difficulty in gaining an entrance, but when, at last, they had broken down the door, had entered the house, and had secured Fowler and his wife, they began a search for the "familiar". And, according to the story, they found it – an old and decrepit man, stark naked, who babbled the words of some devilish incantation which put them all in terror until the minister cried out: "Get thee behind me, Satan," when they rushed at it and bound it with strong cords.

William Fowler and Bessie Wilson were burned as agents of the devil, and, with them, was burned their "familiar". It is said that William Fowler produced something which he called "the king's writ", and which he offered in his defence. But the court refused to look at it, let alone accept it.

As for the house itself, after the burnings, the minister had preached a powerful sermon on the text, "We will destroy this place... and the Lord hath sent us to destroy it." Whereupon all the people had marched out to Balfother and, with crowbars and irons, had pulled down the house, stone by stone, scattering the stones over the land. And yet, apparently, the sight of good cut freestone was too much for the people of a later time. According to MacGregor, many of the stones of Balfother were still to be seen in some of the walls in Kilchonan.

*

We left the knowledgeable MacGregor and we drove from Aberfeldy in silence.

"What a horrible story," said Barnet, at last.

"Yes," agreed Mackinnon. "One of far too many. Horrible. And yet," he continued with his historian's eye for dates, "Robert Norrie must have lived to at least the age of 136. Is that possible, Waters?"

"Certainly it's possible," replied Waters, crisply. "All the same, I'm glad that modern medicine has not yet discovered the prescription for Damian's quintessence. Old age is already a social problem, without further complications from an elixir of life."

"But," I cried, impatiently, "can any of you explain how I came to the House of Balfother when the house was no longer there, and how Robert Norrie came to visit me when Robert Norrie had long been dead."

No one answered me. And I know that no one ever will.

1971

THE DERELICT TRACK

Dorothy K. Haynes

Dorothy Kate Haynes (1918–1987) was born in Lanark, a Scottish town rich in history and tradition. King David I made Lanark a royal burgh in the twelfth century, and it was here that William Wallace led an uprising against the English in 1297. For the first ten years of her life, Haynes lived in Lanark with her twin brother, before the children were sent to Aberlour Orphanage in Moray upon the death of their mother.

Haynes's experiences at the orphanage were formative. Although generally positive, her time there certainly influenced her writing's tendency towards the uncanny, and she would later recall the ghost stories she heard and the eerie songs the girls would sing together. Editor Craig Lamont notes in his introduction to the British Library's recent collection of Haynes's weird tales that her narratives concerning children are "haunted by the spectre of Aberlour".

It is a young boy, Teddy, who is at the heart of "The Derelict Track", a tale that skilfully blends domestic tensions with an unsettling strangeness. Having returned to Lanark, Haynes was a regular contributor to anthologies of supernatural fiction, such as *The Seventh Ghost Book* in which this story first appeared, as well as writing articles for *The Scotsman*. Haynes published *Haste Ye Back*, a well-regarded memoir focused upon her time at Aberlour, in 1973.

The boy kicked open the front door, and stood, with the sun at his back, shadowed against the light. Seen like this, he was a caricature of boyhood, the jeans wrinkling over his shoes, the shirt pulled out at the waist, the tuft of hair sticking up from the double crown. A second later he was over the threshold, lit up into features and colour, the jeans faded blue, and his eyes the shade of grey which people associate, peculiarly, with truth.

"Mum!" he shouted, dumping a heavy box on the hall table. "Mum, look what I've got!"

His mother came through from the kitchen, her hands smudged with flour. "I don't see why you have to stand and bawl, Teddy," she said; and then, seeing the box, pushing the flower arrangement out of place, "Where on earth did you get all *that*?"

"Out at the Camp Station," he said, rattling about, pulling out bits and pieces. "Look, a telephone!" He held it up, a real receiver, and spoke into it, muffling the tone expertly.

"Teddy!" She stood helpless, with her floury hands in front of her. "You've no business bringing all that junk in here."

"It's all right, mum." He held one hand over the mouthpiece of the telephone, as if interrupting a conversation. "They said we could take it. They're just throwing it out, anyway."

"Who's 'they'?"

"The men taking up the track. Kenny and me were walking along the line – "

"You shouldn't be on the line at all. It's dangerous."

"Oh, *mum*!" His face held the exasperation of youth talking to those who will not listen. "It's as safe as the road. Safer. We were walking along the sleepers, and some men were in the signal box, and they said if there was anything we wanted we'd to take it, only we'd to keep our mouths shut."

"There you are. You'll get yourselves into trouble, and he knows it."

"It's not that." Teddy put the telephone down, his voice pleading. "It's just that he knows there's lots of boys would love to get all these things – "

"What else have you got beside the telephone? And where do you think you're going to put it all?"

"I'll find somewhere. Look, old timetables. And here's a poster. And records – it tells you all about looking after the oil lamps, and what to do about level crossings. And I've got a nameplate! I can screw it on to my bedroom door."

"You'll do nothing of the sort. You'll put it all tidily, understand? That is, if I let you keep it."

He slid his arm under the huge box, and began to climb the stairs, looking at his mother cautiously, over the banisters. "Dad'll like to see them when he comes in," he suggested.

"*When* he comes in," she repeated, echoing him, making even that into an argument. "I doubt if your father's got time for any of us nowadays."

His father, for once, was in promptly. The car tyres sprayed the gravel, his brief case lay in the hall, and they all sat down to supper together.

"Dad," said Teddy, "I got – "

"Leave your father alone, dear," said his mother automatically. "He's tired."

His father never answered. He cut up his food and lifted it to his mouth, he dabbed his lips and stirred his tea, and now and again he sighed. Once he spoke, rubbing his eyes wearily. "Keep the boy quiet tonight, Vera, will you? I've brought some work back with me."

"Couldn't it wait? You're never home, you work all weekend. Surely for once you could let it stand till the morning."

"I can't. Foster's off, and Jones is leaving next week. You've no idea, Vera. Things aren't too good. I don't like to bring my worries home with me, but – "

"Wait a minute. Go up and play with your train things, Teddy. I'll come up and have a look at them afterwards."

It was odd, she thought, how her husband made her aware of her inadequacies towards Teddy, just as Teddy made her aware of her inadequacies towards her husband. She loved the boy, but his demands impinged on her responsibilities towards William. She knew very well that William worked too hard, that he paid what was perhaps too high a price for their house, a little larger than they needed, their car, a Rover where a mini might have done, and all the etceteras which guise themselves as necessities as soon as the income jumps.

She was not ready to volunteer for a lower standard of living. Her worry took the form of an obsessive participation in his moods, together with an irritation at the moods themselves. She would try to stand between him and the child's clamour for attention; but let *him* voice a desire for peace, or a complaint about Teddy's interruptions, and she was suddenly guiltily maternal. She saw the boy as deprived and lonely, and she would go out of her way to comfort him, offering to read to him in bed, or trying to draw him into a conversation she had cut short earlier.

Now she went up to his bedroom, where he was sitting with his papers strewn all over the carpet. Gingerly, she picked up the brown and spotted papers, the dog-eared rule books, and all the paraphernalia of a derelict station. She could understand what it must mean to a boy, even as she shuddered at the clutter. "Put some of your posters on the walls," she said. "Daddy will see them later, when he's got time. Once he's got his work off his mind."

When the boy came in late for meals, his hands dirty and his face smudged, his father jumped on him about punctuality, and his mother defended him protectively. "Look, William, the boy's on holiday. It's summer. What do you want him to do? Hang about the house getting under my feet all day?"

"I just want him to be on time. He's always going on about his railway trains and timetables. Do you think you could run a railway if the trains only turned up when they thought fit?"

"That's different altogether."

Relations between them had deteriorated since the spring, and the boy was the bone they quarrelled over. Teddy himself never argued, never complained. Every day he went to the derelict station, and every evening came back with a souvenir, a rusty lamp, a few pebbles, a wad of coloured tickets. His bedroom was beginning to look like a shrine dedicated to the decline of British Rail.

"You don't *mind* me going, mum?" he said. "So long as I don't mess the place up too much?"

"*I* don't mind," she said, off-hand and abstracted. "So long as you watch what you're doing." She went out of her way now to let him indulge himself, cutting him sandwiches and giving him money for lemonade. "Some for Kenny too," she said, loading him up with food, giving him no excuse to come back. It was as if she wanted him to stay away all day.

She told herself that she was doing what was best for him, keeping him away from anything which might puzzle or worry him. You never knew, with children. He spoke very little at meals, conditioned by his father's moods, but one evening he might let something slip. He had already mentioned something about George Mortimer, and his father said "Who? Oh, Mortimer?" and paid no more attention. But once was enough.

Luckily, the weather was good. Luckily, her husband was busy. The child would suspect nothing. All he cared for was his precious railway, and the sad process which was reducing the station to ruin. And all William cared for was his work. George Mortimer was interested in *her*, interested enough to be willing to take Teddy "if anything happened."

"Don't you think you're in too much of a hurry?" she said, enjoying herself, luxuriating, but not wanting to rush things. "What makes you think Teddy would want to go with you?"

"I know kids," he answered. "They'll go with anybody who's good to them."

Towards the end of the summer, Teddy stopped bringing things home. "Are you tired of the station, then?" his mother asked, relieved that the flood of salvage had been halted, but worrying in case his interest had declined. She did not want him hanging about the house for the last week or two that remained.

The boy shook his head. "There's nothing more to take," he said.

"But you still go there, every day?"

He nodded and left the room. It was becoming difficult, these days, to talk to him. She was playing a tense, dreadful game, a mean game, trying to carry on gay conversations with Teddy, leaving his father to join in, or not, as he pleased. "Look," she was saying in effect, "*we* get on well together. We need no-one else. If you want to shut yourself out, go ahead. It's entirely up to you."

The only thing was, Teddy would not co-operate. And William took the wind out of her sails by butting in and nagging the boy about his manners. "Sit up, Teddy. Open your mouth when you speak. Good Heavens, if that's the best you can do, it's time you were back at school."

One could not say that he was not conscious of his son. The child was there, like an itch, or an irritation. "But he takes no real interest," the mother thought. "I'm the one who worries about him. I'm the one who knows him."

But did she? He went about in the evenings with his brows down and his mouth buttoned up, and at night he curled up in bed with Teddy the Second in his arms. Teddy was his old brown bear, relegated to the drawer because "big boys don't take teddies to bed." Now he was installed again, clutched passionately through sleep. In the morning, he prepared for his day at the station with less glee than he prepared for school. "I'm worried about Teddy," his mother said. "He seems to have something on his mind. It's as if he were sulking."

"What?" His father looked up, abstracted, one finger marking the place in his papers.

"I said I'm worried about Teddy. Something's bothering him."

"Well, find out what it is, then. You're his mother. You're with him all day."

The only one she could confide in was George Mortimer. He should know about people, she thought. He's a lawyer. But Mortimer was no more help than her husband.

"Does he know about us?"

"No, I don't think so. How could he? He knows you drop in and out, but what of it? You're a friend of the family."

"The holidays last too long. He'll be better when he's back at school."

But before school started they had to send for the doctor. Teddy came in early one evening, his eyes too bright, his voice high and strained. He picked at the cushions as he started to talk.

"Mum. Mum, something... horrible happened at the station today."

"What was it? Did someone...?" Her mind went wild with lewd imaginings, old men luring boys among the derelict sheds, dreadful revelations of age to innocence. "I never liked you going to that place. If it wasn't for Kenny going with you – "

"He doesn't go now. He got fed up."

"Well, then, why do *you* go? What do you *do* there all day?" She asked, but she did not really want to know. The answer frightened her.

"I look at the trains."

"Trains? But there aren't any. You told me they took up the track."

"Yes." He looked puzzled, but intense. "I know. But – this train comes every day. At the same time. And the people – it's the same people every day. Oh mummy, the same people!" He laid his head on his arms and began to sob, and she stroked his head, tender at last with fear.

"What about the people, dear? What's wrong with them?"

"It's – it's not the *ordinary* people. It's this man and woman. They... when the train comes in, this awful old fashioned train, they're standing up, as if they're ready to get out, but when it stops it's only the lady who gets on to the platform. The man wants to come too, but somehow... she doesn't seem to want him. It's as if she's sending him away. He looks at her, and she turns her head, and then the train starts, and he goes further and further away, and it's so sad – " He sobbed again, and his mother gave a little laugh, nervous and unconvinced.

"You're just imagining it, Teddy. You've got this station on the brain. You'll have to stop going there, that's all."

"But it's *true*, mummy. It happens every day. And the poor man – "

"What about the lady? What's she like?"

"She doesn't care," said Teddy.

"Well... I don't know. I'll have to talk to your father about it."

"Ridiculous," said his father. "You shouldn't have encouraged him to go there in the first place. Give him a damn good hiding if this goes on. That's what he needs."

George Mortimer was more eager to please. "I'd see a doctor, if I were you. He's a nice kid, Vera. Sensitive. It would worry me, if he was mine."

"It worries me," she said.

"Obviously, there's something on his mind," said the doctor, seeing how reluctant the child was to talk, how any probing upset him. "He's very much disturbed. I'll give him a sedative, but I may want someone else to have a look at him. Has he been to this station since he told you about it?"

"No. I haven't allowed him."

"Well, maybe you should let him go as usual. And you go along with him. Try to see what he sees. Watch how he reacts. He might let slip something that shows us how his mind works."

"Well, I'll try," she said dubiously.

*

"Of course I'll take you," said Mortimer, ruffling Teddy's hair, and giving him a playful punch. He finished his tea and stood up, leading the boy out to the car with one arm round his shoulders. "You don't mind me coming, Teddy?"

Teddy shook his head.

"It's such a distance to walk," explained his mother. "I don't see why William has to take the car every day. It means I can't go anywhere."

"I just wondered if you wouldn't be better on your own."

"*I* think I'd be better with as many... witnesses as possible."

The Camp Station had been built in the days of the Militia, when soldiers came to train at the summer camp on the moors. For years it had stood empty and unused, but its rails had been kept bright by the trains passing through to the coast. Now, in a summer, the whole line had been reduced to nothing more than a country lane.

It was amazing, thought Vera, how remote, how far away it seemed. Teddy led her through the broken gate and up the steep incline with both pride and apprehension. This was his territory, his sanctuary where he had spent his summer.

"See?" he said.

It was quiet, sad, summer ending in a drift of seeded willowherb and thistledown. The track came out of a cutting, between green slopes tangled with rasps and brambles, but there was no track now, only grass barred by the marks of the sleepers. The platform was green with moss, and weeds sprouted through the concrete, long nettles leaning against the fences; and at the end of the track was a signal box, an empty brown structure with broken windows, both pathetic and absurd.

"Is that where you got the stuff, Teddy?"

"Yes."

"Well... there isn't much left now, is there?"

He didn't answer. He was holding her hand – he hadn't done *that* for a long time – and looking about him uneasily. Hot and still, the sun came straight down, with a tired yellowish tinge. Autumn was tinting everything, the ragged rowans with their bright berries, the faint rust showing on burned leaves. There was a distant sound of machinery from the sand quarry where the soldiers' tents used to stand.

"It's quiet, isn't it? I don't see what you do here, day after day."

He held her hand tighter. She could feel it sweat through her glove, and her face was pale. "What is it, Teddy?" she asked, as he began to tremble.

He looked up at her in sick panic, and his mouth was too dry for him to speak properly.

"It's coming. Can't you hear it?"

She licked her own dry lips and swallowed. Perhaps there was something... a tremor in the ground, a faint pulsing? But the traffic on the roads was heavy, and the quarry machinery went on and on, unheard until you listened.

Suddenly he screamed, and pulled her backwards. "Hey, steady!" said Mortimer, holding him by the shoulders, trying to make him keep a grip on himself. But Teddy was hanging on to his mother, staring into the cutting, his eyes following Heaven knows what as it came nearer and nearer and halted, apparently a few feet away. "Mummy, *look*!" he sobbed at her. "Don't you *see*? She's getting off, she's going away, and she doesn't care. And he – "

Afterwards, she could not explain exactly what she had seen, or swear that she had seen anything; but for a long second, drawn out in agony like the long seconds of labour, she saw, or... experienced the train, a long, heavy train, dull maroon, the windows bloomed with railway smoke, the carriage smelling of dust and stale tobacco. Sound flashed through her mind, but it was *silent* sound, as in a dream, steam and wheels turning, and the flat crash of slamming doors.

She could not say how the people were dressed. George would have made out a case for her imagining it all, cross examining her and beating her down... but George was miles away in another world, and quite unable to help her. Surely she saw... she had a sense of people gliding and dissolving, brushing past but not touching her... this woman now, nearer, part of her, almost, was solid as a dressmaker's dummy, but the man who leaned from the train, pleading – she felt his sorrow – was more nebulous. Really, she couldn't stand – she shook her head. Why was she here? She felt George Mortimer beside her, puzzled, one arm out to steady her, and she leaned on him with relief. Then Teddy screamed again, and jerked her awake in one palpitating leap.

"Daddy! Oh, Daddy!"

There was nothing there. He had wrenched his hand free, as if she could no longer comfort him, and he was staring wildly after the train – what train? The mauve drift of floss and down whirled by like snow, disturbed by a sudden wind, but there was nothing there, only empty sun on the broken tar and nettles.

She did not know whether there was hate in his eyes or only reproach, as he beat at her in the rage of sudden understanding. "He wanted you, and you went away..."

"Do you think...?" asked Mortimer, one eyebrow cocked, guilty, but brash as ever. Man to man, he put a hand on Teddy's shoulder. "Come on, son. I think it's time we went home now."

"No!" The child hurled himself from the platform, and began to race down the green track, frantic, chasing a train, a ghost, a love – who was to know what? He ran along the railbed in the late yellow sun, through the fuzz and floss of summer dying. No words could reach him, no reasoning. The down settled, the quarry machinery pounded on, and a robin landed lightly as a rowan berry where the rails had been. But as Vera stared, she could feel the train running on and on in her body, running like doom down the long track where her son had gone, and where she dared not follow.

1979

ABOVE THE WORLD

Ramsey Campbell

The career of Ramsey Campbell (b. 1946) has taken in over 60 years of writing – he published his first weird tale in a collection for Arkham House at the age of 16. That story, like others that would follow, is set in the shared fictional universe of the Cthulhu Mythos, a world inspired by the works of H. P. Lovecraft. Growing up in blitz-scarred Liverpool, Campbell was an avid reader, coming across his first Lovecraft tale in an anthology while still at primary school.

Having authored over 30 novels and numerous short stories, Campbell is regarded as one of the greatest living exponents of horror and weird fiction – in 2015 he received the World Fantasy Award's Life Award, a prize previously presented to Susan Cooper, Stephen King and Ray Bradbury. "Above the World" was first published in the anthology *Whispers II* in 1979. In his collection *Alone with the Horrors*, Campbell notes that the story "derived much of its imagery and setting from my one wholly positive, not to mention visionary, LSD experience."

The Bishop of Barf cited in Campbell's tale is a whitewashed human-like rock. It stands about half-way up Barf Fell, a shoulder of Lord's Seat, which rises above Bassenthwaite Lake in Cumbria. Visible from the road below, the rock marks the site where, according to colourful legend, the Bishop of Derry met his end in 1783. Local lore recounts that the bishop fell from his horse while attempting to ride to the summit of Barf following a drunken bet made at the Swan Hotel. The pub's staff resolved to paint the rock each year in commemoration, and since the closure of the Swan the tradition has been carried out by the local mountain rescue team. Wainwright's route up Barf is now strongly discouraged by the same team, following several call outs to rescue hikers amidst loose scree and broken crags. A safer route to the summits of Lord's Seat and Barf can be found on the Visit Keswick website.

Nobody was at Reception when Knox came downstairs. The dinner-gong hung mute in its frame; napkin pyramids guarded dining-tables; in the lounge, chairs sat emptily. Nothing moved except fish in the aquarium, fluorescent gleams amid water that bubbled like lemonade. The visitors' book lay open on the counter. He riffled the pages idly, seeking his previous visit. A Manchester address caught his attention: but the name wasn't his – not any longer. The names were those of his wife and the man.

It took him a moment to realise. They must have been married by then. So the man's name had been Tooley, had it? Knox hadn't cared to know. He was pleased to find that he felt nothing but curiosity. Why had she returned here – for a kind of second honeymoon, to exorcise her memories of him?

When he emerged, it was raining. That ought to wash the fells clean of all but the dedicated walkers; he might be alone up there – no perambulatory radios, no families marking their path with trailing children. Above the hotel mist wandered among the pines, which grew pale and blurred, a spiky frieze of grey, then solidified, regaining their green. High on the scree slope, the Bishop of Barf protruded like a single deformed tooth.

The sight seemed to halt time, to turn it back. He had never left the Swan Hotel. In a moment Wendy would run out, having had to go back for her camera or her rucksack or something. "I wasn't long, was I? The bus hasn't gone, has it? Oh dear, I'm sorry." Of course these impressions were nonsense: he'd moved on, developed since his marriage, defined himself more clearly – but it cheered him that his memories were cool, disinterested. Life advanced relentlessly, powered by change. The Bishop shone white only because climbers painted the pinnacle each year, climbing the steep scree with buckets of whitewash from the Swan.

Here came the bus. It would be stuffed with wet campers slow as turtles, their backs burdened with tubular scaffolding and enormous rucksacks. Only once had he suffered such a ride. Had nothing changed? Not the Swan, the local food, the unobtrusive service, the long white seventeenth-century building which had so charmed Wendy. He had a table to himself; if you wanted to be left alone, nobody would bother you. Tonight there would be venison, which he hadn't tasted since his honeymoon. He'd returned determined to enjoy the Swan and the walks, determined not to let memories deny him those pleasures – and he'd found his qualms were groundless.

He strode down the Keswick road. Rain rushed over Bassenthwaite Lake and tapped on the hood of his cagoule. Why did the stone wall ahead seem significant? Had Wendy halted there once, because the wall was singing? "Oh look, aren't they beautiful." As he stooped towards the crevice, a cluster of hungry beaks had sprung out of the darkness, gaping. The glimpse had unnerved him: the inexorable growth of life, sprouting everywhere, even in stone. Moss choked the silent crevice now.

Somehow that image set him wondering where Wendy and the man had died. Mist had caught them, high on one or other of the fells; they'd died of exposure. That much he had heard from a friend of Wendy's, who had grown aloof from him and who had seemed to blame him for entrusting Wendy to an inexperienced climber – as if Knox should have taken care of her even after the marriage! He hadn't asked for details. He'd felt relieved when Wendy had announced that she'd found someone else. Habit, familiarity and introversion had screened them from each other well before they'd separated.

He was passing a camp in a field. He hadn't slept in a tent since early in his marriage, and then only under protest. Rain slithered down bright canvas. The muffled voices of a man and a woman paced him from tent to tent. Irrationally, he peered between the tents to glimpse them – but it must be a radio programme. Though the voices sounded intensely engrossed in discussion, he could distinguish not a word. The camp looked deserted. Everyone must be under canvas, or walking.

By the time he reached Braithwaite village, the rain had stopped. Clouds paraded the sky; infrequent gaps let out June sunlight, which touched the heights of the surrounding fells. He made for the cafe at the foot of the Whinlatter Pass – not because Wendy had loved the little house, its homemade cakes and its shelves of books, but for something to read: he would let chance choose his reading. But the shop was closed. Beside it Coledale Beck pursued its wordless watery monologue.

Should he climb Grisedale Pike? He remembered the view from the summit, of Braithwaite and Keswick the colours of pigeons, white and grey amid the palette of fields. But climbers were toiling upwards towards the intermittent sun. Sometimes the spectacle of plodding walkers, fell boots creaking, sticks shoving at the ground, red faces puffing like trains in distress, made his climb seem a mechanical compulsion, absurd and mindless. Suppose the height was occupied by a class of children, heading like lemmings for the edge?

He'd go back to Barf: that would be lonely – unless one had Mr Wainwright's guidebook, Barf appeared unclimbable. Returning through the village, he passed Braithwaite post office. That had delighted Wendy – a house just like the other small white houses in the row, except for the counter and grille in the front hall, beside the stairs. A postcard came fluttering down the garden path. Was that a stamp on its corner, or a patch of moss? Momentarily he thought he recognised the handwriting – but whose did it resemble? A breeze turned the card like a page. Where a picture might have been there was a covering of moss, which looked vaguely like a blurred view of two figures huddled together. The card slid by him, into the gutter, and lodged trembling in a grid, brandishing its message. Impulsively he made a grab for it – but before he could read the writing, the card fell between the bars.

He returned to the road to Thornthwaite. A sheen of sunlight clung to the macadam brows; hedges dripped dazzling silver. The voices still wandered about the deserted campsite, though now they sounded distant and echoing. Though their words remained inaudible, they seemed to be calling a name through the tents.

At Thornthwaite, only the hotel outshone the Bishop. As Knox glanced towards the coaching inn, Wendy appeared in his bedroom window. Of course it was a chambermaid – but the shock reverberated through him, for all at once he realised that he was staying in the room which he had shared with Wendy. Surely the proprietress of the Swan couldn't have intended this; it must be coincidence. Memories surged, disconcertingly vivid – collapsing happily on the bed after a day's walking, making love, not having to wake alone in the early hours. Just now, trudging along the road, he'd thought of going upstairs to rest. Abruptly he decided to spend the afternoon in walking.

Neither the hard road nor the soggy margin of Bassenthwaite Lake tempted him. He'd climb Barf, as he had intended. He didn't need Mr Wainwright's book; he knew the way. Wendy had loved those handwritten guidebooks; she'd loved searching through them for the self-portrait of Mr Wainwright which was always hidden among the hand-drawn views – there he was, in Harris tweed, overlooking Lanthwaite Wood. No, Knox didn't need those books today.

The beginning of the path through Beckstones larch plantation was easy. Soon he was climbing beside Beckstones Gill, his ears full of its intricate liquid clamour as the stream tumbled helplessly downhill, confined in its rocky groove. But the path grew steep. Surely it must have been elsewhere that Wendy had run ahead, mocking his slowness, while he puffed and cursed. By now most of his memories resembled anecdotes he'd overheard or had been told – blurred, lacking important details, sometimes contradictory.

He rested. Around him larches swayed numerous limbs, engrossed in their tethered dance. His breath eased; he ceased to be uncomfortably aware of his pulse. He stumped upwards, over the path of scattered slate. On both sides of him, ferns protruded from decay. Their highest leaves were bound into a ball, like green caterpillars on stalks.

A small rock-face blocked the path. He had to scramble across to the continuation. Lichen made the roots of trees indistinguishable from the rock. His foot slipped; he slithered, banging his elbow, clutching for handholds. Good Lord, the slope was short, at worst he would turn his ankle, he could still grab hold of rock, in any case someone was coming, he could hear voices vague as the stream's rush that obscured them. At last he was sure he was safe, though at the cost of a bruised hip. He sat and cursed his pounding heart. He didn't care who heard him – but perhaps nobody did, for the owners of the voices never appeared.

He struggled upwards. The larches gave way to spruce firs. Fallen trunks splintered like bone hindered his progress. How far had he still to climb? He must have laboured half a mile by now; it felt like more. The forest had grown oppressive. Elaborate lichens swelled brittle branches; everywhere he looked, life burgeoned parasitically, consuming the earth and the forest, a constant and ruthless renewal. He was sweating, and the clammy chill of the place failed to cool him.

Silence seized him. He could hear only the restless creaking of trees. For a long time he had been unable to glimpse the Swan; the sky was invisible too, except in fragments caged by branches. All at once, as he climbed between close banks of mossy earth and rock, he yearned to reach the open. He felt suffocated, as though the omnipresent lichen were thick fog. He forced himself onwards, panting harshly.

Pain halted him – pain that transfixed his heart and paralysed his limbs with shock. His head felt swollen, burning, deafened by blood. Beyond that uproar, were there voices? Could he cry for help? But he felt that he might never draw another breath.

As suddenly as it had attacked him, the pain was gone, though he felt as if it had burned a hollow where his heart had been. He slumped against rock. His ears rang as though metal had been clapped over them. Oh God, the doctor had been right; he must take things easy. But if he had to forgo rambling, he would have nothing left that was worthwhile. At last he groped upwards out of the dank trough of earth, though he was still light-headed and unsure of his footing. The path felt distant and vague.

He reached the edge of the forest without further mishap. Beyond it, Beckstones Gill rushed over broken stones. The sky was layered with grey clouds. Across the stream, on the rise to the summit, bracken shone amid heather.

He crossed the stream and climbed the path. Below him the heathery slope plunged towards the small valley. A few crumbs of boats floated on Bassenthwaite. A constant quivering ran downhill through the heather; the wind dragged at his cagoule, whose fluttering deafened him. He felt unnervingly vulnerable, at the mercy of the gusts. His face had turned cold as bone. Sheep dodged away from him. Their swiftness made his battle with the air seem ridiculous, frustrating. He had lost all sense of time before he reached the summit – where he halted, entranced. At last his toil had meaning.

The world seemed laid out for him. Light and shadow drifted stately over the fells, which reached towards clouds no vaster than they. Across Bassenthwaite, fells higher than his own were steps on the ascent to Skiddaw, on whose deceptively gentle outline gleamed patches of snow. A few dots, too distant to have limbs, crept along that ridge. The fells glowed with all the colours of foliage, grass, heather, bracken, except where vast tracts of rock broke through. Drifts of shadow half absorbed the colours; occasional sunlight renewed them.

The landscape was melting; he had to blink. Was he weeping, or had the wind stung his eyes? He couldn't tell; the vastness had charmed away his sense of himself. He felt calm, absolutely unselfconscious. He watched light advancing through Beckstones Plantation, possessing each successive rank of foliage. When he gazed across the lake again, that sight had transfigured the landscape.

Which lake was that on the horizon? He had never before noticed it. It lay like a fragment of slate, framed by two fells dark as storms – but above it, clouds were opening. Blue sky shone through the tangle of grey; veils of light descended from the ragged gap. The lake began to glow from within, intensely calm. Beyond it fields and trees grew clear, minute and luminous. Yes, he was weeping.

After a while he sat on a rock. Its coldness was indistinguishable from his own stony chill. He must go down shortly. He gazed out for a last view. The fells looked smooth, alluringly gentle; valleys were trickles of rock. He held up his finger for a red bus to crawl along. Closer to him, red dots were scurrying; ladybirds, condemned to explore the maze of grass-blades, to change course at each intersection. Their mindless urgency dismayed him.

They drew his gaze to the heather. He gazed deep into a tangled clump, at the breathtaking variety of colours, the intricacies of growth. As many must be hidden in each patch of heather: depths empty of meaning, and intended for no eye. All around him plants reproduced shapes endlessly: striving for perfection, or compelled to repeat themselves without end? If his gaze had been microscopic, he would have seen the repetitions of atomic particles, mindlessly clinging and building, possessed by the compulsion of matter to form patterns.

Suddenly it frightened him – he couldn't tell why. He felt unsafe. Perhaps it was the mass of cloud which had closed overhead like a stone lid. The colours of the summit had turned lurid, threatening. He headed back towards the wood. The faces of sheep gleamed like bone – he had never noticed before how they resembled munching skulls. A group of heads, chewing mechanically, glared white against the sky and kept their gaze on him.

He was glad to cross the stream, though he couldn't feel the water. He must hurry down before he grew colder. The hush of the woods embraced him. Had a sheep followed him? No, it was only the cry of a decaying trunk. He slipped quickly down the path, which his feet hardly seemed to touch.

The movement of silver-green lattices caged him. Branches and shadows swayed everywhere, entangled. The tips of some of the firs were luminously new. Winds stalked the depths of the forest, great vague forms on creaking stilts. Scents of growth and decay accompanied him. When he grabbed a branch to make sure of his footing, it broke, scattering flakes of lichen.

Again the forest grew too vivid; the trees seemed victims of the processes of growth, sucked dry by the lichen which at the same time lent them an elaborate patina of life. Wherever he looked, the forest seemed unbearably intricate. How, among all that, could he glimpse initials? Somehow they had seized his attention before he knew what they were. They were carved on a cracked and wrinkled tree: Wendy's initials and the man's.

Or were they? Perhaps they were only cracks in the bark. Of course she and the man might well have climbed up here – but the more Knox squinted, the less clear the letters seemed. He couldn't recapture the angle of vision at which they had looked unmistakable.

He was still pacing back and forth before the trunk, as though trapped in a ritual, when stealthy movement made him turn. Was it the shifting of grey trees beneath the lowering largely unseen sky? No – it was a cloud or mist, descending swiftly from the summit, through the woods.

He glanced ahead for the path – and, with a shock that seemed to leave him hollow, realised that it was not there. Nor was it visible behind him as far back as the wall of mist. His reluctant fascination with the forest had lured him astray. He strode back towards the mist, hushing his doubts. Surely the path couldn't be far. But the mist felt thick as icy water, and blinded him. He found himself slithering on decay towards a fall which, though invisible, threatened to be steep. A grab at a crumbling trunk saved him; but when he'd struggled onto safer ground, he could only retreat towards the tree which he had thought was inscribed.

He must press on, outdistancing the mist, and try to head downwards. Wasn't there a forest road below, quite close? But whenever he found an easy slope, it would become abruptly dangerous, often blocked by treacherous splintered logs. He was approaching panic. As much as anything, the hollow at the centre of himself dismayed him. He had intended to welcome it when it had grown there, in his marriage and afterwards; it had seemed safe, invulnerable. Now he found he had few inner resources with which to sustain himself.

The mist was only yards away. It had swallowed all the faint sounds of the wood. If he could only hear the stream, or better still a human voice, a vehicle on the forest road – if only he had gone back to the hotel for his whistle and compass – But there was a sound. Something was blundering towards him. Why was he indefinably distressed, rather than heartened?

Perhaps because the mist obscured it as it scuttled down the slope towards him; perhaps because it sounded too small for an adult human being, too swift, too lopsided. He thought of a child stumbling blindly down the decayed slope. But what child would be so voiceless? As it tumbled limping through the mist, Knox suppressed an urge to flee. He saw the object stagger against a misty root, and collapse there. Before he had ventured forward he saw that it was only a rucksack.

Yet he couldn't quite feel relieved. The rucksack was old, discoloured and patched with decay; mist drained it of colour. Where had it come from? Who had abandoned it, and why? It still moved feebly, as though inhabited. Of course there was a wind: the mist was billowing. Nevertheless he preferred not to go closer. The blurred tentative movements of the overgrown sack were unpleasant, somehow.

Still, perhaps the incident was opportune. It had made him glance upwards for an explanation. He found none – but he caught sight of a summit against the clouds. It wasn't Barf, for between the confusion of trees he could just distinguish two cairns, set close together. If he could reach them, he ought to be able to see his way more clearly. Was he hearing muffled voices up there? He hoped so, but hadn't time to listen.

He wasn't safe yet. The mist had slowed, but was still pursuing him. The slope above him was too steep to climb. He retreated between the trees, avoiding slippery roots which glistened dull silver, glancing upwards constantly for signs of the path. For a while he lost sight of the unknown summit. Only a glimpse of the cairns against the darkening sky mitigated his panic. Were they cairns, or figures sitting together? No, they were the wrong colour for people.

Above him the slope grew steeper. Worse, twilight was settling like mist into the woods. He glared downhill, but the fall was dim and precipitous; there was no sign of a road, only the grey web of innumerable branches. He groped onwards, careless of his footing, desperate to glimpse a way. Surely a path must lead to the cairns. But would he reach it before dark? Could he heave himself up the slope now, using trees for handholds? Wait: wasn't that a path ahead, trailing down between the firs? He stumbled forward, afraid to run in case he slipped. He reached out to grab a tree, to lever himself past its trap of roots. But his fingers recoiled – the encrusted glimmering bark looked unnervingly like a face.

He refused to be reminded of anyone. He clung to the hollow within himself and fought off memories. Yet, as he passed close to the next tree, he seemed to glimpse the hint of a face composed of cracks in the bark, and of twilight. His imagination was conspiring with the dimness, that was all – but why, as he grasped a trunk to thrust himself onwards, did each patch of lichen seem to suggest a face? The more closely he peered, enraged by his fears, the smaller and more numerous the swarming faces seemed. Were there many different faces, or many versions of a couple? Their expressions, though vague, seemed numerous and disturbing.

For a moment he was sure that he couldn't back away – that he must watch until the light was entirely gone, must glimpse faces yet smaller and clearer and more numerous. Panic hurled him away from the lichen and sent him scrabbling upwards. His fingers dug into decay; ferns writhed and snapped when he grabbed them; the surrounding dimness teemed with faces. He kicked himself footholds, gouged the earth with his heels. He clutched at roots, which flaked, moist and chill. More than once he slithered back into the massing darkness. But his panic refused to be defeated. At last, as twilight merged the forest into an indistinguishable crowd of dimness, he scrambled up a slope that had commenced to be gentle, to the edge of the trees.

As soon as he had done so, his triumph collapsed beneath dismay. Even if he glimpsed a path from the summit, night would engulf it before he could make his way down. The sky was blackening. Against it loomed two hunched forms, heads turned to him. Suddenly joy seized him. He could hear voices – surely the sound was more than the muttering of wind. The two forms were human. They must know their way down, and he could join them.

He scrambled upwards. Beyond the trees, the slope grew steep again; but the heather provided easy holds, though his clambering felt almost vertical. The voices had ceased; perhaps they had heard him. But when he glanced up, the figures hadn't moved. A foot higher, and he saw that the faces turned to him were patches of moss; the figures were cairns, after all. It didn't matter: companionship waited at the summit; he'd heard voices, he was sure that he'd heard them, please let him have done so. And indeed, as he struggled up the last yards of the slope, the two grey figures rose with a squeaking and rattling of slate, and advanced heavily towards him.

1984

REDCAP

Lisa Tuttle

Lisa Tuttle (b. 1952) grew up in Texas and developed a love of science fiction, fantasy and horror at a young age, editing and contributing to fanzines in high school and while studying at Syracuse University. She published her first story in 1972 and continued to write fiction while working as a journalist on the Texas newspaper the *Austin American-Statesman*. After moving to Britain in 1980, she began to write fiction full-time, publishing novels (including *Windhaven*, a collaboration with George R. R. Martin) and short stories – "The Bone Flute" won the Nebula Award for Best Short Story in 1982. "Redcap" was first published in the September 1984 edition of *The Magazine of Fantasy & Science Fiction*.

Tuttle now lives in Scotland and "Redcap" is rooted in a knowledge of the Scottish Borders. In *Literary Hauntings*, the writer R. B. Russell (whose story follows Tuttle's in this collection) notes that it was a trip to Hermitage Castle in Roxburghshire that inspired Tuttle's distinctly creepy tale. The titular redcap is a malevolent goblin said to haunt lonely fortresses and ruined towers along the Anglo-Scottish border. After her visit, Tuttle read that local folklore tells of one such creature being kept as a familiar by the castle's evil master, Lord Soulis. The forbidding structure is now looked after by Historic Environment Scotland and is usually open to visitors between April and September each year.

Off the main road, Carter walked into silence. Wonderful, he thought, to find such solitude in crowded, civilized Britain. It was like traveling back in time. The peaceful border country was especially appealing after two hot weeks of sight-seeing in London.

According to his guidebook, the castle should be less than a mile away, but he could see nothing but dark green conifer forest on both sides of the road.

"A haunted, uncanny, wicked place," the girl in the pub last night had called it. Carter wasn't superstitious, but he liked hearing her talk. To provoke her he said he intended to camp out in the castle ruins.

"You'll never!" she cried in alarm. "Oh, no, once you see it for your own self, you'd never want to pass the night there. It's a wicked place. The stones are soaked with blood."

The old lord who built the castle had been a sorcerer, she told him, who kidnapped and murdered babies. He used his magic to terrorize the local people and pile up treasure. Finally, for his sins, he was boiled in oil.

"So he's dead," said Carter. "His ghost can't hurt me."

"It's not the old lord you need to be afraid of – but Redcap. Redcap still guards the treasure, as his master bid him. And Redcap will never die."

Carter rounded a bend and saw the castle, the top of it projecting through the trees: jagged black stone, sharp edged as the teeth in a monster's gaping mouth.

The silence suddenly seemed unnatural. There were no birds singing, and no breeze stirred. The only sound was the low mutter of rushing water from somewhere out of sight.

Carter shifted the weight of his bedroll, trying to ignore the tension in the pit of his stomach, the sudden reluctance to continue. In his mind's eye he could see the goblin the girl had described to him, see it as clearly as he saw the ragged stone jaws of the castle: a stocky, powerful little man with long yellow teeth and glowing red eyes. The girl's voice rang in his ears, a voice straight out of the bloody, fearful past: "His cap is red because he dyes it in the blood of his victims."

A car passed, a sudden flash of color, noise, and dust heading toward the main road. Five minutes earlier Carter would have resented it, but now, even though it made him jump, he was glad to be reminded so forcibly of the twentieth century.

He looked at the cloudless sky, remembering his plan to sleep out, to save money, unless the weather turned. Still, there were probably laws against camping on government property. He didn't have to keep a drunken boast made to a girl he would never see again. He walked on, and the castle was hidden by the forest.

A narrow, fast-flowing river churned and bubbled over rocks to his right, rushing down the hillside to follow the course of the road. The trees thinned, and there, on the other side of the river, stood the castle.

It was not the ruin he had imagined, although it was roofless. The walls – dark, weather-streaked stone – looked as solid as the day they were built. It was a high, square, sturdy fortress, not very large. The "teeth" were jagged crenellations rising to a point at the top of each side.

As he approached, Carter saw an elderly couple standing beside a white car parked on the grassy verge. He nodded at them as he passed, going through the wooden gate and up the path. Behind him he heard the sound of a car being started and driven away, and he felt the silence descend upon him once more.

A wooden shed with a Department of the Environment sign on it marked the end of the path. On a campstool in front of the door sat a grey-haired, heavyset man in khaki.

"Hello," Carter said. "Not too late, am I?"

The guard looked him carefully up and down, then shook his head. "Not too late. We're open until sunset, by law, but no one ever comes that late. No one wants to be caught here after dark."

Carter grinned. "You mean ghosts?"

"No, I don't mean ghosts."

"I met this girl last night," Carter said. "She seemed to think this place was haunted. She said a lot of people had been murdered here."

"That's true enough."

"She said that at night their screams and cries could still be heard." The man shrugged. "I've never seen any ghosts. Or heard them."

"You've been here at night?"

"Of course. It's my duty to look after the place. I've nothing to fear."

Carter fumbled in his pocket for change. "I'll take a ticket and... is there a book about the castle? A history?"

"No, and there should be. I could write one myself, if I had the gift for writing. I know more about this castle than anyone else alive, and that includes all your book-writing history professors! I could tell you some stories..."

"Maybe when I come out," said Carter. "I'm interested in history."

The guard looked at him again, a little too searchingly for Carter's taste. "What've you got in that rucksack?"

"Just – things," he said defensively.

"Must be heavy, carrying it around all day. Why don't you take it off and leave it here while you look around the castle? You needn't worry. I'll look after it for you. It will be safe with me."

It would have seemed ungracious to refuse, Carter thought, almost an insult. Besides, his few valuables – passport, money, camera – were in his pockets or slung around his neck. And as he shrugged off the backpack and handed it over, he realized it had become a burden. It was a relief to move unencumbered. "Hey, thanks a lot. I won't be too long."

"Take your time," said the guard. "I'll wait for you."

Carter walked up toward the castle, feeling uneasy. No doubt about it, the place had an evil atmosphere. He couldn't put his finger on a reason – it just seemed to be in the air. Probably some places were naturally like that, due to negative ions or underground water, he thought; or maybe there was something in the idea that violent deeds left a trace behind. He wondered if the guard felt it, working here every day as he did. Was he immune to it, or had he learned to ignore it?

The heavy wooden door on one side was locked, but on the other an identical door had been wedged open with a lump of stone. Entering, Carter saw that the interior was less well preserved than he had expected. Walls had crumbled away in places, and chunks of rock littered the earth floor. Wooden beams and floorboards had long since deteriorated, like the roof, so stone stairways rose to emptiness. Carter liked the look of the steps climbing to nothing, and took several photographs from different angles. He investigated odd corners and climbed up and down, taking more pictures and enjoying himself, forgetting that odd prickling sensation in the interest of the moment. Outside, he took shots of the ruin from all sides and finally, reluctantly, went back to the guard's hut.

"Like it?"

"You bet! That old well especially. I only wish I could have seen it when it was being used, you know, how people lived in it. How long was it occupied?"

The guard rattled off names and dates, giving a potted history that Carter barely took in. He was noticing the length of the shadows on the grass, and wondering how soon it would be dark.

"Uh, sorry to interrupt," Carter said. "But I need to find a place to stay the night. You wouldn't happen to know of anybody around here who does bed and breakfast?"

The man stared at him. "Nobody lives around here. Did you see anybody on your way? No, they wouldn't build their houses too close to the castle – not *this* castle. Out of fear. But why do you want to pay for a bed when you've got your kit with you? It will be a fine, dry night, and the moon full. When I saw you coming up the path, I said to myself, there's one who'll be asking permission to camp out. Mind you, I couldn't let you stay inside the actual castle. I'll lock that up proper before I go home, as I always do. But I don't mind if you want to sleep outside the walls."

"No, not tonight," Carter said. "I do sleep out a lot, but I don't have any food with me, so I'll have to hike to the nearest village for a meal, and then I won't feel like coming back all this way." He felt pleased with himself for coming up with such a good excuse.

"Ah, so you are afraid." The beginning of a satisfied smile appeared.

The guard's expression annoyed Carter. "I'm *not* afraid. I don't believe in ghosts."

"It wasn't ghosts I meant. It wasn't ghosts killed the last ones."

"The last ones?"

"The last who spent the night here. They didn't believe in ghosts either, that man and that woman with their tent and their Primus stove and their – "

"When was that?" Dimly, he recalled something the girl in the pub told him. He'd found it hard, listening to her, to judge how long ago the things she spoke of had happened.

"Oh, five years ago. You hadn't heard of it? A shocking thing, in all the papers... but I suppose in America you have enough of your own murders without importing ours."

"Who killed them?"

"Who, indeed? Their throats were slit with a knife."

"A robber?"

"No robber."

Carter glanced at the sun, low and glinting redly through the trees. "Look," he said. "I'm sure it's an interesting story, but I would like to find a place to stay tonight – "

"But not here, eh? Not on Redcap's ground."

"Redcap!"

"Aye, Redcap. He carries the keys and guards the treasure just as the old lord set him to do. Still here, still killing strangers to dye his cap."

"I've heard the legend," Carter said. "Very colorful. But I don't believe in the supernatural, in ghosts and goblins. The reason I don't want to stay has nothing to do with Redcap, or the people who were murdered here five years ago."

"You'd believe if you saw them. If you saw what *I* saw."

"You saw them. After they were dead?"

"Oh, yes." The guard nodded. "I could tell you a story..."

"I need to get started walking. I don't want to miss dinner," Carter said, ignoring the tickle of interest the man's words had stirred in him.

"Don't worry about it," the guard said. "There's a farmhouse not too far from here where they know me. If I take you to them, they'll give you a bed for the night and even cook you supper. Mrs B's a fair cook, too. Just wait for me." He touched the keys hanging at his belt. "The sun's setting and I must lock up. No one else will come now. Wait here for me."

Carter watched the man walk away, feeling the urge to run for it. But where would he run? He remembered that long stretch of forest road behind him. He didn't know what lay ahead, but the guard had offered to take him to a farmhouse. How silly to run away from a good offer, to pay attention to that irrational prickling down his back.

He stepped into the wooden hut and looked around. It was tiny, but the walls had been fitted with built-in shelves, and it was well equipped for a man who must wait here all day. There was an electric kettle, mugs, a teapot, a box of tea bags, a bottle half-full of milk, a small sack of sugar, a roll of digestive biscuits, a radio, some magazines and books, a deck of cards, boxed jigsaw puzzles, extra clothes – all the comforts of home. His own gear was on the floor beside the wall, and as he knelt down beside it, something caught his eye, glinting on a shelf, out of place among a pile of clothing. Without thinking, Carter reached out.

It was a knife, he thought at first, but then he had it in his hand and could see that it was only the hilt. It was a heavy, ornate, iron hilt without a blade. It looked very old, the sort of thing Carter could imagine seeing in a museum, behind glass, the blade reconstructed in plaster, with a typed card giving its history.

Suddenly nervous, Carter thrust the hilt to the back of the shelf, hiding it, and stood up. Through the open door he saw the guard approaching.

"Sit there," the man said, nudging his campstool farther onto the path. "I'll make us a cup of tea before we go. I never set out for home without a cup of tea inside me."

"Maybe you could give me directions," Carter said, edging past. "Just tell me where – "

"I said I'd take you, and I will. Now sit. I've got another stool for me."

Carter looked at the looming dark mass of the castle and wished himself elsewhere, but he sat down.

"I was telling you about the murders," the guard said some minutes later, handing Carter a steaming cup and settling down beside him. "It was a married couple, as I said, and a child. The boy wasn't their own. They'd taken him on out of charity. It came out later that his real father had been done for murder. Of course, I didn't know that at the time, but afterward it made sense of something she said, about not believing in heredity. She believed in the socializing process, and she was going to socialize that boy good and proper, make him into a weedy little vegetarian pacifist.

"That's what *they* were, you see. Or at least, she was. She did all the talking. Did she talk! When I gave them permission to stay the night, of course I told them about Redcap. I had to ask them if they knew – it wouldn't have been right to let them stay, unknowing.

"She as much as called me simple to my face. Went on about reason and logic, didn't want the boy to hear such nonsense.

"I felt sorry for the kid, I can tell you, having to put up with all that from her. While those two were setting up camp, I had a chat with the boy. I gave him a biscuit – not like these, I had chocolate-covered ones that day – and would you believe it? He scoffed half the roll. And he ate up my stories, too. He'd never heard the like all about magic and murder. He thought history was dull, dry dates. In his house they didn't believe in fairy stories, which meant no comics, no television, no *fun*. He took it all very serious. He didn't know how to laugh, I don't think.

"After I told him about Redcap, he didn't want to stay. He had more sense than his people, but of course they wouldn't listen to him. No matter what he said, they would stay. That woman was furious with me for putting nonsense into his head, as she put it. She said no one had ever lied to him before; she believed in telling children the truth and only the truth. The last thing I heard as I left was her telling him to stop crying and forget the silly stories that bad man had told him, and to put on his pajamas, and not to forget it was damp out, so he must wear his socks and his nightcap as well. His nightcap! I ask you...

"I was the one who found them, of course, in the morning." He stared into the shadows, as if seeing it all again.

Carter looked into his untasted tea, feeling his heart pounding with a kind of sick excitement. The silence stretched on, lengthening like the shadows, and he finally had to ask.

"How... how exactly did you find them?"

"I saw the woman first – the man was in the tent. I saw her lying on the ground, all bloody, and the kid crouching over her. I thought he was trying to help her, at first. Then I saw what it was. He had his little nightcap in his hands, and he was dipping it into the wound in her throat.

"He looked up at me, holding it up. 'I'm making it like *his*,' he said. 'Red, just like his.'"

Carter could almost feel the darkness thickening the air around them, wrapping them in silence. He had to clench his teeth to keep from shivering. "What... what about the police?"

"I had to call them, of course. The boy was their only witness, but also their only suspect. They didn't believe the story about a little man with glowing red eyes and long yellow teeth, with a red cap pulled down over his long, shaggy hair. If this person had cut two throats, why had he left the boy untouched?

"He had the answer. He held out his nightcap, stiff with his mother's blood. 'I was wearing this,' he said. 'It was just like his. He grinned at me, and he touched his cap and pointed to mine. Then he disappeared. He left me because he thought we were the same. Because of the cap. He thought I was like him.' And he smiled, so pleased to have worked it out.

"But the police don't go for stories about people who disappear. And he was their only suspect, even though he wasn't really strong enough to have cut a throat like that – the woman had struggled, and she was a big, strong woman, too. But they ignored that because it was simpler to keep it in the family. There was just one problem."

The tenor of the man's voice changed, and Carter looked at him. In the last, late rays of the setting sun, the guard's eyes glowed a deep, dangerous red. Carter stared and could not look away.

"The murder weapon. They never found it. They never found my knife." He grinned, showing long, yellow teeth.

And then it was really dark.

1992

THE PHARISEES' GLASS

R. B. Russell

R. B. Russell is a writer of novels, short stories and non-fiction. Since 1990 he has co-run Tartarus Press, an imprint that has done much to preserve and raise the profile of the weird fiction canon. Russell is also a noted authority on the life and work of the master of the strange story, Robert Aickman, publishing a biography of the author in 2022. "The Pharisees' Glass", a story in the tradition of the Welsh author and mystic Arthur Machen, was first published in the journal *Aklo* in 1992.

Central to Russell's tale is the enigmatic, 72-metre-tall Long Man of Wilmington, a figure dominating the slopes of Windover Hill in East Sussex. From a distance, the stark outline of the Long Man's form, holding an upright pole in each hand, appears to be cut from the chalk of the hill itself. The fact that the figure is now composed of painted breeze blocks, rather than Sussex earth alone, does little to detract from the impressive, beguiling sight that confronts the visitor.

Countless theories have been put forward to explain the Long Man of Wilmington, from Alfred Watkins' thought that he represents a surveyor involved in ley-line construction (see Jacqueline Simpson's story later in this collection), to the idea that he is a Neolithic marker of the constellation Orion. However, recent archaeology suggests a Tudor or Stuart date for the hill figure's creation, which would make him significantly younger than his counterparts at Uffington and Cerne Abbas. Regardless of age, the giant on Windover Hill continues to attract those who, like the character of Goring in "The Pharisees' Glass", feel a connection to this beautiful, mysterious part of the South Downs.

We seek wonder in all the wrong places. There are few areas left on the earth where exploration will yield anything fantastic, and science destroys all sense of awe with its need to explain and find "systems" for everything. Psychologists, perhaps, look in the right direction, but not in quite the right way.

No, strangeness is to be found where we least expect it, and one evening last summer I was rewarded in my search among unlikely places. I had been walking on an errand for a friend, the significance of which has little bearing on the tale I am about to relate. I found myself in a quiet public house in a southern suburb of a northern city, and I suppose that I had been seeking adventure.

I had strayed from the paths that I knew. I had an address but had decided that I should be able to find it without a map. There was no urgency in the matter, and I was absently turning left here into an interesting avenue, and right there through occasional park grounds. The city is known for the hills on which it is built, and often there would be a steep winding alley or diving path that demanded to be explored.

The afternoon wore on, and knowing that I must have been close to the area I sought I asked a passerby if he knew of the quiet cul-de-sac that I was after. It was getting dark now and I decided to make my way there as directly as possible. In the event I was distracted by a delightful walk alongside an old canal, and when I eventually found myself on the right road night was with me.

The errand was eventually run; and faced with the walk back I decided that before I set off I would visit the local pub previously recommended by my friend.

"The Bull" was almost empty, despite the warmth and the hospitality offered there and the late hour on this Saturday evening. It was not an old pub, and I am glad to say that it lacked the fake beams and horse-brasses that breweries often impose these days. I ordered a glass of stout.

"You're from down South, then?" asked the rotund landlord while the pint was pouring.

"Yes, originally. I've been up here for five years now. Moved up from Sussex."

"Sussex, eh? Isn't Eastbourne in Sussex?"

"Yes, but I hail from Lewes."

"Well, Mr Goring over there is from Eastbourne." He nodded to a middle-aged man sat on his own, set behind a pint of bitter.

I paid for my drink and walked over to the gentleman. Usually I find it impossible to initiate a conversation with a stranger in a pub, but he was a fellow exile.

"The barman tells me you're from Sussex," I introduced myself. He looked up at me and I was embarrassed to note that I had interrupted him. He had been correcting what appeared to be a small pile of essays.

"I come from that way myself," I continued, feeling profoundly awkward. "Where in Sussex were you?"

"Do you know Wilmington?" he asked quietly. I nodded. "Well, that's the nearest village. I lived in a cottage about a mile from there. And you?"

"Not far away then – Lewes. How long ago was it that you moved up here?"

"Oh, a year or so now, I reckon. Just after the hurricane."

"Really, that must have been something?" I asked if he minded if I sat with him. "I still haven't been able to get down there. Will I find it much changed?"

"Well, yes, but I don't rightly know if I can say how much. I left just a few days afterwards. There was a hell of a lot of work to do. You wouldn't believe just how many trees have gone. Though it's pretty surprising how many stayed up as well."

"I've been sent photographs by relatives. It looks as though it was pretty devastating."

"It was quite remarkable. I don't suppose that anyone in Sussex or Kent, or Hampshire for that matter, will ever forget last October."

He remembered back.

"I was woken in the early hours by the wind," he told me. "It was a kind of constant low roaring. If it wasn't the wind that woke me it may have been the tiles falling from the roof, or the sound of the roof itself straining under the pressure. You see, all other less immediate sounds were lost in that one mighty roar."

"Are we right to call it a hurricane though?"

"I wouldn't like to say myself, but as I peered through my front door, holding onto it tightly, there was no rain and it was unnaturally warm. It was more than just a gale. And it was quite terrifying, mainly because I felt so isolated. I lived on my own at the time, and it was as though I was the only living thing on the face of an earth gone quite mad.

"With daylight and the dropping of the wind the feeling of isolation didn't diminish, although I was able to meet up with others in the village. Everybody in the area who could be found got together to help each other in makeshift repairs. With all the roads blocked by the fallen trees there was a general, almost unspoken, feeling that we were the last folk left in the world.

"The first result of the destruction to impress me was the great size of the trees as they lay all about. It was prophesied at the time that the smell of wood smoke would be with us for the rest of the autumn and winter into the new year. The earth was ripped and scarred. Yes, things had changed quite fundamentally."

"In what way?" I asked.

"No," he laughed. "I've made it all sound far more interesting than it is. There's nothing at all to tell. It's just the changes wrought in a place so dear to me. You couldn't possibly understand."

"Why couldn't I? Yes, I come from Lewes; it's a big town, but I hold the Downs just as dear."

"It's more to me than that," Goring explained. "There is something almost mystical about the South Downs. It's something that can be seen and felt. It's a retention of the memory of their ancient past." He stopped while he considered whether to continue. "I don't know what it is, but the flinty paths and tracks in the chalk were made by the remotest of our ancestors. And the mists that steal in from the sea have been doing so ever since our island was separated from the land mass that we now call Europe.

"I can't say how it is for you, but it's something that anyone who has been brought up in the area should know. I've felt it since I was a young child. The knowledge of the Downs became mine from the very first time that I was allowed to roam those rolling grassy hills alone. They're beyond all doubt the nearest point on earth to the heavens, and the wooded valleys hide secrets that stem from the very bowels of the earth."

Goring was again quiet. I was unsure whether I should say anything.

"Well," he admitted, "the changes were fundamental to me. Time casts doubts in your mind as to reality, but I wish that I was as sceptical of my tale as I know that you are going to be."

He paused, considered, and continued. "It was the first evening after the hurricane and we were all in the village when someone asked if anyone had seen Daniel Pettit. I didn't know much about the old boy other than that he was reputed to be an unsociable so-and-so. He lived on a small-holding on the other side of the village to me. Anyhow, I was delegated to go and check on the man. It turned out that he had been injured in the storm, though not seriously so.

"Now this old boy, God help his soul, must have been seventy-odd. I soon found out that he knew the matters of the countryside like nobody else that I've ever had the pleasure of meeting before.

"I could say that we were kindred souls, but I suppose it would be more truthful to suggest that we were both as mad as each other.

"And his small-holding! It must have been a hundred years behind the times a century ago. He couldn't have kept it going with any economic success if it weren't for some strange religious community on the Sussex-Kent border who bought most of his produce at the higher prices he was forced to charge just to stay in business.

"Now until I introduced myself to Daniel Pettit I didn't think that the countryside, nature and natural things were appreciated by people as I appreciated them."

Goring paused, remembering.

"And he was most sociable. We talked, quite understandably, of the hurricane. Now, everybody was talking about the weather, but he could talk of the elements and their impossible-to-understand moods with a passion that I'd never heard before. He was almost poetic. He suggested as real, though, the strangest things and ideas, phenomena that I have guessed at only in the wildest flights of fancy.

It may sound as though I'm exaggerating, but I was captivated by him and his veiled, often inadvertent hints of knowledge of things that should be beyond our mortal ken. He became almost metaphysical at times, but he brought the conversation back to more material things for my sake."

Goring had been waxing quite lyrical, loudly in fact, and he noticed that the landlord was endeavouring to listen to the conversation. He lowered his voice, after a pointed glance in the direction of the bar.

"As we sat at his kitchen table in his small and ancient cottage, our conversation became almost outrageously mystical, although I was sceptical about many of the old man's claims. He told me of dormant;. and latent powers in those South Downs. The fairies or 'Pharisees', as Sussex folk called them, were not to be dismissed as imagination, he claimed. No, they were not the pretty gauze-petticoated and winged fancies of the Victorians. Those were just an attempt to make ridiculous and inoffensive the strange and often cruel things that are to be found in certain secret places.

"'Cruel?' I asked, 'or evil?' No, that was just a fallacy, he said, just as was the idea that they could sometimes be good. These powers, entities perhaps, Pharisees, are beyond our perception. We mean little to them with our petty and inward aims and ideals. Thus they transcend good and evil. Can we really say, old Mr Pettit asked, that a nettle is evil because it would sting us? We enjoy flowers and call them good, but they aren't there just for us to look upon. Mankind is too wrapped up in itself and will not acknowledge that nature moves in accord with its own laws, laws that do not necessarily have to be understood by man."

At this point Goring stopped, and I went to the bar to buy us both further drinks. The pub was filling up with people and smoke, and I was worried that Goring would not continue his story. However, as soon as I sat down he resumed his tale.

"Anyway, I was happy to accept his arguments, and he considered my own views. He agreed with much that I said, but curiously he dismissed or suggested alterations to other things in such a way as could only be explained by the stubbornness of age or, as I believed was unlikely, first hand esoteric knowledge based on unbelievable observation.

"There was very little left of the elderflower wine that he had opened. I declared that I too held the conviction that there were powers beyond our comprehension. Perhaps, I suggested, they manifest themselves in ways that we cannot understand, but explain in prosaic terms that are naturally limited by our lack of knowledge and understanding. I found it hard to believe his tacit assumption that fairies, or Pharisees, little people, gnomes, pixies, water or wood spirits, whatever one calls them, actually existed. That was, I said, unless he had seen them himself."

Goring paused for effect.

"Old Daniel Pettit laughed, and shook me somewhat by admitting that he had seen them all, knew them, and many more that I could not ever hope to name. Of course I didn't think him entirely serious, but there was something earnest in his manner. He said that I was contradicting myself by denying the validity of an argument I claimed to believe.

"I defended myself by saying that without proof, actually seeing such things before my own eyes, I could never really believe any of it.

"Now, young man," Goring addressed me. "Mr Pettit was faced with much the same dilemma as myself when you asked me for this tale. You see, I was asking him to show me these wonderful things that he claimed. I can't offer any proof to you now, and at that time I didn't believe he could offer me any either.

"With voice hushed in awe and a little because of the drink, Pettit then offered to show me what he had been able to see, what he claimed he could still see when he chose to do so.

"Now, I admitted that I would be most interested, but still cast doubts. The old man grinned and asked me to wait while he fetched something down from upstairs. I was, meanwhile, to prepare myself for a short walk. And also, he said, to prepare for an experience known to but a few.

"Despite the obvious theatricals a strange thrill ran through me, and also a certain apprehension. It was probably nothing more than a combination of the drink and the queer eloquence of the old man that had unnerved me. I couldn't believe that he was about to reveal to me the existence of something that I had often dreamed of but which I knew instinctively to be beyond our reach. Only now did I realise just how tired I was after the exertion of the clearing up that day. I wanted to use this as an excuse not to follow the old man out into the darkness.

"I looked around the warm kitchen with its heavy though functional air that confirmed Daniel Pettit's status as a bachelor. I could hear him moving around upstairs. After a minute's eerie silence during which all I could hear was the settling of the fire in the Aga, his slow tread descended the stairs and he came back into the room. His look was now grave and he was holding something carefully, almost reverently, in his hands. I had no idea what it could be.

"He was obviously determined to carry this charade through to the end, but what, I wondered, would this end be. He led the way out into the small garden and locked the door behind us. I followed him into and down the lane. We had to clamber over a fair few trees, with him all the time carefully keeping hold of his precious object. The destruction that the hurricane had wrought was all the more disheartening in the dark. The great bodies of the fallen trees loomed up dark and helpless against the sky.

"We crossed a couple of fields and were beginning to climb a small slope when I realised the old fellow's motive. He was clearly attempting, in his inebriation, to frighten me. It was indeed an appropriate setting and time, with all the natural order of things visibly in ruin around us. And there can be, with little imagination, as you yourself must know, an almost occult aspect in the Downs at night. I know that I'm saying all this with hindsight, but it was almost as if something malignant lurked within those dark, rounded hills. Until recently this was the countryside that I loved so much, but in that hour I would have preferred to be in any one of those tatty seaside towns along the coast that I usually so hate. The nearness of something man-made would have eased my soul at that moment. Yes. Pettit had succeeded in frightening me, especially when he talked now of the 'Long Man' who reared up ahead of us, his outline shining weirdly in the moonlight."

Goring offered to buy me another drink, his glass being empty. Annoyed that he had stopped the tale I insisted that I get it for him, and topped up my own. When I returned to his table he asked me what I knew about the Long Man of Wilmington.

I had to admit that I knew precious little of the chalk-carved giant other than that it was the largest representation of a human figure known.

Goring admitted that he too had known little about it. In his youth a local magazine had attempted to clear up the mystery of the history and origins of the figure. Its various inconclusive conjectures, however, had merely confirmed his belief that none should ever know the secret of its origin. Wilmington's "lazy" monks were one possibility, but more realistically the Romans and the Celts were put forward as being the responsible parties. The Long Man had changed in certain small details over the more recent years, without a doubt, but how much had it altered before any of the records of its appearance had been preserved, Goring asked. There were many suggested sources for its origin, but perhaps all the suggested peoples had in fact inherited the giant? Perhaps its origins lie with a race of which history is ignorant?

"The Long Man stood before me," Goring continued, "then, as always, a mystery. My companion stopped at the top of a rise and with disconcerting solemnity assured me that what he was about to show me was not a delusion, that anything I saw was not the result of brain fever or imagination or alcohol.

"So saying he unwrapped the parcel and produced a small wooden frame, roughly four inches square and having within it a piece of dark glass backed by a thin piece of board.

"'This,' said Daniel Pettit, 'is the Pharisees' Glass. And through it one may view the wonders of nature, nature as it really is beyond the veil that we imposed when we fell from Eden. This is nature as we should really know it.'

"Unsure and stalling I asked where he had obtained the glass and he said that the Pharisees had presented it to him themselves. 'So,' I asked, thinking that I had seen a flaw in his story, 'you were able to see these Pharisees before you were actually given the Glass?'

"'Not properly, no,' he replied. 'They were indistinct though I knew them to be there. I was out seeing to my animals during the storm when something struck me, and I suppose that I was knocked out. I had a wonderful dream in which the Pharisees told me where to find the Glass.'

"Pettit said that he didn't come around till morning. He immediately went out and found the Glass exactly where the Pharisees had said it would be. Apparently a huge old oak had been uprooted and had torn up a large white stone with it. On the stone was a square piece of dark glass. He had then come back home and spent the afternoon making the frame for it.

"Uncertainly, I asked if I could look through it and he agreed. He said that such wonder should be shared, but warned me first that such devices were not without their dangers. He would remove the board at the back, and I was to look through the Glass from one side only. On no account should I attempt to view through it from the other side. Pettit reckoned that the Pharisees in his dream had told him that if he was tempted to look from the wrong side then he would not be able to view through the Glass again, and never would he be able to view the world in the way he had before. He said that he would keep their trust.

"The board was then removed and I saw through the Pharisees' Glass a world unknown yet weirdly familiar. The Glass was at first dark, cloudy, but then a light slowly played through it so that I was able to see, although it was night. There was a supernal light over everything that I had once known, and a beauty and complexity in everyday things that the most colourful of imaginations could never hope to dream of. And this light was totally alien in its hues, colours so unknown that I am quite unable to recall them now. I can remember only my reaction to what I saw. Those who claim to have seen such things as these with the aid of drugs have caused debate as to whether they have experienced a vision or a delusion. Do they see what is really there, or are they fancies created by the drugged mind? I have never taken such drugs and can't compare what others see with what I beheld, but I knew, and still believe that what I witnessed was real. When I eventually withdrew my gaze, reluctantly, I had no doubts as to the validity of what I had viewed.

"I was almost euphoric. To think that so much exists in dimensions running concurrent with ours. That it exists and influences us and is yet unseen and guessed at by but a pathetic few who are dismissed as dreamers!

"My hand trembled, I was unable to speak. I held the Glass out to Pettit but it slipped from the wooden frame. He cursed me, but then saw that it lay unbroken on the grass. He lifted it gently from the earth and peered at it in the darkness. He turned to me as if to speak, and I saw that his expression was one of profound realisation and horror. Never can a face have ever registered such abject fear. Every feature was contorted beyond anything that I could have thought possible. His eyes bulged and saliva frothed from his lips. His face was dark, and with one violent spasm he jerked back and lay outstretched on the ground. He didn't move.

"After a year or so now I am sure that, as in the tales, Pettit had 'seen Pan'; he had seen nature as it really is, in all its awful and terrible wonder."

"Doesn't 'seeing Pan' mean the same as seeing the spirit world?"

"It depends on what you call the spirit world. The old man may have been right when he said that nature does not know good and evil, though as we interpret it there are always the two sides. There is a profound and wonderful brilliance in nature, and there are also depths loathsome and unbelievably foul. What makes the one so magnificent and the other so terrifying is their complete and deep rooted indifference to man."

Goring had stopped. When talking he had been animated but now looked tired. I said nothing, for what could I say?

"Any doubts that I may have had about this were impossible after what I saw next," Goring resumed. "The action of violently throwing the Glass away, throwing it in fear and disgust, meant drawing it to myself before hurling it back. As I did so I caught a fleeting glimpse through it. It was so momentary that it shouldn't even have registered on the retina of my eye, though I must say that recollection is mercifully blurred. Like Pettit I suppose that I too 'saw Pan'."

Goring laughed loudly. There was more than a hint of madness in his laugh, attracting attention to both of us. He smiled, composing himself.

"I have looked upon something far worse than that mythological creature. I have seen the Long Man of Wilmington for what it really is. Through the Pharisees' Glass I saw him as he was originally depicted in the chalk upon the venerable South Downs. He wasn't holding staves as he does today – he was standing in an open doorway, guarding what is beyond."

Goring rose, obviously impatient to leave.

"Young man," he told me. "It was no ordeal telling you that much of the story, but there is no way that you will ever learn from me that which I saw, or fancied that I saw, through that gateway."

Goring left The Bull hurriedly.

2002

DRAGON PATH

Jacqueline Simpson

Jacqueline Simpson (b. 1930) is an award-winning folklorist and former president of the Folklore Society. After studying English Literature and Old Icelandic at London University, she began her writing career in the 1960s with a particular focus on the folk tales and legends of Scandinavia. Simpson co-authored the indispensable *Dictionary of English Folklore* with Steve Roud in 2003, before publishing *Lore of the Land* with Jennifer Westwood in 2006 – a fascinating, exhaustive guide to England's legends. Simpson also writes supernatural fiction, with her stories to date collected in 2018's *Where Are the Bones? and Other Stories*. "Dragon Path" first appeared in *All Hallows*, the magazine of the Ghost Story Society, in June 2002.

The story takes place on Cornwall's Bodmin Moor, an area notably rich in legend. Not far from the stone circles of the Hurlers, on Stowe's Hill, stands the remarkable Cheesewring, a granite tor which has taken on a fantastical shape due to millennia of weathering. Rillaton Barrow, also mentioned in the story, lies close by. The marvellous Rillaton gold cup was unearthed when the barrow was excavated, and, for a while, stood on George V's dressing table holding his collar studs. It can now be found in the British Museum.

Bodmin Moor is also dear to ley line enthusiasts, an idea that Simpson incorporates into her tale. Alfred Watkins proposed ley lines in the 1920s as straight lines connecting venerable sites in the landscape. The idea had fallen from fashion by the Second World War, but received a boost in the countercultural world of the 1960s and beyond. Here leys were given a mystical twist (Watkins had thought of them as, essentially, trackways) as conduits of earth energy that had been tapped into by the ancients. John Michell's *The View Over Atlantis* proposed the St Michael Line mentioned by Simpson – an enormous ley of "dragon current" which incorporates key sites on an alignment across England. Many of these places have associations with dragons, such as churches named for the dragon-slaying archangel St Michael.

"God, I'm thirsty!" The young man flopped down in the shade of the rock, hauled off his backpack, and dug out a can of Coke. He flicked the ring-pull away, and drank.

"Hey, pick that thing up, Geoff!" said his companion sharply.

"Oh, for God's sake, what's the matter now? Am I polluting Holy Mother Earth? Am I annoying the pixies? Pick it up yourself, Mick, if it bothers you."

"That," said Mick in tones of elaborate patience, "is the way that fires get started. When the moors are dry, you only need for the sun to catch on a bit of metal or glass – "

Geoff groaned, but didn't move. Neither did Mick, but he glared at Geoff and at the ring-pull. The two girls had also reached the rock by now and stood listening, one anxious, one amused. The anxious one picked up the ring-pull and slipped it into her pocket, glancing hopefully at Mick for approval; he gave her a nod, but his eyes were on Geoff, and on the other, prettier, girl, who had joined him in the patch of shade. Grinning, Geoff passed his can to her, and she drank with a casualness which hinted at other sharings, other intimacies.

"Boy, did I need that!" Then, licking her lips and flashing a brilliant smile at Mick, "Well, here we are, and there's your Cheesewring, so tell us what it's all about. I can't wait to hear!"

An answering smile lit up Mick's tense features. "This is a sacred landscape, Julia – one of the best, almost unspoilt. Over there – "

"Over *there*," said Geoff, waving his hand grandly in the opposite direction, "is a bloody great quarry. Disused, I grant you, but not sacred and unspoilt. Not virgin soil unploughed."

"Shut up," said Julia, stifling a giggle, "I want to hear this."

"So do I," said the anxious girl, whose name was Anne. "Mick knows such a lot about the earth."

Mick's interrupted lecture resumed. "Over there, as you see, is the Cheesewring. Seven round slabs, perfectly balanced on top of each other, nothing else like it in the world. The scientists," (there was acid scorn in the word) "being scientists, will tell you it's natural, it just happened that way. But as Cornishmen, we've always known better. We knew there was power in the stones; we knew people had put them up there for a good reason, like Stonehenge. So we made up stories to pass on the message, stories which make sense to us, but not to you outsiders."

Geoff gave a loud yawn. "OK, do your Mystic Celt stuff if you must. But you're no more a Celt than I am. Yeah, I know your name's Trelawney, but it's over two hundred years since your revered Cornish ancestor came to London, as you told me yourself, so how many of his magical genes do you think you've got? Come to that, one of my great-grans was an Irish tweeny who hadn't brains enough to say no to the boss's son. Maybe if I had enough Guinness in me I'd see leprechauns."

"I said, shut up!" said Julia, kicking him. "I like Mick's stories."

"OK, OK, it's listen-with-mother time, if that's how you want it. Sitting comfortably, pet?"

He slid his arm around her, but she pulled away, her eyes on Mick. "Go on, tell us. What do they say about the Cheesewring?"

"It *moves*. That top stone there, it turns round three times when it hears the cock crow. Now, if you say that's just silly, it's you that's the fool, because stories like that are a code. The storytellers, they kept the secret knowledge alive, and now we've found out what it was. It's amazing, but it's been proved, over and over again. The Cheesewring is a powerhouse, like Stonehenge, like Avebury – there were hundreds of them, powerhouses built to store earth energies five thousand years ago, so the currents could flow along the leys – even now, any good dowser feels it – and you know what, Julia? Here, right here where we are sitting, we're on the biggest ley of all – St Michael's Line – the Dragon Path!"

He jumped up and began pointing at the horizon with his blackthorn stick, pacing up and down and talking faster and faster. "It comes from St Michael's Mount, and all the churches it goes through are St Michael's too – he's the greatest of the angels, he's my patron of course – and here we have the Cheesewring, and the Hurlers, and then away it goes to the northeast, straight to Glastonbury Tor itself, and on to Avebury, and out across England, straight as a die, to Bury St Edmunds and the North Sea! It's just amazing, and such power!"

Anne went over to him and took his arm. As she moved, she thought she saw Julia and Geoff catch each other's eye, and certainly Geoff grinned. "Come back over here, Mick," she coaxed. "We can't hear properly if you keep moving around. So, why is it called the Dragon Path?"

"Dragons are earth currents, they guard the power, the wisdom. The Chinese knew this, and where the dragons went, they called their paths the Dragon Lines. It's not true, you know, what the Church says, that Michael *killed* the dragon; they go together, like yin and yang – neither makes sense alone. And

Druids worshipped snakes, and the avenues at Avebury made it a Serpent Temple."

"I think all this is rather scary," Anne said.

"That's because you don't understand it. Julia's beginning to see, aren't you, Julia?"

"I think it's absolutely *magic*," she agreed at once. "Of course I don't understand it the way you do, Mick, but you're so good at explaining, and I think I do sense the power of the ley, just a little. I'd like another story, please. Did the Druids have anything to do with the Cheesewring?"

Now why, thought Anne, were Geoff and Julia sitting closer than ever? Why did they look so eager? And had Geoff just winked slightly? But already Mick was talking, his eyes fixed on Julia, willing her to share his vision.

"There was a Druid who kept watch here. They say he always sat on the same rock, and it's still called the Druid's Chair, and if anybody – "

He stopped dead, his eyes fixed and his mouth half open. The others waited.

"Geoff," said Mick in a voice quivering with excitement, "what did you say the minute we got here? Do you remember what you said? I do."

"Er... Was it about wanting a Coke?"

"Yes! You said you were thirsty. It's amazing!"

"I was thirsty too," said Julia. "Just suddenly thirsty, don't know why."

"It fits, it all fits. This Druid, if anybody came and said they were thirsty, he'd give them a drink in a gold cup which nobody could ever empty, which of course means he gave them enlightenment, and this went on for years and years till one day some man who was out hunting stole the cup and rode off with it, but his horse threw him and he broke his neck on the rocks. And he was buried over there in Rillaton Barrow, and the cup was buried with him. But of course we're still thirsty, we still need wisdom..."

"I never heard such crap. Beats me how anyone with even half a brain can believe a word of it," said Geoff.

"Well, that's where you're wrong, and I'll prove it. This is one case where the old tales *have* been proved true, and it's really wonderful what happened. For centuries everyone round here had known about this Druid's cup, and where it was buried, and then along came the archaeologists and opened up Rillaton Barrow, and bingo! A prehistoric gold cup! So even the high and mighty scientists – hey, what's up? What've I said? What's up, Julia?"

But Julia was laughing too much to answer, clutching Geoff's arm, burying her face in his shoulder, shrieking with giggles. Geoff was grinning from ear to ear.

"Listen to this, mate, and next time, do your homework before you go round boring the pants off everyone. What date was the dig at Rillaton Barrow?"

But Mick, struggling for words, could only stutter.

"I'll tell you when, 1818, that's when. And do you know when that fine tale you told us was first told. Do you? Do you?"

"It's a f-f-f-olktale, there's no f-f-f-irst time for f-folktales..."

"Oh, but in this case there is, you f-f-f-olksy p-p-p-prat! Nobody ever mentioned it before 1899, when it popped up in a book by the Reverend Sabine Baring-Gould, and that means there was eighty years for the story to grow in *after* the wondrous cup was found. What's more, the Reverend gent could have helped it grow a bit himself – a little more padding for his umpteenth book, you know.

So much for your ancient lore and its amazing confirmation. Don't believe me? Show him the Xerox, Julia."

Still giggling, Julia scrambled to her feet and held out a sheet of paper: "We found this really good book on British legends, and Geoff said – "

"God damn him to Hell, what do I care what Geoff said? But you, Julia, you said you were thirsty, you said you could sense the ley, so why are you siding with him? Why?"

It was Geoff who answered: "You still don't get it, do you? We were winding you up, weren't we? We've had Celtic Mysteries and Celtic Magic and Celtic Mumbo-jumbo till it's coming out of our ears and enough's enough. So we set you up good and proper, but it's for your own good, really. What you need, Mick, is not so many leys and a few more lays, know what I mean? But not with my Julia, if you don't mind, mate."

Anne shrieked: "Stop it, will you? Don't speak to him like that, it's not fair! You know he's been sick. You bitch, Julia, you absolute bitch! Just stop laughing, and *look* at him!"

For Mick was standing rigid, his hands clenched on his stick. Slowly, his lips drew back in a snarl and his eyes rolled up, showing the whites. He swayed, but did not fall.

Mist, white mist over Bodmin Moor. And circling figures, hooded, tall, blue-cloaked. Harps, deep-voiced choirs. No, not harps, drums. A weird chesty chant. Furs, masks, feather cloaks. Torches flaring. Come to me, come. I need your power. Stags looming through the mist, stags with human voices. Men with stags' heads. Stag-man, man-stag. I need your power.

Take the power, son. It is already yours. It runs in your blood. Show them the power and wisdom of a Druid.

Mick drew a deep, rasping breath, and his contorted face relaxed abruptly. "Nice one, Geoff, nice one, Julia. Thanks for the fun.

And thanks for your pity, Anne, but it's not needed. Now come over to the Cheesewring, where I'll show you something. Not tell you, show you."

"I said we've had enough," Geoff began, but Mick turned steady, cold eyes on him, and to his own utter bewilderment Geoff felt all words and laughter drain away, leaving just one thought: to obey Mick in everything. Meekly he headed for the rocks, walking a few paces behind Mick, the girls, similarly compelled, trailing behind him. As they drew nearer, the darkly looming pile seemed more unstable, more threatening. Mick vaulted onto one of the lower boulders, while the others lined up awkwardly below, silent, like prisoners before a judge.

"It would be very interesting, don't you agree, to know how many adders there are on Bodmin Moor? A piece of scientific, factual research, just up your street, Geoff. And yours, Julia – oh, silly me, I forgot you don't like snakes. Funny, isn't it, I've always liked them, in all my lives. And now I have this fancy to know how many there are on the Moor... Well, say something, can't you, have you all swallowed your tongues?"

No answer. No movement.

Mick slid down from the boulder and walked round them, staring at each in turn. "I take it you all agree. Now, this is how it's done. You see my stick? It's Irish blackthorn, same as St Patrick had, and we all know, don't we, how snakes feel about *that.* So if the three of you stand *quite* still – thank you – while I just draw a little circle round, like so, and leave the stick upright at the edge, like so, we can begin. There's nothing to it – I just whistle for them."

In a flash he leaped back onto the Cheesewring, swinging up from rock to rock till he stood on the topmost slab. Putting two fingers in his mouth, he whistled, shrill notes that ran through strange discords till the human ear could no longer follow them, though the air shook with their power. Then, as abruptly, he folded his legs into a yogic pose, and sat motionless.

"You may talk while we're waiting," said Mick.

Released from their mental bonds, they broke into a babble of questions and exclamations, dominated by Geoff's angry "Waiting for what? I'm bloody well not waiting!" as he strode off – only to stumble backwards with a yelp of pain, as if he had walked headlong into a glass door. A moment later, Anne and Julia too struck the invisible barrier. Mick watched them running to and fro, until repeated experience forced them to accept the incredible fact that they were imprisoned within a nine-foot circle whose circumference was defined by the faintly glowing track left by Mick's stick. The stick itself stood sentinel, slightly vibrating its tip barely piercing the soil.

"That's what's doing it! Pull it out!" cried Julia, as she and Geoff lunged simultaneously at the stick. Both screamed and recoiled, their arms cramping uncontrollably as fiery waves shot up from fingertips to armpit. The stick's oscillations, momentarily disturbed, resumed their rhythm.

"Earth energies, if you believe in such things, might do that," commented Mick, while Julia collapsed on the ground in tears and Geoff swore. "And now, take a good look round. Nature is so comforting, don't you think?"

"God damn it, man, don't be so bloody patronising. Drop your stupid game, can't you? You look like bloody Peter Pan, stuck up there on your heap of stones."

"I said, look round. Look at the path, the grass, the heath. Look."

Despite himself, Geoff obeyed. Anne was already pressing face and hands against the solid air at the circle's further edge, staring across the moor. Even Julia, still whimpering and nursing her burnt hand, lifted her head to look – and hastily scrambled to her feet, for a tuft of grass had parted to reveal the brownish, diamond-patterned head of a small viper barely a yard away. Anne too cried out, pointing up the path. There were two more snakes, no, three, rapidly twisting their way among the granite chips towards the circle, while further off there were glimpses of movement among rock slabs and scrubby heath.

Julia flung herself into Geoff's arms. "Get me out of here, get me out! Snakes, oh Christ, I hate them, I can't stand it!"

"Don't panic, pet. It's hypnotism, that's all it is. There are no snakes here, I promise you. The bastard has hypnotised us, but he can't keep it up for ever. We'll break free, and then, by God, what I won't do to him!"

But even as he spoke, more vipers came gliding swiftly towards the circle, where they halted, pressing noses and flickering tongues against it, coiling and rearing up, hissing and striking at the line of power. The three humans clung together in the centre.

"If I were you," Mick's voice cut through their outcry, "I wouldn't be trying to break free. Believe me, you are safer inside than outside, for the moment."

"Send them away, Mick," pleaded Anne. "You called them, you can send them back."

There was no reply.

Julia fell to her knees. "Oh Mick, we didn't mean anything, it was just a joke, we're sorry, look, I'm apologising," she wailed. "Go on, Geoff, say you're sorry too."

"It's only hypnotism," he muttered, but added reluctantly, "Well, if that's what it takes to get us out... for your sake, pet... I'm sorry, Mick."

Mick did not answer. There were many more vipers now, making an unbroken ring, and in places mounting each other in tangled heaps.

"Mick," said Anne, struggling to sound calm, "this can't go on, and you've proved your point. We believe in your power, in the Dragon Path, the Druid's cup, everything. How much longer before you let us go?"

"By my reckoning," came the cold voice, "there are seventy-eight here so far. Now you will, I'm sure, agree that in an area like Bodmin Moor (how many square miles would you say it is?) there are more than seventy-eight adders, not to mention grass-snakes. I have summoned every serpent on the Moor, but it may take several hours for the distant ones to reach us. Luckily, summer days are long. It will probably still be daylight when the tally is complete."

"And... and then?"

"Why, then I take down the barrier, obviously."

Momentary relief, followed by incredulous horror, and wild protests. Time passed, and the wall of writhing, flickering reptile bodies grew higher. Julia, who had vomited violently, lay curled in a tight ball, shivering and moaning. Geoff's threats and oaths had given way to humble pleading, even tears; but in vain; now he sat helpless, head in hands. Anne stared, stony faced, at the sun-drenched moorland, where still light glistened, every now and then, on the scaly backs of yet more approaching serpents. Then abruptly she looked up once more at Mick's motionless figure.

"I can see why you want those two to die, but why me, Mick? I listened to you, I believed in you, I thought the world of you. I didn't know what they were planning – how could you ever imagine I'd want to make a fool of you, Mick? Let me out, please, please.

Do what you like to them, but please... Oh Mick, can't you answer me? I'm your friend."

"I know exactly how much of a friend you are, Anne. You had no part in the joke, that's true, but why? Because you think I'm 'sick'. 'Don't laugh at him, he's sick,' you said. 'Sick' means 'crazy' doesn't it, my dear friend, Anne? You thought I'm crazy, so now you must learn your lesson like the others."

More time, more grass-snakes and vipers. They were piled up to the level of Anne's shoulders now; soon there would be nothing to look at but seething snakes, the sky, the looming Cheesewring, and Mick's silent, watchful form. No sound but Julia's moans, which Geoff's occasional murmurs of comfort could not quieten.

Suddenly Geoff raised his head. "God, how stupid can one get? We must be bewitched, I think. Look here, Julia, Anne, this is a famous beauty spot, right? There are people around, walkers, climbers, picnickers, right? We shout, they come, and someone can do something – get rid of the snakes, if they're real, or knock Mick out, or shoot him, the raving maniac, or whatever. So let's shout, girls."

"Well done," came the mocking voice from the rocks, "you've achieved a thought. Rather late in the day, but better late than never. Now for another. We've been here – what, two hours? Three? Time goes so fast when one has fun – So why has no-one seen or heard you yet? No ideas? Dear me, time for another little lesson."

Even as he spoke the landscape faded, the air turned chill, and beyond the wall of snakes they saw a second wall of thick grey mist which swirled around them, blotting everything from their sight, though directly overhead the sky remained clear.

"That," said Mick, "is the famous Druidic mist. Everyone heading for the Cheesewring on this lovely sunny afternoon ran into it, and most turned back at once – these sudden changes of weather make the Moor so treacherous, you know. For the few hardy souls who did press on, I prepared a good strong stench of rotting sheep. No-one has come within half a mile of us, and no-one will, I guarantee. And anyway, what makes you think soundwaves would go through my barrier if I chose to stop them?"

He waited for an answer, but heard only incoherent sounds of terror and despair. The mist rolled back and dissolved, and once again his victims saw him, standing upright now, poised on the capstone, turning to scan the moors on every side.

"Two thousand, one hundred and forty-one are here, and no more in sight. Every serpent on Bodmin Moor has heard me. It is time to finish the game."

As he stretched out his hand, the blackthorn stick uprooted itself amid a shower of greenish sparks and cartwheeled up the rocks into his grasp. Simultaneously the snakes surged forward. For a few moments there were screams, as three struggling, staggering forms tried to shake off the creatures which swarmed over them. Then they lay still and silent.

From his high perch Mick watched contentedly as the vipers began to glide away, abandoning the bodies and scattering over the moor.

Then, on the western skyline, his glance caught a distant but massive movement, as if the earth were rising and falling in great rounded waves; with it came a deep rhythmic pulse, felt in the bones rather than with the ear. Shielding his eyes from the sun, he saw at the centre of the disturbance something dark and narrow approaching rapidly, while to either side, bushes and boulders swayed like small yachts tossed in the wake of a speedboat. In a few moments he could see more; the thing was dark, yes, and tall; it was rising from the ground yet driving forward, cutting through it, like a periscope through waves, like a swan's neck, like...

With an exultant cry he stretched his arms towards it: "Dragon! Dragon of the Ley! Earth Shaker, Guardian of the Wisdom! Did you too hear my summons? Truly, my power is greater than I knew. Yet I should have known, for I am Michael – we belong together, you and I – Earth Dragon and Druid Lord!"

With unaltered speed it hurtled towards him, then at the foot of the Cheesewring it stopped dead. Coil upon glistening coil, it drew itself up until the swaying head was level with Mick's face, its scales shimmering in iridescent patterns of darkest blue and green. Cold eyes, moon pale. A purple, flickering tongue. Mick gazed, entranced.

Then the jaws opened, and hissing breath enveloped him, filling his lungs with sulphurous fumes. The head drew back, then lunged, striking obliquely at the topmost slab of rock, so that it spun with dizzying speed and sent Mick hurtling to the ground. Lying broken-backed across a boulder, racked by the choking of his seared lungs he did not see the Dragon whip its huge form back into the earth, though he felt the tremor of its going. The Druid mist closed over him, bringing mocking voices:

Power we gave you, for a while – wisdom we could not give.

He did not die till dawn.

2014

ON ILKLEY MOOR

Alison Littlewood

Alison Littlewood grew up in the South Yorkshire town of Penistone and attended Northumbria University, where she studied for a joint English and History degree. She has written several novels exploring Gothic and folkloric themes, and has contributed to a number of anthologies, winning the 2014 Shirley Jackson Award for Short Fiction for her story "The Dog's Home".

"On Ilkley Moor", first published in *Terror Tales of Yorkshire*, is an eerie story of friendship, betrayal and guilt whose events begin at Ilkley's Cow and Calf pub. A short distance from the pub, the imposing millstone grit outcrop and boulder of the Cow and Calf provide a popular starting point for moorland walks. Rombald's Moor is the name given to the wider landscape of which Ilkley Moor forms a part, and, as Littlewood's character of Inchy tells us, it was the giant Rombald who gave the Cow and Calf their current form. Rombald is one of several giants who populate Yorkshire legend as shapers of the landscape – others include Wade (father of Wayland the Smith), said to be the builder of the causeway found in the North York Moors.

The prehistoric rock art mentioned in Littlewood's story is scattered across Rombald's Moor, with over 400 stones featuring enigmatic "cup and ring" carvings identified to date. The Friends of Ilkley Moor website has Ordnance Survey map references for several of the most notable carved stones, alongside details of walks taking in key sites dating from the Neolithic to the Victorian period.

It wasn't until I turned off the main road and up towards the moors that it really struck me that this had been my home. There was that old sound, the wind billowing its way across the tops and down into the valley; it was like a sound out of memory, but the way it buffeted the car was real enough. I reached out and turned up the radio, but in my mind it was another tune I heard, different lyrics:

Wheear 'ast tha bin since ah saw thee?

I smiled. Where indeed? I hadn't felt the need to come back since Dad had died, and that was years ago. I had my own place now, my own job; my training was done, my school days long behind me. I'd never thought to see Inchy – Warren Hinchliffe – again. I jabbed at the radio, turning it off, and listened to the sound of the wind coming over the tops. Up there were swathes of green, patched with the lighter shades of dead grass and the darker growth of heather, the purple flowers dimmed under a cloudy sky. And grey paths wound through it all, leading nowhere, or so it had seemed when we were small.

I remembered what Inchy had said on the phone: *It'd be just what I need.* I had the impression that he'd been prepared for my rejection. He'd just lost his job, he said, nothing special, just helping out on a farm, but now it had ended: *I need summat to help me start ower.* And he'd waited in silence, and the old guilt had crept from his end of the line to mine.

Wheear 'ast tha bin since ah saw thee?

I'd been miles away, while he had stayed, along with the memory of what had passed between us, the thing we had done. I pushed the thought away. I'd started again long ago; the least I could do was help Inchy do the same. I dropped down the slope and saw the pub – *The Cow and Calf* – named for the giant outcrops of millstone grit that could just be seen at the edge of the moor. I slowed, and pulled into the car park.

Inchy was propping up the bar. I recognised him at once, though he wasn't so much taller than me as I'd remembered, and he'd been working on a beer gut since I'd been away. He didn't smile when he saw me, didn't act surprised, didn't say "How've you been?"; he just nodded to where a pint stood at his elbow.

"I was going to have a Coke – "

"You might as well 'ave it. Get it dahn thee neck, Andy." And then, belatedly: "All right, mate?"

"Not bad." I grinned at him before taking a drink. It was cold, but more welcome than I'd expected.

He grinned back and drained what was left of his own pint. "Lad's day out, and all that. Get you out o' t' city furra bit. God's own country."

I tried not to let him see how the beer was going straight to my head. "My dad always called it that."

"Aye, well, 's changed a bit round 'ere since them days. 'S all posh folk in Ilkley now – more accountants and bankers than you can shake a stick at."

I kept quiet, taking another sip. He knew what I did for a living, didn't he? I was already wondering if this had been a good idea.

"Not locals. Not like us. Remember 'ow we'd go off looking for frogspawn an' that, in t' streams?"

I smiled. I did remember.

"They don't do that these days. Now it's all off to ballet in their fancy Land Rovers, or walking their labra-fucking-doodles. They sink a hundred quid on designer wellies and chuck a hissy fit if they get 'em mucky. Well, we'd best go, mate."

He pulled on an army surplus jacket and nodded at my padded coat. "Cragface, eh?"

"Craghoppers." I shrugged and bent to tighten the laces on my hiking boots, only then realising how clean they were. They'd been more than a hundred quid, but they were guaranteed comfy out of the box, and I hadn't been walking in a long time. When I straightened I expected Inchy to narrow his eyes or make some comment, but he didn't; he only nodded.

"We'd best get off then," he said.

Once we got walking, it was just like the old days. Inchy had always led the way then too; he was a few months older than me but he'd always been taller, and he seemed more so now he was higher up the hillside. The wind barrelled off the slope, flattening the grass, and we leaned into it. The path led steadily upward past the side of the old quarry and it felt as if I was fifteen again, playing hooky from school, led astray by "that boy," as my mum used to call him. She'd even correct me if I said his nickname – *Hinchy*, she'd insist – but he was never called that; no one ever said their aitches, not round here, not then.

The old song started to run through my mind as we climbed higher:

On Ilkla Moor baht'at...

We used to sing it for a joke and it seemed more than ever like one now, with the wind raging around us. How on earth could anyone have kept a hat on their head? The wind was cold too, chilling my ears and the nape of my neck. *Tha's bahn to catch thy deeath o' cowd*, we'd sung. I paused and pulled up my hood, holding it in place, the fabric buffeting about my head. It was loud, and at first I didn't realise that Inchy had spoken.

"Cow n' Calf."

He pointed down at the quarry, towards the two huge boulders. The Calf stood away on its own, the Cow jutting from a longer crag. Beyond them was more moor and fields and little villages and all the long grey sky watching over it all.

"Bet you never knew t' legend," he said. "There was this giant, see. Rombald. He ran off from 'is wife – dunno what 'ed done – an' 'e stamped on them rocks and split t' Calf off from t' Cow. Course, it never looked like no bloody Cow n' Calf to me."

I laughed. "Me neither. I could never work out why they called it that."

"Aye, well." Another pause. "'E split summat up, anyroad."

I stared after him as he started to walk, seeing only his back, the dull green of his coat blending into the landscape. I wasn't sure he'd said what I thought I'd heard. I blinked the idea away. He hadn't meant anything; it was only the rocks he'd been speaking of. I shrugged and started after him, climbing higher, away from the quarry and the pub and the view behind it.

As we laughed over the old days, I started to remember them in a way I hadn't for a long time. The further I'd gone, the hazier the memories had become; now Inchy brought them back. I remembered trying to smoke a cig he'd nicked from his old man's pocket;

unscrewing people's gates on Mischief Night; and coming up here, to the moor. That, most of all, and I remember the way it felt, as if anyone in the world could look up and see us and know what we were up to, and yet hidden too, as if we were a hundred miles from anything.

We fell quiet. There was only the sound of the wind and the rustle of our coats, and I started to drift, and I heard the old song once more in my mind:

Tha's been a cooartin' Mary Jane
On Ilkla Moor baht 'at...

I pulled a face. There were things I wanted to remember and things I didn't, and this was one of the things I didn't.

It was Inchy who'd got a girlfriend first. Of course it was; he was taller than me, and harder, and he always seemed so much older, even though the difference between us was small. And Joan was the best of them, the one all the lads fancied. It wasn't long before they started going out, and Inchy suddenly didn't have so much time for fishing or wandering or anything else.

She was pretty, Joan Chapman. Her long dark hair was never tied back and she had a pale oval face and, what all the lads thought but wouldn't say in front of Inchy, the best pair of tits in school. She had a laugh like a drain and sparkles – it sounded corny even now, but she did – she had sparkles in her eyes. She looked like she was going somewhere, but of course she never did; she hadn't gone anywhere, had never even become any older than we were then. But I hadn't had to think about that, or not too much, because by then I'd been leaving. I was wondering how far that was true of Inchy when he said, "'Ere: I wanted to do summat. For *'er*."

"You what?"

He turned and I saw that his face was white. It came as a shock to see the way he kept blinking, as if he was trying to hold something back.

He pulled something from his pocket. I stared at it. It was a candle. I didn't know what on earth he was thinking: it wasn't something I wanted to remember, and anyway, a *candle* for God's sake, just as if the wind wasn't howling over the tops like the very devil. And it was daylight, even if it was thin and mean, the clouds heavy and grey.

"I thought we could," he said. "Old time's sake. Finish it, you know? Just summat to..."

Start ower, I thought. I felt suddenly sick, the beer uneasy in my belly. I didn't want to agree, but I found myself saying, "All right."

"Serious?" He brightened at once and I suddenly felt as if I was the older one. I nodded and he went on, towards another grey rock, this one overhanging the hillside as if at any moment it would tumble to the valley below.

The Pancake Stone was balanced on a small grey outcrop, its position precarious, and yet it had remained there for years. Its name had never seemed quite right; it was flat on top but it looked to me more like an anvil, pointing out over the empty air. Ancient markings were carved into it, cup and ring formations, some almost joining so they looked like part of a larger pattern that had long since been lost.

"Here," he said.

"Inch, I'm not sure – "

The look he gave me was so hurt I didn't say anything else. Anger I could have understood, but this, from him, was worse. He took the candle and set it into one of the cups, but it wouldn't hold. He jammed it instead into a crack in the rock and pulled a matchbox from his pocket. The wind almost took it from him. He struck a match and it blew out at once. He swore under his breath and the wind whipped the curse away.

"Ne'er mind," he said. "I brought summat else."

He fiddled in his pockets and took out a small plastic bottle. Carefully, he tipped some of the liquid it held into one of the cups. "'S what they were for, they reckon," he said. "Lighting fires."

I looked at the rock. I wasn't sure anyone knew what the patterns were for, not really, but I somehow felt there must be more to it than that.

This time he threw the match down as soon as it sparked and as the liquid caught, flaring, he jerked away from it. The flame became invisible almost at once.

"I 'eard," he said, "this place behind t' rock – Green Crag – they used t' call it land o' the dead. They did rites, an' that."

I pulled a face. I didn't know where he was getting this stuff. For all I knew, he was making it up. This trip was a mistake, I knew that now.

Tha's been a cooartin' my lass Joan...

I shook my head, trying to clear it. I felt my guilt stirring, rising into the air with the flame that was already dying, dead and gone like...

"This is wheear she did it," he said.

I whipped around to face him. "What?"

"Oppened a vein. Right 'ere. Laid 'ersel' down on t' rock, an' she – "

"No. She *didn't*."

He half-turned to stare at the stone, just as if he could still see the fire burning there, as if anybody could.

I took deep breaths. He had to be lying. I'd heard she'd killed herself – of course I did, everybody knew, everybody knew everything in a place like this – but I'd imagined her doing it in the bath, lying down, putting her wrist under the water before she sliced –

But I *hadn't* known, had I? Because I'd left. I'd gone away to college because I couldn't wait to turn my back on it; I hadn't *wanted* to know.

And now he'd brought me here. Inchy had brought me back.

Tha's been a cooartin' my lass Joan

Baht thee trahsers on...

The voice in my head, adding the extra line so beloved of schoolboys, had become mocking. No: accusing.

It hadn't been my fault. I'd told myself that so many times. I may have gone after her, *set my cap at her* as my mum would have put it, but it was Joan who'd decided: it was her choice. And when she realised it was a mistake, when we'd split and she tried to go back to Inchy and he wouldn't have her – that wasn't my fault either, was it? He'd been happy enough to have me back, as a friend. I'd often wondered how he could bring himself to forgive me but not her, but friendship was like that, wasn't it? It was for keeps. It was for *ever.*

Now I looked into his face and I found myself wondering who the hell he was; who he had ever been.

"I would've bought her a ring," he said, his voice distant. "If she 'adn't – I mean, I know we was young. But I would 'ave. Eventually."

I went on staring. I realised my mouth had fallen open and I closed it again. When he didn't say anything else I tried to find words, but there were none. All I could think was: *He said he didn't care.* He'd said she was just a lass and she didn't matter, not really.

He'd laughed at her when she tried to win him back. He told folk she'd let anyone lift her skirt and he called her a slag, even when she cried to his face. If he hadn't told me he wasn't bothered, if I'd known –

But I looked at him now and I *did* know. Of course he couldn't forgive her. He hadn't been able to forgive her because of how deep the hurt went, and I saw now that time hadn't eased it, only weathered it, carving the grooves deeper.

When he turned, it didn't come as a surprise to see that he was crying.

"Inchy. I – I'm going back to the pub," I said, and I backed away.

"'Ang on." He looked startled.

"I didn't ask for this. Look, I said I was sorry. I *am* sorry. But this – " I raised my hands and let them fall again.

"Look, I din't mean nowt. But this is why we came, in't it? We did that to 'er, thee an' me, and it seemed right, that's all. It's done now. I've said what I want to say, an' that's it. No more, all right? It's ower."

"Is it, Inchy?"

He rubbed a hand over his eyes and he smiled. If it hadn't been for that smile, I would have turned and gone back then and there, but I didn't; I looked at him for a long time, neither of us wavering, and then I nodded and I stayed.

"Rombald's missus dropped that," Inchy said. I looked at the odd cairn set into the wiry grass. It was made of grey stones of similar sizes, forming a low, rough circle. It reminded me of a plate with an indentation in the middle.

"Skirtful o' Stones," he added. "She were runnin' after 'im, see, when 'e put 'is size nines through t' Cow n' Calf. And then she dropped all t' stones she were carryin' and made this circle. Dun't know 'er name. Nubody did."

I gave him a sharp look, but there didn't seem to be any hidden meaning in what he said. He seemed to have put Joan out of his mind; he'd been striding out with new energy, his cheeks reddened by the continual assault of the wind. It was me that couldn't stop thinking about her.

I opened my mouth to ask why the giant's wife was running after him, but realised I didn't want to know. I had an image in my mind: me and Inchy heading off up Curly Hill on one of our expeditions, and Joan catching up with us; the look she'd had on her face when she pulled on Inchy's arm. The look on her face after he'd brushed her off. She hadn't been angry. If she'd been carrying something then, a skirtful of stones, I imagine she'd have just dropped everything too; she'd have let it all go.

I started walking, pulling my hood tighter. The wind was full in my face, chilling my eyes and my skin. It felt like little knives. I walked faster. I probably deserved it.

But Inchy had deserved it too. I felt a stab of anger. He was the one who'd let her go, wasn't he?

I was leading the way, though I hadn't asked where we were headed. I didn't suppose it mattered. I wasn't even looking at the moor, not really, I was looking into the past, and I could see Joan's face as clear as anything. It struck me now that she had always been a little like the moor: half-ordinary, something that was just *there*, but half-wild too, her hair always flying and in knots, something unfathomable in her eyes.

I wondered if it was still there when she died.

I almost felt I could hear that lilting song again, and the words crept across the moor:

Then we shall 'ave to bury thee...

I shook my head, spoke without turning. "Inchy, did you hear something?"

He didn't reply.

"Inchy?"

His voice, when it came, was gruff. "Nowt but the wind. And you know what, mate? Me name's *Warren.*"

I was only half-listening. He was right, it *was* only the wind, but it sounded as if there were voices in it. I was sure, at some point in the past, I'd heard it called a devil wind; now I thought I knew why, only it sounded less like a devil than a host of demons crying together.

Bury thee, bury thee...

I shook my head. I was tired and wishing I was a hundred miles away, back in my old life – no, my *new* life – and that bloody wind just wouldn't ease up. I was allowing the past and other people's mistakes and yes, my own, to get to me. It was only then that Inchy's words sank in.

Me name's Warren...

I whirled around. He wasn't there.

I scanned the hillside, knowing how the dull green of his jacket would have faded into it. It wasn't any use. Inchy had gone.

Bastard.

I took a few steps back the way I had come, looking for any sign of another living being, and I saw none. Despite the wind, I felt hot all over. He'd lured me out here and then ditched me, an act of petty revenge, and why – because he'd lost his job, was jealous all over again?

I squinted into the cold air. He surely couldn't have passed out of sight so quickly. But it occurred to me that maybe he wasn't out of sight. He might be crouching in the grass, hiding in his green coat, but somehow it didn't feel like that. The place felt empty. He'd already scarpered, heading back to the warm pub and leaving me to freeze. No doubt, when I got there, I'd find he'd let my tyres down too. Well, good luck to him. He was going nowhere, someone who hadn't even had the nous to grab the girl he'd cared about and hold onto her.

The sky was heavier than ever and everything had darkened, taking on the colours of a storm. In the distance the space between earth and sky was streaked black with rain. It seemed to echo something inside of me.

I could try and blame Inchy all I liked, but the knowledge squirmed in my gut: *it was my fault.* It had always been my fault, not because I went after her, because I fancied her, but because the reason I'd gone after her was that Inchy had had her first.

He had always been taller than me. He was always tougher. He was the one who smoked without chucking his guts up, back when smoking was something cool. I pictured him in the pub, clutching his pint glass with his yellowing fingers, and I imagined the rot creeping inside him.

But I'd been the one who set out to destroy something. I was the one who'd *thought* about it, something Inchy never seemed to do, not back then. Now it seemed that had changed. I could hardly blame him.

It didn't matter. All I had to do was retrace my steps and get out of here, leave it all behind, just as I had before. I turned a full circle. All around me was purple heather, long grass bowing in the wind, and bared grey earth. It looked as if there were paths everywhere, radiating like the spokes of a wheel. My belly contracted as I realised I was no longer sure which way I'd come. But it should be easy, shouldn't it? All I had to do was head downhill. Except now I appeared to be standing at the summit of a crag. That couldn't be right, could it? *Everywhere* was downhill.

My mouth felt dry. I cursed Inchy for the alcohol I'd had earlier. It was confusing my mind, clouding my judgement. Still, I couldn't stay here; I'd pick a direction and get moving. I'd soon know if I was going the wrong way. Scowling at the moor, wondering if Inchy was still out there, watching, I started to walk.

As I went, the old tune became the background to my steps, the refrain to my thoughts. I remembered us singing it, the story of comic cannibalism where the man caught his deeath o' cowd, was buried and eaten by worms, which were eaten by ducks, which were eaten by the people.

Then t'worms'll come an eyt thee up...

That had seemed the funniest line of all. It wasn't so funny now.

Then we shall all 'ave etten thee. On Ilkla Moor baht 'at...

I never knew who the "we" in the song was supposed to be, the singers or someone else, and now I wondered.

I stopped walking and frowned. I didn't think this could be the right way. The moor all looked the same, flat and bleak and with nothing to relieve the monotony, and across everything, that merciless scouring wind.

I remembered I should be walking away from it, the wind behind me, but it seemed to be coming from all directions; whichever way I turned it blustered and spat in my face. My cheeks were numb, all feeling long since faded. I turned and started to walk back the way I had just come. As I did, it started to rain.

*

I'd forgotten how bloody miserable the moor could be. Even the air seemed grey and it was hard to keep my eyes open; I squinted against the rain. It lashed my hood, drowning everything in a loud patter. *Fuck this.* The sooner I got off the moor the better. I tried to move quicker and my boots slid on the wet, slicked-down grass. I landed on my arse, pushed myself up, went on again. I could hardly see at all. I found I was muttering the words of the song, over and over:

Tha's bahn to catch thy death...

I realised what I was saying and shut my mouth. I'd be off this hill soon, then I could dry off in the pub before heading home. I'd have the heater on full blast. I'd be too hot then, and I wouldn't bloody care.

It was then that I saw the light.

It hung there on the other side of the rain, a faint yellow glow, and I realised: it was *her* light, it was the Pancake Stone, and I was back after all. It had to be. It had somehow kept burning and soon I'd be there; I'd see all the lights of Ilkley and Ben Rhydding shining out from the valley, calling me back. I hunched myself against the rain and hurried towards it.

The light flickered in and out of existence. One moment I'd think I was getting closer and then there it was, in the distance again. I must be going in a circle. Or I was seeing things. Whatever it was, I couldn't seem to find it. And all the time the rain kept coming down and the sky was growing darker.

I tilted my head, allowing my hood to fall back, and let the rain find my face. It was dead cold and I cursed, pulling my hood back up, though it wasn't any use; the rain was inside it. I shivered and turned. The light was still there, but it was behind me now. I didn't know how I'd got turned around but I started off again, unable to tell if I was going up a rise or heading slightly downhill. The light kept moving. It bobbed and wavered, confusing my eyes. I had to reach it soon. The moor couldn't be that big. If I just kept going in a straight line, sooner or later, I had to reach its edge.

It was Inchy, it had to be. He'd hidden a lamp out here and he was taunting me with it, and I had to give it to him, he was *fast.* One minute it was off to the left, the next, away to my right. I'd tried to keep straight but somehow I'd found myself following anyway, being drawn this way and that. Well, enough; I wasn't playing any longer. I was cold and wet and tired.

There was a large boulder in front of me and I leaned against it, slicking water from my coat. The rain was easing off at last. I knew I couldn't stay here for long; cold was spreading from the rock, finding its way inside my skin. Still, I couldn't quite bring myself to move. I stayed while the rain reduced to a light patter and then I felt something, almost as if the rock at my back had trembled, and a moment later I heard it: a dull, hollow boom ringing out across the moor. I reached out and touched the rock, and thought I could still feel it, a faint resonance that took a while to fade.

A few seconds later, the sound came again. I froze, listening. It had to be thunder, didn't it? It could take on all sorts of odd sounds, out here. It's just that, for a moment, it had made me think of footsteps: the footsteps of a giant, echoing in my ears.

Damn Inchy. It was his stories, playing on my imagination. Stones and giants, old legends that wouldn't die. The Cow and Calf, where were they now? And something flashed across my mind, something I'd heard long ago, that there had been a Bull once too, a rock bigger than any of them that was broken up and carried off for building. No one ever seemed sure if it was true or not and it was odd to think that something so large could simply disappear, out here, and no one could even agree if it had ever existed.

Just as the rain was letting up at last, the wind was rising again. Its voice moaned across the hills and my head began to throb with it, aching behind my eyes.

I forced myself to my feet, my wet jeans sticking to my skin, and set my face to the darkness. It wasn't the rain now, robbing everything of light; soon night would fall. I would be out here all alone, and no one would come to help.

But it wasn't entirely dark. Somewhere ahead and a little to my left was the gentle glow of a light. No: *two* lights, now.

Tha's been a cooartin' my lass Joan...

I must be seeing things. But it was easy, with night hailing at the edges of the world, to believe that both of them were out here with me: Inchy and Joan, walking hand in hand maybe, together again...

I shook my head, trying to dispel the image. It was nonsense, of course. I started walking again, pulling my coat tight around me. I'd be off this moor in no time. I would soon be warm.

Except there seemed to be no end to this place. It was as if I'd walked into some giant land that went on and on. Everywhere I looked was the moor, dark and smudged with shadows that could have been rocks, could have been anything. *The land of the dead*, he'd called it.

It was suddenly easy to imagine the way Joan might have felt when she came up here all alone. The way she would have sat down on an ancient stone, perhaps smoothing a hand over the things that were carved there. And she'd opened a vein, over those cup markings perhaps, the hollows ready to receive what she gave...

And what had the old gods offered in return? What had she asked for as she lay there dying – *me?*

A slow chill spread through my chest.

Then we shall 'ave to bury thee...

Something struck me then, something that had never made any sense before. The last verse of the song, the very last – it was about revenge, wasn't it? Only I'd never understood why. Yes, that was it:

That's wheear we get us ooan back...

The "we" had had their revenge because they'd eaten him, the man who'd courted the girl and caught the cold and been buried and eaten by the worms – but why *our ooan back?* The song never explained what he'd done to them.

But the song was a part of this place. No one even knew who'd written it; it had been sung down the ages. Now, with the light failing and no one in sight and nothing around for miles, it almost felt as if it had been intended for this moment. It repeated itself inside my mind, but the intonation was different:

That's *wheear we get us ooan back. On Ilkla Moor baht 'at...*

I shuddered. *Here*, that's where it would be. This was where Joan would come to me, to thank me properly for what I'd done. She'd come with the rain and the wind in her hair, her eyes all a-sparkle in the dark.

I let out an odd sound and started to hurry onward, stumbling in my haste. I realised I was singing as I went, and I knew it was crazy but I couldn't stop. I sang the words faster and faster, no inflection in them now at all, not thinking about what they meant or where they had come from, and I stumbled and slipped and for a time, everything was dark.

When I woke, the cold was bone-deep. I was lying on something hard and I touched it, feeling whorls and dips beneath my fingers, and I pushed myself up. My head swam. I was lying on a grey rock that was partially hidden in the ground, and I must have hit my head on it because there was something dark that looked like blood. I looked at the cups and the rings, delineated more clearly than any I had yet seen. I thought of Joan, of her blood. How much had she given? Perhaps this would help. It was an offering, a libation: *something*. Perhaps it would be enough.

I lay back, not caring that the ground was hard. It wasn't dark any longer, I realised. It wasn't dark and the wind had fallen still, its voices silenced. I was still on the moor but now it was beautiful. The moon had risen and stars were sprinkled across the sky, sparkling like eyes, watching me. I imagined staying here forever, just looking up at them and letting everything slip away.

Then the sound came again, a long, ringing echo as of giant footsteps, and the earth shook beneath me.

I think I smiled. And I remembered another line that we used to add to the song when we were small:

On Ilkla Moor baht 'at

Wheear's that?

The words seemed to whisper in my mind: *Wheear's that?* And I looked into the sky with its infinite stars and I realised I was no longer sure.

ALSO AVAILABLE BY WEIRD WALK

A remarkable blood-soaked stranger upends the lives of two Lake District ramblers; a lonely tavern offers its guests something much more disturbing than a post-walk pint; a night hike on the Fens takes a terrifying turn when the fog rolls in.

From the darkly humorous to the chillingly sinister, tales of the haunted trail are as old as time. We have always travelled on foot and our worst fears have often accompanied us. Whether walking for pleasure or necessity, the ramblers of these classic stories trip across unseen boundaries, plotting routes towards the numinous, the uncanny and the plain evil.

Featuring fourteen pieces from an intrepid band of writers including Robert Aickman, Charlotte Riddell, M. R. James and many more, this new anthology is a haunting trail mate, guiding you into the wild unknown.

ALSO AVAILABLE

A seaside honeymoon holiday is plagued by the mystery of bells which never stop ringing – and the uncanny force which answers the call. The echoes of undying druidic rites spell disaster at a Norfolk golf course. An ancient relic found on the Suffolk coast summons a relentless spectral pursuer to its discoverer.

Welcome to East Anglia, one of the heartlands of British strange and ghostly fiction whose mind-stretching expanses, wide, yawning skies and disorientating tidal fens have bewitched generations of writers.

Unearthing seventeen short tales set in Norfolk, Essex, Suffolk and Cambridgeshire from the 1900s to the 2010s, Edward Parnell's selection unites eternal classics by M. R. James, Robert Aickman and Marjorie Bowen with modern chillers from Daisy Johnson and Matthew Holness to offer a sweeping view across the dark horizons of East Anglia's eeriest literature.

For more Tales of the Weird titles
visit the British Library Shop (shop.bl.uk)

We welcome any suggestions, corrections or feedback you may have, and will aim to respond to all items addressed to the following:

The Editor (Tales of the Weird), British Library Publishing,
The British Library, 96 Euston Road, London NW1 2DB

We also welcome enquiries through our social media accounts, @BL_Publishing.